Watching ~~Edie~~

Camilla Way was formerly an editor on the style magazine *Arena*, and has written for *Stylist*, *Elle* and the *Guardian*.

She first became interested in the theme of toxic female friendships and the question of whether we can ever, truly, escape our past after hearing a news story about a teenage friendship that went horribly wrong.

Camilla is now a full-time writer and lives in south-east London with her partner and twin boys.

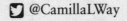 @CamillaLWay

By Camilla Way

The Dead of Summer
Little Bird

Watching Edie

CAMILLA WAY

HARPER

HarperCollins
P U B L I S H E R S
Since 1817

Harper
An imprint of HarperCollins*Publishers*
1 London Bridge Street
London, SE1 9GF

www.harpercollins.co.uk

This paperback edition 2017
1

First published in Great Britain by HarperCollins*Publishers* 2016

A catalogue record for this book
is available from the British Library

ISBN: 978-0-00-815904-7

Set in Sabon by Palimpsest Book Production Limited,
Falkirk, Stirlingshire

Printed and bound in Great Britain by
Clays Ltd, St Ives plc

MIX
Paper from
responsible sources
FSC **FSC™ C007454**
www.fsc.org

FSC™ is a non-profit international organisation established to promote
the responsible management of the world's forests. Products carrying the
FSC label are independently certified to assure consumers that they come
from forests that are managed to meet the social, economic and
ecological needs of present and future generations,
and other controlled sources

Find out more about HarperCollins and the environment at
www.harpercollins.co.uk/green

For Alex

'It's no use going back to yesterday, because I was a different person then.'
Alice's Adventures in Wonderland,
Lewis Carroll

PART ONE

After

Outside my kitchen window the long afternoon empties of light. I look at London stretched out far below, my dripping hands held poised above the sink. The doorbell rings, one long high peal; the broken intercom vibrates. The view from up here, it's incredible, like you're flying. Deptford and Greenwich, New Cross and Erith, then the river, and beyond that there's the Gherkin, over there's the Shard. From my top-floor flat here on Telegraph Hill you can see forever and as usual it calms me, soothes me: how big it is, how small I am, how far from where I used to be.

The doorbell rings more urgently – whoever it is putting their finger on the buzzer and holding it there. The night hovers.

At first I used to see Heather everywhere. Connor too, of course. From the corner of my eye I'd catch a

3

glimpse of one or the other of them, and there'd be that sharp, cold lurch that would leave me sick and shaken long after I'd realized that it had been an illusion; just a stranger with similar hair or the same way of walking. Whenever it happened I'd go somewhere busy and lose myself amongst the crowds, roaming the south-east London streets until I'd reassured myself that all that was very far away and long ago. A small West Midlands town a million miles from here. And the doorbell rings and rings as I'd always known it would one day.

I live on the top floor of a large, ugly Victorian building, and there are lots of us squashed in here side by side, in our small, draughty little flats. Housing Association, most of us. And when I wedge my door open with a shoe and go down to answer the bell, past four floors of white doors marked with brass letters, the early evening sounds seep from beneath each one: a baby crying, a telly's laughter, a couple arguing; the lives of strangers.

I'm entirely unprepared for what's waiting for me beyond the heavy wide front door and when I open it the world seems to tilt and I have to grip the door frame to stop myself from falling. Because there she is, standing on my doorstep staring back at me. There, after all this time, is Heather.

And I have imagined this, dreamed of this, dreaded this, so many hundreds of times for so many years that the reality is both entirely surreal and anticlimactic. I see and hear life continuing on this ordinary London

4

street on this ordinary afternoon – cars and people passing, children playing down the street, a dog barking – as if from far away, and as I stare into her face the sour taste of fear creeps around the back of my tongue. I open my mouth but no words come and we stand in silence for a while, two thirty-three-year-old versions of the girls we'd once been.

It's she who speaks first. 'Hello, Edie,' she says.

And then she does the unthinkable. She steps across the threshold (my heart jumping as she looms so close), wraps me in her arms and hugs me. I stand there rigid, enclosed, as memories slam into me: the wiry feel of her hair as it brushes against my cheek, that weird fried onions smell her clothes always had, her tall, heavy presence. My mind is empty, I am only my heart knocking in my throat and now she's following me into the hallway *no no no this is just one of your dreams* and up the stairs, past all the other doors with their brass letters and their chipped paint and we're at the top and I'm watching my hand as it pushes open my door and we're here inside my kitchen *no no no no no*, and we're sitting down at my table, and I'm staring into the face I'd once hoped never to see again for the rest of my life.

Neither of us speak at first and I'm filled with longing for my quiet, solitary life within these three cramped rooms of moments before. The tap drips, the seconds pass, the browning tendrils of my spider plant shiver on the windowsill. I get up so I don't have to look at her, and I turn away and grip the work surface. With my

5

back to her like this, I manage to speak. 'How'd you find me then?' I ask and when she doesn't answer I turn and see that she's gazing around the room, peering across the hallway to the narrow lounge with its fold-down bed.

'Hmm?' she says vaguely. 'Oh.' She looks at me. 'Your mum. Still lives in your old place, doesn't she.'

And I nod, although I hadn't known, because Mum and I haven't spoken in years and in that instant I'm back there, in the old Fremton house. We're in the kitchen, the strip light flickering, the blackness outside making mirrors of the windows. I'm crying and telling Mum everything, every single thing about what happened that night, as if telling her might stop the screaming in my head, clear the pictures from my mind. I tell her about Heather and Connor and what they did but it's like I'm telling her about some horror film or a nightmare I've had. I listen to myself say the words and I can't believe that what I'm saying is true. I don't stop talking until I've told her every last detail, and when I've finished, I reach for her, but Mum's body is rigid and her face grey with shock. She backs away from me, and never, never again in my life do I want someone to look at me the way she does then.

When she speaks she spits out her words like stones. 'Go to bed, Edith,' she says. 'And don't ever talk to me about this again. Do you hear me? I never want to hear about this again.' She turns her back then, staring at the window and I see her pinched, awful face reflected

6

in the glass. The next morning I get up before dawn, take some money from her purse and catch the train to my Uncle Geoff's in Erith, and I never go back there again.

I'm stunned by what Heather has told me: that my mother had my address to give her amazes me. My uncle never knew what caused the rift between us and always hoped that we would one day reconcile, so the fact he passed it on to her is no surprise. But that Mum had actually written it down and kept it safe somewhere is a revelation.

I suddenly feel exhaustion roll over me in waves, but I force myself to ask, 'What do you want, Heather? Why have you come here now?' Because I always knew, really, that this moment would come. Hadn't I dreamt about it night after night, woken in the small hours sick with the fear of it, looked over my shoulder certain it was approaching, out there somewhere, getting steadily closer?

She doesn't answer at first. On the table in front of her she's put her bag: a black woollen knitted thing with a chipped plastic button. Clinging to the wool are bits of fluff, crumbs, and lots of little ginger hairs – cat hairs, maybe. Her small hazel eyes peer at me beneath sparse pale lashes; she wears no make-up except for an incongruous smear of bright-pink lipstick that looks like it should be on someone else's face. In the silence a woman's voice drifts up to us from the street, *Terry . . . Terry . . . Terrrrrrr-eeeeeee . . .* and we listen to it dwindle and die, and at that moment the darkness over London pounces, that sad, final instant where daylight vanishes, the electric lights of the city suddenly strong, and I hear a faint tremor of hurt and reproach in Heather's voice as she says, 'Nothing. I don't want anything. I just wanted to see you.'

I try to make sense of this, my mind confusedly grasping at various possible explanations, but then she starts to speak again, and she says – with loneliness like an open wound, so raw and familiar that I have to turn my eyes from it – 'You were my best friend.'

'Yes,' I whisper. And because I have no idea what else to do I get up and put the kettle on and I make some tea while Heather talks, for all the world as though this is an ordinary visit – two old friends catching up: how she lives in Birmingham now ('We moved not long after you left'), the newsagent's where she works part-time.

As she talks I take in little glances. Such an ordinary-looking woman. A bit on the large side, her chubby hands folded in front of her on the table, her soft Welsh accent, her shoulder-length hair, her eager smile. 'Do you still live with your mum and dad?' I ask, for something to say, falling in with the game she's playing, if that's what this is. And she nods. Yes, I think – it would be hard, even now, to imagine her coping without them. She was never stupid, Heather, not backwards or anything like that – in fact she'd always done well at school. But despite her cleverness there'd always been an inexplicable something missing somehow, an innocence that made her vulnerable, too easily led astray. I sit down in the chair next to her. 'Heather,' I say quickly, before I lose my nerve, 'Heather, what do you want?'

Instead of answering, she reaches over and, taking me by surprise, gently pulls a strand of my hair between her fingers. 'Still so pretty, Edie,' she says, dreamily. 'You haven't changed a bit.' And I can't help it: I flinch so obviously that I have to get to my feet, clattering the tea things together in the sink, her eyes boring into my back.

'Can I see your flat?' she asks, and when I nod she goes and stands at the door to my tiny living room. I follow her, and together we look in at the cramped, dusty mess, the fold-down bed, the rail of clothes, the crappy, second-hand telly. 'It's lovely,' she says in a hushed voice, 'you're so lucky,' and I have to stifle a sudden desire to laugh. If you had asked me at sixteen what sort of person I would become, what sort of life my future self might lead, I would never have pictured this.

It occurs to me that she must have found her way to London by herself, before making her way through the city to get here, and I'm both impressed and horrified by this. The thought hits me that she might expect to stay the night, and the idea is so awful that I blurt, 'Heather, I'm sorry but I have to go out, I have to go out soon and it's been so nice to see you again but I really do have to—'

Her face falls. 'Oh.' She looks around the room

wistfully, disappointment etched into her face. 'Maybe I could stay here until you get back.'

She eyes my sofa hopefully and I try very hard to keep the panic from my voice as I lie, 'I'm going away for a few days actually, with friends,' and I begin to steer her back towards the kitchen. 'I'm sorry.' Reluctantly she nods and follows me to where she's left her coat and bag. I watch her, my heart sinking, knowing I should relent. She's only been here fifteen minutes after all. But I stand there as she puts her coat on, and I say nothing.

'Can I have your number?' she asks. 'I could phone you and then next time we could spend the day or even the weekend together.' There's such longing in her eyes that I feel myself nodding hopelessly, and she rummages eagerly in her bag. I watch her, my arms folded tightly, as she slowly punches my name into her mobile.

She looks up expectantly, but my posture or the angle in which I'm standing reveals something to her and as realization dawns, her mouth gapes. 'You're pregnant!' she says.

For the briefest moment I see something in her eyes that makes me shudder, though I don't know why – just for a second something else peeps out at me from behind her hazel stare. My hands fly defensively to my belly and an image, gone almost before it's there, of Heri's face flickers across my mind. I don't reply.

'Well,' she says after a silence, 'congratulations. How lovely.' As she continues to gaze at me her pupils twitch intently, and sensing that she's about to ask more questions, I rattle off my number and watch as she punches it in, agonizingly slowly, until finally I open the door, say goodbye as warmly as I know how, and at last she turns to leave. But before she does she stops and pauses and says very softly, 'Do you remember the quarry, Edie? How we used to go up there together, all of us?'

I feel momentarily light-headed, a wave of nausea washes over me, and when I speak my voice is barely a whisper. 'Yes.'

She nods. 'Me too. I think about it all the time.' And then she leaves, her sensible lace-ups clattering upon the staircase as she retreats lower and lower. I lean against the wall, weak with relief, until from far below I hear the front door's heavy slam as she closes it behind her, like a jailor.

Before

Year 11 leavers' day, and everywhere you look girls are writing on each other's shirts in felt-tip pen, drinking from Coke cans I think they've filled with something else, throwing flour bombs out of top-floor windows. I sit on the bench below the library window and watch. They're all going up to the rec later to get drunk – I'd heard them talking about it in the loos. They hadn't asked me, but I don't really mind because Mum always worries if I'm back late. I see Nicola Gates over by the water fountain, but she turns away when I wave.

And that's when I first see Edie. Walking across the forecourt in the direction of the main doors. As I watch, her face appearing then disappearing behind others in the crowd, she stops, her eyes squinting up at the building before darting around herself again and then finally landing upon me. I hold my breath. I don't think I've ever seen anyone so pretty before, not in real life.

Then there she is, standing right in front of me, and at first I'm too distracted by all the different parts of her to take in what she's saying: the smell of the leather jacket she's carrying over her arm, mixed with something else, something soft and appley, her eyes, big and golden brown with lots of black eyeliner, pale mauve varnish on her nails. In the hollow of her clavicle is a little gold locket with a tiny green stone in the middle. If you were to put your finger beneath it you'd feel the jump jump jump of her pulse.

'Sorry,' I say. 'What?'

She smiles. 'The office. Where is it?' Her voice is clear and sure with a northern accent – Manchester maybe.

Of all the people she could have stopped to ask, she'd picked me. I get to my feet. 'I'm going that way myself,' I tell her, though I wasn't. 'I'll walk with you if you like.'

She nods, shrugs. 'Yeah, OK. Ta.'

As we walk, I see Sheridan Alsop and Amy Carter standing by the water fountain. They stop talking and watch us as we pass. I have a mad impulse to link my arm through hers, this stranger who walks beside me, and I imagine us strolling along like that, arm in arm like best friends. How amazed Amy and Sheridan would be to see that! I don't though, of course. People don't like it when you do that sort of thing, I've realized.

'My name's Heather,' I tell her instead.

14

'I'm Edie. Well, Edith really. But how lame's that?' She looks around herself then shakes her head, 'Bloody hell, this place.'

'Yeah,' I say. 'I know! Totally lame, isn't it? Are you going to come to school here then?'

She nods. 'Starting my A-levels in September.'

'I'm doing my A-levels here too! What're you studying? I'm taking Biology and Maths and Chemistry. I was going to do a language as well but Mum and Dad said it was pointless because it's not what I need to read Medicine at uni. Best to concentrate on just the three. What with all my volunteering work and everything too. I'm going to be a doctor one day and—' I stop myself, my mouth snapping shut. I always talk too much, Mum says. I bite my lip, waiting for Edie to look at me the way the other girls do.

But she doesn't, she only smiles again. Her long brown hair swings in front of her face and she pushes it away, tucking it behind her ear. 'I'm doing Art,' she tells me. 'And photography. I'm going to go to art college in London. Saint Martins probably,' she adds with breezy certainty. And she explains that she's recently moved down here to Fremton from Manchester with her mum. She has this way of talking, like she's a bit bored by everything, looking around herself like she finds it all a bit of a joke, but all the while glancing back at me, including me as if I'm in on the joke too. It's nice. I could stare at her for hours.

We've already reached the office, even though I'd

taken her the long way round. 'It's in here,' I say, and I'm about to tell her that I'll wait for her, that I'll show her around after if she wants, but she's already moving away. 'OK. Thanks, yeah?' she says. 'See you later.'

The door swings shut behind her. Edie. *Eedee*. I turn the word over and over in my mind on the walk home, trying it out for size, tucking it away for safekeeping like it's a precious locket on a fine gold chain.

'Heather . . . *Heather* . . . HEATHER!' My head snaps upwards and I look around my bedroom in a daze. How long had it been this time? 'Heather!' My mother's voice, its note of irritation rising as she calls me from the kitchen, propels me to my feet. I look around myself for clues. I'm dressed in my school uniform, my bag of books by my desk. It's light outside, but definitely an evening sort of light, I think. Slowly it comes back to me. It had been the last day of term before exams started. I had returned home from school and come up here to begin my revision and then . . . it must have just happened, the way it sometimes does, and I never know why. Almost as though I fall asleep while I'm wide awake. It usually happens when I'm upset or angry, like the time with Daniel Jones, the boy who'd bullied me all through primary. I hadn't even known I'd hit him till I saw the blood. A jumble of my classmates' voices, past and present, crowds in on me, mingling to make one long mocking hiss. *What's wrong with you? Why do you stare like that? Weirdo. Fucking freak.* I shake my head to clear it.

16

My dad collects clocks and there are hundreds of them in our house all ticking at once, like the air is shivering, chattering its teeth. I listen, and sure enough after a few moments, there it is: the clanging jangle of dings and dongs as they all strike the hour at once. I count to seven. Teatime, then. My mother's never late. The thought of her downstairs sat at the kitchen table waiting to begin grace jolts me into action. 'Coming!' I shout. 'I'm coming!'

Downstairs, Dad sits at the kitchen table reading aloud from a newspaper article about geological engineering. Mum moves around the kitchen not listening to him, transferring plates of food from the worktop to the table in front of us. I watch her, trying to gauge her mood, but she puts the last plate down and without looking at me, sits and begins to pray.

Sometimes Mum reminds me of the lake where we used to go camping back home in Wales. I'd wade through its water on hot summer days, occasionally chancing upon inexplicable pockets of ice-cold, before blundering further into a shallower, warmer patch. I'd stay there for as long as possible, wallowing in the sunny warmth until the touch of slimy seaweed or the thought of eels or dead fish slipping past my ankles would make me panic and press on. Being with Mum is like that sometimes: you never know where the cold pockets are, or what's there waiting for you in the warmer spells.

'Heather!' My mother stops mid-prayer and I realize too late that I'd been absent-mindedly picking at the tomato salad.

'Sorry,' I say, and feel myself redden.

Sometimes I do this thing to help me sleep: pretend that everything's as it was before, that I am six again and Lydia three, and we're all still OK. I imagine Lydia's hand in mine as we run together in the garden of our old house and hear her laughter as I fall asleep.

As if to rescue me from my thoughts the face of the girl I'd met that afternoon pops into my head, and I feel a sort of light, lifting in my heart. *Edie*.

Fremton's a horrible town. I shouldn't say that, but it's true. We moved here from Wales when I was ten – a fresh start, Mum said. After what happened, people in our village who I'd known all my life suddenly looked differently at me when I passed them in the street, or else swooped down on my parents like big black greedy crows, cawing sympathy, pecking for answers.

Eventually Mum and Dad stopped doing the things they used to do. Slowly, bit by bit, Mum pulled out of choir practice, her book group, organizing school fetes. Except for church on Sundays, she barely left the house at all. Dad carried on teaching at the boys' school across the valley but at home he found refuge in his study, mending his clocks and reading his books. I guess from the outside it might have looked like we were shutting out the world to find comfort in each other, but it wasn't like that at all. My mum and dad cleaved like a stricken tree, me like a lost squirrel hopping between the two halves. Dad had never looked at me in the same way after it happened and Mum didn't either, but it was different with her. With Mum I knew in my heart that she wished it was Lydia who had come home safe and sound that day, not me.

So when they told me one evening after supper that Dad had been offered a new job in an English town 160 miles away, that it meant a promotion and a bigger house, I knew the real reason for the move: we would be going somewhere nobody knew about us, about what had happened, and what it meant. And a month later here we were. But nothing changed, not really. My mum found a new church to go to, but apart from that she still hardly ever leaves the house. These days her focus is on me. My schoolwork, my weight, my piano practice, my future. She's trying to make me better, I think.

Now that the exams are over I have seven empty weeks to fill, so when I'm not helping Mum around the house or doing my volunteering work there's nothing much else to do but walk. Fremton's right next to the motorway, so wherever you are you can hear it, the never-ending rush of traffic on its way to somewhere else. The whole town feels like it's been forgotten somehow, like everyone upped sticks and left years ago. There's a canal that runs through the middle but no one goes down there very much and the shops in the square are mostly empty since the superstore opened on the Wrexham road. There's a big statue of a miner in the centre of the square, carrying a sack of coals on his back, but someone's spray-painted a big orange willy on his head. Then there's just streets and streets of council houses till you get to the Pembroke Estate, three high towers pushed right up against the motorway, like they're standing guard, warning outsiders away.

Wherever I go I look out for Edie, my eyes scanning the faces I pass, hoping that one day one of them will be hers. I think about her smile and her brown eyes and how nice she'd been to me and I wonder what she's doing and where she lives, whether she's bored or by herself like me. Then, out of the blue, I see her again. I'm walking home through the square when I spy her sitting on a bench by the statue, smoking a cigarette. I stop in a shop doorway to watch her. She's wearing a short denim skirt and her legs are long and tanned, stretched out in front of her, a silver chain around one ankle. Her hair hangs loose around her shoulders and she smokes her cigarette like she's deep in thought. She looks beautiful. It's as if she shines against the greyness of this town, I think, like she's full of light. I hesitate before half raising my hand to wave and I'm about to call her name when someone cuts across in front of me and reaches her first. My hand falls to my side, her name catching in my throat.

I can't see him properly, whoever he is, this person who's come between the two of us. I only know that his effect on her is instant, her face and neck flushing pink, her eyes wide and bright. She listens to what he says, laughs and glances away, but only for a second, as though her eyes can't quite help being drawn back to him. And then he sits down next to her, so close that their arms touch. He says something and she shakes her head, a smile hovering upon her lips, and I don't know what it is, this strange heat that's there in the crackling, held-breath space between them, I only know that it has no place for me.

As quickly as it began, it's over. He leans in close and murmurs one last thing in her ear that makes two red spots appear high on her cheeks before he gets up and walks away. I get a clearer look at him now. He's dressed in tracksuit bottoms, a zipped-up jacket with a hood. He's about twenty or so and very handsome, I suppose, though I don't like his face at all, its roughness and its smile that shows he knows she's watching him still. I wait for a few moments more, in the shadow of the shop's doorway, before I take a breath and go to her.

When I'm there, standing in front of her, saying her name, she looks at me so strangely, as though she hardly knows where she is, tearing her eyes from his retreating back and blinking up at me. 'Edie?' I say again, and the moment lengthens until, at last, her expression clears and she smiles and says, 'Oh, hiya! Heather, right?' and my heart somersaults with relief.

After

A new family's moving into one of the ground-floor flats today. I stand by the window and watch them; a couple of teenage lads lugging furniture from a van, while a small, ginger, tattooed woman shouts directions from the kerb. As I watch, she raises her arm to point at something and her top rides up to reveal a long, red scar running the entire width of her back and I find myself wondering how she got it, what could possibly have happened to leave such an awful wound behind. Best part of an hour it takes them, the two, grim-faced boys towering over their mother as they traipse back and forth beneath boxes, a sofa, a fridge, watched all the while from the van's front seat by a shining black lump of muscle and teeth that barks and barks and barks.

My hands fall to the warm curve of my belly. The

decision to keep it, the baby, was never consciously made, I just never went through with getting rid of it. I got as far as making the appointment, booking myself in at a clinic, but when the time came for me to put on my coat and take myself to the bus stop, I simply didn't. My coat stayed where it was, I stayed where I was, and the seconds and minutes ticked by until the time had passed, my appointment had been and gone, and the phone with which I could call and reschedule remained untouched. I had never actively wanted a child – motherhood was something that happened to other women, not to me – yet some stubborn, unexamined part of me clung to the life growing in my belly, and it clung stubbornly to me.

The boys carry the last of the boxes from the van and are followed into the building by the woman and the dog. Within minutes I hear the sound of banging coming from the ground floor, the repeated *thwack* of a hammer echoing up the stairwell, and I stay where I am for a while longer, staring out at the street, watching the afternoon traffic pass until the hammering stops and the sound of a drill takes its place.

Heri, my baby's father, was a chef at the restaurant where I waitress. Like me he worked more and longer shifts than everyone else and we were often left to lock up together, sometimes sharing a beer after a long night. He would tell me about his home in Tunisia, about lagoons and deserts and the sirocco winds. I liked him; I liked that he didn't push his nose into my life, never asked questions I didn't want to answer, liked that he was always somehow self-contained and by himself, like me.

The night we spent together was not unexpected, but never repeated. An attraction that had always been there flickering into life one evening and, for no particular reason, acted upon. From the window of his bedsit you could see the floodlit grounds of Charlton Athletic Football Club. 'You see!' he said proudly as we stood looking out. 'The very best seats for free!' He'd shaken his head sadly as he added, 'You English really can't play football.' We drank beer and talked about our corner of south-east London. The only possessions he seemed to own were lined up on the windowsill: a book, a metal tin, some writing paper and pens, a photograph of a woman with a small boy. His clothes were folded neatly on a chair, his bed a single mattress pushed up against the wall.

'You are a strange one,' he said, turning to me, his large, almost black eyes watching me in the half-light. 'So beautiful, work so hard, so quiet.'

I continued to stare out at the illuminated pitch.

'You never talk about yourself,' he went on. 'Why are you not married, not . . .' He shrugged, and when still I didn't reply, he reached over and brushed a strand of hair from my face.

We undressed in the yellow glow of the floodlights, his skin dark and warm against my paleness; a night's comfort. And afterwards our friendship had continued exactly as it had before. When the day came for his wife and little boy to join him over here, I was happy for him and wished him well. He left the restaurant soon after for an office-cleaning job the three could do together and even after I learnt I was pregnant the thought of contacting him never occurred to me.

And the child inside me grows. I don't think about what will happen after it's born; a strange calmness possesses me: what will be will be.

In the weeks following Heather's visit she phones me repeatedly, sometimes several times a day. I never answer. Instead I watch as my mobile vibrates and buzzes, the unfamiliar number flashing on the screen, my stomach twisting queasily. Sometimes she leaves a message, but I delete them all unlistened to. It's six weeks before the calls stop abruptly one day. Life begins to return to normal, the water closing over the disturbance that she'd made, my pregnancy taking over my thoughts once more, leaving no room for anything else, not even her.

But out of the blue like a carefully aimed dart, she pierces my life again. A few days after the woman and her two lads move in downstairs, I spot the postman approaching from my window and go down to collect my mail, expecting an appointment letter from the hospital. As I pass the new tenants' ground-floor flat I hear the sound of bolts being drawn and keys turning in their locks before the door opens a crack, stopped by a heavy thick chain. Someone peers out at me through

26

the slim black gap as I pass. For a few seconds I feel myself being watched until finally the door closes again. I hear the locks turn and the bolts shoot home once more.

Amongst the scattered envelopes lies one that's pink and square. I don't remember ever seeing Heather's handwriting before, but I know instinctively that it's from her. The physical presence of it makes my scalp crawl but I return with it upstairs, carrying it like some dead and rotten thing between my fingertips. There on my kitchen table it sits. I leave it unopened, curling up in a ball on my sofa, my legs tucked beneath me, my arms tight around my bump. The minutes tick by until with quick decisiveness I run into the kitchen, snatch up the envelope and tear it open. Along with a piece of pink notepaper a photograph falls out, landing face down on the floor.

My hands trembling, I pick up the letter and quickly scan the words. *Dear Edie,* it says.

I've tried to phone you loads but I think I've got the wrong number. Can I come back and see you? Here's my number at the top. Please phone me.
   Lots of love from Heather Wilcox. XOXO
   PS. I found this photo of us! LOL! You can keep it if you want!! X

Eventually, reluctantly, I pick up the picture and look

at it. It's of Heather and me. I'm sitting just in front of her by the quarry and I'm smiling up at the camera, holding my hand out as if to defend myself from its lens, my fingers a big pink blur in the foreground. Heather is looking away, staring off down the hill. I'm shocked at how childish we look, our faces plump and stupid with youth. But the picture's not of us, not really. Even though he's the one taking the picture, it's of Connor. He is in the expression in my eyes and in the shadow that streaks across the grass between Heather and me. Connor. In my flat the walls feel a little closer, the air a little harder to breathe. A wave of nausea hits me and I have to run to the sink to vomit up the bile that floods my mouth.

Opening the kitchen window I crawl out on to the flat roof of the neighbour's bedsit below, gulping at the fresh air until the sickness begins to pass. Usually I love to sit out here, high above the city spread out before me in all its noisy, dirty glory, comforted by its vastness and indifference. It's not true what they say about London, that it looks down on the rest of the country – in fact London's barely aware of the England that lies beyond its borders. In its self-absorbed bubble, towns like Fremton and all they represent barely figure, and that has always suited me just fine.

But now, even as the sickness recedes, I see only Connor's face, the moment he'd first approached me in the square, and I feel a reflexive cold punch to my guts. I remember how the sight of him had made the rest of the world vanish, how immediate and physical it had all been. I had never seen anyone so beautiful. He'd asked me for a light, in that quiet voice of his that was like cigarettes, like syrup. Then he'd sat down next to me as if he didn't doubt for a second I'd want him to. I think he asked me what my name was, where I was from. It didn't matter: all I knew was that I'd never ever seen eyes like his before; never in my life had I seen such beautiful green eyes.

I shudder. Far below me is the building's communal garden, full of abandoned furniture and bags of rubbish. As I watch, one of the new lads from the ground-floor flat appears with his dog and it squats down next to a fridge freezer while he waits. The boy, about seventeen or so, tall and well built, smokes a cigarette and fiddles idly with his mobile, oblivious to me up here looking down at him. I will be due at the restaurant soon and I need to catch the bus to another seven-hour shift, earning all the money I can before the baby comes. I make myself get up and, resolving to throw the letter and photo in the bin, crawl back through my kitchen window. But at the sight of them lying there on my table I freeze then barely notice as I sink into a chair.

Beyond my window the light begins to change as the afternoon wears on, an ice-cream van's chimes jangle in the warm, close air, the school-run traffic picks up, slowly, rain begins to fall. But I'm only dimly aware of these things. Despite my best intentions I am entirely back there at the Wrexham quarry, the night before I left for good, memories slamming into me one after another: the confusion and panic, the awful, terrifying screams as everything spiralled out of control. Here in my flat the last seventeen years vanish, meaningless and unreal compared to the tangible, unforgettable horror of that night.

What does Heather want from me now? What could she possibly want from me now?

Heather seems to haunt me in the days and weeks that follow. I imagine I smell her sour, oniony scent wherever I go, I keep glimpsing her from the corner of my eye, or hear her voice amongst others in the street, causing me to turn sharply, seeking her out with a pounding heart, only to find that she isn't there at all.

When my Uncle Geoff phones one day out of the blue, I'm relieved almost to the point of tears when he tells me he's coming round, so grateful am I for the distraction. He sits here now, filling my tiny kitchen with his comforting smell of cologne and cigar smoke, his broad Manchester accent familiar and soothing. I feel his eyes on me, watching me fondly as I make him tea, and for the first time since Heather turned up again, I begin to relax.

'You all right then, Edie love?' he says.

'Yeah, you know. Not bad.'

'Not long till the little one arrives.'

'No, not long now.'

He takes the tea I offer him and says, 'Be the making of you, I reckon. You'll be a great mum, you'll see.'

I smile back at him, touched. 'Thanks, Uncle Geoff.'

'Everything going well with that fella of yours, is it?'

I nod, and we drop each other's gaze. He knows as well as I do there's no fella on the scene, but he's too tactful to say. I've always loved that about him, his unquestioning, steady support. I think about how he'd taken me in when I first arrived on his doorstep at seventeen, how kind he'd been to me, and the memory calms me and gives me strength.

When he leaves again a few hours later, I watch him from my window setting off down the street, and my heart tightens with love for him. He's nearly sixty now and I'd only ever known him as a bachelor, though Mum had told me he'd been married once, years before, to a woman who'd run off and broken his heart. He never speaks about her, but you can somehow see the memory of her there still, in his eyes and his smile, the way they do remain a part of us, those people who have hurt us very deeply, or who we have hurt, never letting us go, not entirely.

Before

In the square, Edie shivers and stands up, squashing with her foot the cigarette she'd been smoking. 'Where're you off to?' she asks, and when I tell her I'm heading home she smiles and says, 'I'll walk with you.' And just like that it's as though the man, whoever he was and whatever went on between them, is forgotten.

'Great,' I say, 'fantastic!'

She bends to pick up her bag, and as she does her skirt rides up to show her knickers. I quickly look away. 'GCSE results will be in pretty soon,' I say hurriedly, as we begin to walk. Her bare arm brushes mine, the fine hairs on both mingling briefly together.

'Yeah? How do you think you did?'

I shrug. 'OK, I guess. I was predicted ten As, so . . .'

She turns to me, wide-eyed. 'Ten As? *Ten As?*' She whistles. 'Wow, brainbox, huh?'

I glance at her, trying to work out if she's saying this in the same way Sheridan Alsop would, as though there's something mystifyingly pathetic about me doing well at school, but then I see her admiring smile and my tummy dips with happiness.

'God, I wish I was clever,' she says a few moments later. 'I did my GCSEs last year. Total disaster! Got to retake some of them while I do my A-levels.' I notice again how nice her voice is. Loud and clear and confident, her words spilling out quickly in her Manchester accent. She's delving into her bag and eventually pulls out another cigarette. She lights it, and offers one to me. 'No?' she says, when I shake my head. 'Very wise. Wish I'd never started.' She laughs, a lovely, warm throaty sound, and says, 'See? Not very bright, am I?' She walks as though she's on springs, her long legs striding, her chin held high. I trudge next to her, feeling too hot, my thighs rubbing together.

Hesitantly I say, 'I could . . . I mean, I could help you, if you want. With your GCSEs – your coursework and stuff.'

She looks at me in surprise. 'For real? That would be amazing!' She bumps her shoulder against mine. 'Seriously, that's really nice of you.'

I bite my lip, trying to contain the smile that's threatening to split my face in two.

We walk in silence for a while but as we leave the square she tells me why she moved to Fremton. 'It's my nan's old place, but she died last year. My mum had a

34

car accident and she can't work any more, so we moved down here to save on rent while she gets better.'

'Oh, I'm sorry about your mum,' I say.

'Don't be,' she replies breezily. 'She'll be fine. She doesn't care about me anyway, and neither does my dad – not that I've seen him for years.'

I'm shocked by her words, how casually she says them – I could never imagine speaking about my own parents like that.

'You're easy to talk to, you know,' she says suddenly.

'Am I?'

'Yeah. Haven't you noticed how most people when you're talking to them are just waiting till it's their turn to speak? You actually listen. It's nice.' Her face darkens and she adds, 'Not that I've had *anyone* to talk to since Mum dragged me away from all my friends – and *she* certainly doesn't give a shit, that's for sure.'

I don't know what to say to this, and we walk in silence until we turn the corner into Heartfields, where I live, and she brightens again. 'How about you, anyway? You lived here long?'

So I tell her about our old village in Wales, and how we moved down here, and though I don't mention Lydia or the way my parents barely speak to each other any more, I somehow find enough to say that we're almost at my house before I realize I haven't stopped talking once. 'Sorry,' I say, putting my hand to my mouth. 'I'm going on and on, aren't I?'

She shrugs. 'So?'

'Mum says you should only speak if you can improve upon the silence.'

'Yeah?' She raises her eyebrows. 'Your mum sounds like a right laugh.'

'No,' I say, surprised. 'No, she's really not.'

She smiles at that, but I'm not sure why.

'Come on,' she puts her arm through mine, 'this your street, is it?'

I hadn't expected Edie to actually want to come home with me, but she follows me up our front path and waits expectantly as I dig around for my keys. 'Wow,' she says. 'Nice house.' And as I look at her I see Edie through my mother's eyes: the make-up and short skirt, the cigarette that she's only now dropping to the ground. Sure enough, as soon as I open the door, Mum appears, stopping in her tracks in the hallway as she looks past me to Edie.

'Mum,' I say nervously, 'this is—' but Edie walks in front of me, giving Mum a big smile. 'Hiya, I'm Edie. I'm going to be starting at Heather's school. Wow,' she adds, gazing around herself, 'look at all those clocks, bet you're never late, are you?'

'Um, no,' my mother replies faintly as I grab hold of Edie's arm.

'Come on,' I say, 'let's go to my room,' and together we run up the stairs, laughter bubbling in my chest, leaving my mum standing by herself in the hall, staring after us.

When I close my bedroom door I look at Edie standing

36

by my bed and feel suddenly shy. 'I love your skirt,' I tell her at last. 'And your hair.' I look down at my own clothes bought for me by Mum. 'I wish I looked like you.'

'Don't be daft,' she says, wandering over to my dressing table and picking up a tube of spot cream. 'You should see me without my make-up.'

'I don't wear any,' I admit. 'I don't know how to do it.'

'I can show you if you want.' She rummages in her bag and pulls out some mascara and lipstick. 'This is all I've got, though. How about you?'

I hesitate, not sure whether to show her at first, but then I figure of all the things I could share with her, all the secrets I could reveal about myself, this one's probably not the worst. I go and lift a shoebox down from the top of my wardrobe and pull off the lid. We both stare down at its contents: a mass of unopened lipsticks, mascaras, foundations and eye shadows. I have everything, in every shade.

Edie whistles. 'Wow. Where'd you get the money for all that?'

'I suppose I . . . well, actually . . . I stole them.' Even as I say the words the feeling I get when I do it comes back to me; the awful, almost sickening fear of how terrible the consequences would be if I were caught somehow only making it more addictive. I never wear any of it, though – it's like I have no desire for it once I've slipped it up my sleeve in Boots.

She's still staring at me open-mouthed. 'What, shop-lifted?' She says it so loudly and sounds so scandalized that I glance at my closed door in alarm.

'Shussh!' I hiss urgently. Our eyes meet and though I have no idea why, we both burst out laughing. And pretty soon we can't seem to stop. The laughter gathers and swells until neither of us can speak, and finally I have to sit on the bed and hold my stomach, barely able to breathe. I have never laughed like this with anyone before. I don't even know exactly what's so funny. Edie flops down next to me and I look at her and I think, *I love you.*

'Come on,' she says, and taking my hand pulls me up off the bed and sits me in front of my dressing-table mirror. She starts with my hair, picking up my brush and running it gently through my thick yellow frizz. I close my eyes. The touch of her hands on me, the slow, patient stroke of the brush, it's all so wonderful, so lovely. I can smell the cigarette smoke on her fingers, a scent of apples when she moves. A hush falls, there's only the ticking of the clocks beyond my closed door and the sound of the bristles against my scalp.

And then, into the silence, she says, 'Did you see that lad I was talking to, in the square?'

I open my eyes. The brush stops. When I look up at her reflection I find her watching me, waiting for a response. 'Yes,' I admit.

'Had you ever seen him before?'

I shake my head.

38

'Me neither. He said his name was Connor.' And by the way she says it, I somehow know that she has longed to say the name out loud, loves the shape and sound of it on her tongue.

There's a silence. 'He seemed to like you,' I offer at last, understanding that it's what she wants, and instantly her face lights up.

'You think?' A strange half-smile plays around her lips as she turns back to her reflection in the mirror, and I can tell that she's no longer here with me, that it's him in the room with her now, not me.

Even before we reach the top of the hill we hear it: the screams and music and the dull roar of generators, loudspeaker voices and a klaxon's wail. And then, there we are, Edie and I, looking down at it all spread out below us, the coloured lights and the big wheel and the people and the caravans and the stalls. A magical, other world transported into the middle of Braxton fields.

Edie nudges me in the ribs and I look down to see a bottle of vodka in her hand. I shake my head but when she grins and thrusts it at me again, something makes me hesitate. Real life recedes and in its place I see spread out below me in the lights and music and laughter a million shimmering possibilities. On impulse I take the bottle from her and swig it back, the liquid choking and burning my throat, making me splutter while Edie laughs. 'Come on,' she says, grabbing my hand, and we run down the hill together, to where the fair waits for us, the vodka trailing excitement through me like a firework.

I can't believe I'm here, that my parents have let me come. I'd walked in on one of their arguments earlier, too excited by Edie's phone call to notice the sound of voices hissing from beneath the closed kitchen door like a gas leak. I think Dad had let me go to make Mum cross. 'For pity's sake, Jennifer, she's sixteen,' he'd said, and I ran to get my coat, not daring to catch Mum's eye, my head already full of Edie and of what we'd do tonight.

And now here we are in the midst of it all: little kids with fluorescent rings around their necks, candy floss and giant cuddly toys and goldfish in bags, groups of lads with cans of beer and girls shrieking on the Hearts and Diamonds. A loudspeaker booms a thudding bass as we stand by a ride called Moon Rocket that sends a cage of screaming people soaring into the air. It's amazing, the colours and noise and lights, but when I turn to Edie I suddenly realize that she's scanning the crowds as if searching for something. 'Are you all right?' I ask her.

She shrugs. 'Yeah, sure. What shall we go on? Have you got any money?' Excitedly I pull out the handful of notes I'd grabbed from my savings box before coming tonight and her eyes widen. 'Christ, Heather,' she laughs. 'You been robbing banks now too?'

We go on everything, running from ride to ride. I don't mind paying for everything at all. I drink more vodka and I laugh and scream as if, were I to stop for a moment, the night might end, the fair and all its possibilities might vanish. But when I notice again Edie's distracted expression I understand with a stab of disappointment that it's him she's looking for, the lad from the square – it's him who she came for tonight. And soon I'm searching him out too, in the gaps between the rides where the fair's bright lights don't quite reach, faces lingering in the shadows, mouths sucking on cigarettes and sipping from cans. Strangers' eyes flickering back at us, but he's not there.

The last ride we go on is the waltzers and we spin round and round, the speed and the motion causing Edie to slide along the plastic seat towards me. I feel her softness and her hard angles as she lands against me, catch the scent of her hair. We're dizzy when we get off, giddy and disorientated and laughing, but I look up and there he is. Standing with some other lads a few metres away, down by the side of the dodgems, huddled over something that they're passing between them. It's him. He's half-turned away from us but it's definitely Connor, and suddenly he looks up, his face flashing red, yellow, purple, green, his eyes scanning the crowds before landing on Edie, dark and steady as the barrels of a gun.

I try to steer her away but I'm too late. Her eyes are locked on his and it's as if he's a magician, a hypnotist, the way she goes to him, as though sleepwalking, as though the rest of the world and all its light and music has vanished. I trail after her and just before she reaches him I pull on her arm. 'What?' she asks, without looking away from him, without dropping his eyes, even for a second.

'It's late. I better go home.'

'OK,' she says, already moving off again. 'I'll see you later, yeah?'

'Aren't you coming?'

'No.' She shrugs off my hand and I feel a sharp slap of rejection. 'Go home,' she says. 'I'm staying here.' And she moves away, to where he's waiting for her. For a moment I watch her go before I turn back through the crowds alone.

After

The floorboards are bare except for a large, colourful rug, the shelves full of paperback books. Somewhere, down the hall, a crackling record plays a song by a man with a scratchy, rasping voice. I sit on the sofa alone, twisting my fingers together, wishing I hadn't come. Above my head, occasional thumps and dragging sounds are interrupted by intermittent swearing: the man who had opened the door to me three minutes ago had clearly forgotten I was coming. 'Won't be long,' he shouts, and I go to the bay window to look out at the street.

This part of New Cross is different from mine. The neat terraced houses have freshly painted front doors in muted shades of green or blue or grey; little olive trees stand neatly outside them in terracotta pots. Down the road a pub that had once been dilapidated for years has tables and hanging baskets out front, where couples drink beer in the sunshine, their babies asleep in expensive buggies. I turn back to the room and look around me, taking in the books, the prints on the walls, the stylish furniture and rugs – the sort of place I'd once imagined myself living, in fact. And I think about that old me as if of a stranger, so certain I'd been that the world would be mine for the taking one day.

At that moment a boy of about five walks into the room. He's mixed race and very lovely looking with a cloud of light brown Afro hair and deep blue eyes. He's gazing at me very seriously, as if unsure whether I'm real or not. 'Hi there,' I say after a silence, just as the man returns, carrying with effort a cot.

'Here you go,' he says, smiling. 'Sorry about that.' He puts his hand on the boy's head and they watch me scrabble about in my bag for my purse.

'Thirty, was it?' I ask.

He nods and takes the money I hand him. 'Cheers. You want me to dismantle it to put in your car, or do you have a van or something?' It's only then that I realize – and the stupidity of it leaves me gaping at him with embarrassment – I had entirely forgotten to think about how I'd get it home.

The child and his father look back at me expectantly. Down the hall, the record comes to an end. 'I don't have a car,' I admit.

He looks at me in surprise, his gaze dropping to my seven-month bump. 'Were you going to carry it home on your back?'

44

And so, several minutes later, despite my many protestations, I find myself sat between the boy, whose name I learn is Stan, and the man who tells me he's called James, in the front seat of a battered pickup truck, being driven home with the cot sliding and rattling behind us. I'm overcome with embarrassment.

'Stop apologizing,' James says. 'It's no trouble, really.'

I glance sideways at him. He's nice enough looking, with very black skin and an attractive, open face, but though he's in his thirties and well spoken, he's wearing a bizarre assortment of clothes: a neon orange jumper with army trousers and paint-splattered boots, his hair cut in peroxide blond tufts. He looks like a student, or a homeless person, I think. During the short drive he's never quiet or still, whistling between his teeth, commenting on other people's driving, asking me questions about when I'm due, what I do, where I'm from, all the while ruffling his son's hair, thumping the horn or drumming his fingers against the steering wheel. I can't think of anything to say to him. He's exhausting and I'm relieved when we reach my building at last.

He jumps out and starts unloading the cot on to the pavement. 'You got someone to help you carry it in?' he asks. 'Which floor do you live on?'

I shrug. 'It's OK. I can manage.'

He looks at me and I see it dawn on him that there's no one to help. 'Don't be silly,' he says. 'I'll give you a hand.'

45

And I feel hemmed in by his persistence, his insistence on helping me. I wish he would leave the cot and me alone here on the street. But up the three flights of stairs he follows me, carrying the cot awkwardly, swearing under his breath each time he bangs it against his shin, the little boy trailing after us.

When I open the door to my flat, the threadbare carpet, the old, ugly furniture and the dirty paintwork look suddenly much worse than they did half an hour before. 'Put it anywhere,' I say. He hoists it through into the lounge, knocking a shelf and sending its contents scattering, magazines and old bills and a dozen or so loose pages of drawings falling at our feet. I kneel down, hurriedly grabbing at the pictures and stuffing them back into the folder. But it's too late: he plucks one from where it landed on his foot and begins examining it. 'These yours?' he asks, and I feel my face begin to burn, so painful is it to have this stranger – anyone at all – look at my sketches; my inky landscapes peopled by their spindly ghosts.

I hold out my hand to take it from him, but he's still engrossed. 'This is actually really good,' he says slowly, and then he looks at me, his expression different now, curious, reassessing. 'Do you paint too, or just draw?' he asks, 'Because I—'

But I snatch the drawing from his hand. 'No, I don't do anything,' I say, stuffing it back into the folder and moving away.

There's a brief, surprised silence. I look at the door.

'Right,' he says stiffly. 'Sorry,' and he takes his son's hand and starts to leave.

'Thanks for the cot,' I manage to mumble when they reach the door, and he smiles again his easy smile.

'No problem.' It's a nice smile, and for a second or two I allow myself to return it, until Connor's face flashes across my mind and I turn away with a thumping heart, busying myself with the scattered papers while they let themselves out, closing the door behind them.

As my belly grows I find myself thinking increasingly of my mum. I wonder what she felt like being pregnant with me, whether she felt as scared as I do, whether she loved me right away. She was only seventeen when I was born and for as long as I can remember we fought and bickered like sisters. I was six when my dad walked out and I blamed her for his leaving. And yet, in my heart, I always knew we loved each other, a part of me understanding that the passion with which we hurt each other came from something strong enough to withstand the blows we inflicted. Looking back, I guess I always felt that we would have time to work things out eventually, not imagining what was to come; that we would one day have to cut all ties and never speak again.

When I first came to London and lived with Uncle Geoff I would hear him sometimes on the phone to her, passing on news of how I was doing. Sometimes, when he thought I was out of earshot, I would hear him asking her to talk to me, but she never would and I never picked up the phone myself. I don't blame her for cutting me off, because I left her no choice, not really. If I'd stayed she would have had to have done something, told someone about what happened that night, so by turning her back she was protecting me in a way. And I think, now, that by confessing to her, I was looking for her to force an end to it all – to put a stop to Connor and me.

And still I dream about Heather. Night after night my sleeping mind replays what happened between us in Fremton. I see us at the quarry, all of us: Heather and me, Connor and Niall, Rabbit and Boyo and Tully and the rest. Even the same music is playing on the car stereo and I see again the sinking sun as it stains the quarry's water red and gold. In the small hours when I wake, breathless and panicky after reliving it all again, I try to make sense of Heather's behaviour when she visited me. How she'd acted as though nothing had happened back then, as though we were just old friends catching up. Sometimes, in the long sleepless hours before dawn, I wonder if I'd imagined it all, been mistaken somehow in the part she played that night – perhaps time and memory had played tricks, distorted things. But even before the thought has properly formed I know that I'm deluding myself. Whatever it is that Heather wants from me now, nothing can change that.

I'm on my way to the hospital and letting myself out of the front door when the new tenant, the ginger woman from the ground-floor flat, arrives on the steps in front of me, and I look at her with curiosity as I hold the door open for her. She's very thin and covered in tattoos – a tapestry of names and patterns and hearts and flowers that seems to cover every inch of her. I smile but she doesn't look at me and though I'm not sure what it is about her that makes me want to talk to her I tentatively clear my throat and say, 'Hi, I'm Edie, I live—' But she only nods curtly in response, avoiding my gaze and turning her back on me abruptly as she lets herself into her flat, closing the door behind her. I stare after her, before beginning the long, slow process of getting myself to the hospital.

These days I'm more belly than person; a bump on legs, as if I, or the person I was, has been entirely replaced by my unborn child. And the rest of the world seems to collude in this. In the street, elderly women reach out with narrowed, hungry eyes to touch my belly as though, Buddha-like, it might bring them luck. At my hospital visits I wait, obedient and detached as I'm weighed and measured and scanned and tested, and I feel entirely separate from the life that's growing inside me. I faithfully attend every appointment and read every leaflet and booklet that's pressed on me, but if I try to imagine the baby inside me I find that I can't. When the midwife asks me if I want to know the gender I shake my head in panic, because I only know that I have one wish: I hope with all my heart that it isn't a girl.

The bus takes me through New Cross towards Camberwell, winding through narrow back roads then

49

on to Peckham High Street, past dusty, sun-baked shop-fronts, the jumbled mixture of Georgian terraces and council blocks, strings of nail bars and chicken shops and newly arrived delis and fashionable bars. When we reach Denmark Hill twenty minutes later, the sprawl of King's College Hospital looms to my right, the low Victorian red bricks of the Maudsley psychiatric unit to my left. I get off at the busy intersection and begin to head towards the maternity unit.

Just as I'm turning into the main entrance I glance across the road and freeze. A woman is standing at the bus stop, turned away and half concealed by the waiting queue of people, but her hair and build and posture is so like Heather's that my stomach plummets with fright. I crane my neck but a bus pulls up obscuring my view and though I wait, my mouth dry, my heart knocking, by the time it's moved on again the queue has halved and the woman I'd seen has gone. I stand there for a long time, fear twisting in my gut. But surely it wasn't her. It couldn't possibly be. Just another in a long line of lookalikes I've spotted over the years – my mind playing tricks again, that's all. I tell myself to get a grip, the baby gives a hefty kick to my bladder and I hurry on my way.

Today the antenatal waiting room is busy and nearly every orange plastic chair is taken. A small wall-mounted TV shows a daytime property programme, its sound turned low. Women in various stages of pregnancy come and go, each clutching identical blue cardboard folders and occasionally trailing a toddler, a boyfriend or a husband in various states of boredom, excitement or fear. I take the one remaining seat, next to an exhausted-looking Irish woman who nags her four children to get up off the floor, stop fighting, be quiet. I check my ticket. Thirty-nine. The LED screen flashes number twenty-one. I sigh and along with nearly everyone else pull out my iPhone and turn it on.

But a small commotion at the door causes me to look up. A heavily pregnant teenage girl waddles in wearing tracksuit bottoms and flip-flops and shouting at a lad behind her. 'Fuck off,' she screams, 'Fuck off, right? I don't want you here. I don't fucking want you here!' The lad says nothing, his head bowed. They sit on opposite sides of the room, he with his chin almost on his chest, her glaring furiously at him. And as I watch, he looks up and makes brief eye contact with me. He is, I realize, about twenty, the same age Connor was when I first met him, though they are nothing alike – the wounded, vulnerable expression of this stranger is nothing you'd ever have seen on Connor's face.

In that instant I'm transported back to the night of the fair, the night it all began. I see Connor staring at me across the fairground, feel again the electric charge of excitement. I'd walked towards him and said his name and he'd thrown away his cigarette and nodded. I'd felt suddenly shy and for something to do had taken a swig of the vodka before passing it to him.

'I saw you,' he said, when he'd drunk some. 'On the

51

waltzers, with the fat girl,' and I'd shivered at the thought of him watching me without me knowing it, those sea-green eyes on me. He'd looked away, and I'd started to panic because he might go: he might walk away and I didn't know how or when I'd see him again. So I'd blurted the first thing that came to me. 'Want to go on a ride?' and he'd smiled; it broke across his face, a beautiful smile, wide and sudden and with such sweetness it had taken my breath away.

In the waiting room the Irish woman gathers up her children and heads towards one of the consulting rooms, but I'm barely aware of my surroundings now, lost as I am in the memory of that night. The big wheel had taken us up into the dark sky, his jeans rough against my bare leg, dark hairs on his arms and stubble on his cheek and a faint smell of sweat and aftershave and cigarettes and something deeper and more pungent, something masculine, indefinable. A man, he was, *a proper man*, and excitement had fizzed inside me as I'd drunk in his long lashes, the curve of his skull, the line of his neck, and I'd had to sit on my hands to stop myself from touching him.

He pulled a spliff from his pocket and lit it, before turning and squinting at me through the smoke. When he'd passed it to me I'd sucked it down and the hit was instantaneous, mixing with the vodka in dizzying waves, and I'd closed my eyes, then felt the suddenness of his lips on mine, hot and soft and hard, dry and wet, his tongue pushing into my mouth. I touched him, my fingers

52

beneath his jacket eager, hungry, running them over the fabric of his T-shirt, feeling the skin and muscle and flesh of him. Even though I was so nervous I could hardly breathe, I couldn't stop myself, had no shame, no self-control as I kissed him, ran my lips against his jaw, buried my nose in his neck, breathing him in.

What little I'd done with lads before had been nothing like this. I left that old me there, behind the last tree at the end of the playing fields in Withington, and took a leap into something else, something new. He was touching me too, his hands rough and careless over my chest, beneath my skirt, parting my thighs, slipping his hand beneath my knickers, and the bit of me that would normally smack his fingers away, tell him to get lost, was silenced. I was only feeling and sensation, the big wheel carrying us round and round as I trembled into his neck, not wanting him to stop.

In the hospital waiting room a large West Indian woman touches my arm. 'Is that you, honey?' she asks, nodding at the number flashing on the wall.

'Oh,' I say, 'Yeah. Thank you.' And I gather up my things, pull myself laboriously to my feet and walk towards my midwife's room.

Before

Edie lives in Tyner's Cross, the bit of Fremton between the Pembroke Estate and the rest of the town. A scattering of cul-de-sacs and council houses and new builds, as though Fremton proper had emptied out its pockets one day and this rag-bag jumble was what had tumbled out. We get to Edie's street, a row of small, pebble-dashed houses with falling-down fences, front yards strewn with junk and weeds, and she glances at me. 'Not like round your way, is it? Mind you, our old place wasn't much better.' She sighs, then says, 'One day I'm going to be rich, Heather. I'm going to move to London, go to Saint Martins and become an amazing artist. I'm going to have a gorgeous flat, and people will go to galleries and buy my pictures for millions,' she laughs, as though she's only joking, but I feel a rush of admiration. I want to tell her that I believe her, that it sounds amazing and that I think she could do anything if she set her mind to it, but before I can speak we've stopped outside a house with a peeling yellow front door and Edie's pulling a key from her bag.

At that moment it swings open and a short, stocky woman comes out. She stops abruptly when she sees us, her small eyes flickering over me without interest before turning eagerly on Edie. 'Ah,' she says, 'There you are, Edith.' She takes a step forward and puts a hand on Edie's arm, standing very close. Her hungry smile shows a mouth full of sharp little teeth. 'I'd been wondering where you'd got to. How are you? Everything OK?'

Edie gently releases herself. 'Fine thanks, Janine.' She shoots me a look; 'Mum's physio,' she explains.

The woman nods. 'You look after your mum now. We'll have her up and about in no time.' Her gaze lingers on Edie, hot and slippery.

'Right you are,' Edie says. 'See you next time.' And together we hurry through into the hallway, Edie laughing into her hand as soon as she closes the door. 'Yuk,' she says, and though I roll my eyes and nod, unease shifts inside me, an unpleasant memory of playground taunts, an ugly word to describe shameful, unnatural things. I force myself to rid the woman from my mind as I follow Edie down the hall.

The living room is small and cluttered and I drink it all in eagerly, not wanting to miss even the smallest detail. 'It's basically mostly my nan's old stuff,' Edie tells me carelessly, but I think it's lovely. Little china ornaments on every surface, flowery wallpaper and a thick, swirly brown carpet and a green sofa with a matching foot stool. A vase of plastic flowers on the brown-tiled mantelpiece. It's untidy and stuffy and smells of burnt dust and cats, but I know instantly I'd rather live here than my house any day.

Edie throws her keys on the coffee table. 'Mum,' she calls, 'I'm back.'

A woman walks slowly in on crutches and I remember how Edie had told me her mum had been in a car accident. Even in her nightclothes she looks beautiful, so glamorous and young, with make-up and long hair and a pink silky dressing gown very different from the one my mum's usually buttoned up in. She glances at me and smiles briefly but before I can say anything she looks past me and says to Edie accusingly, 'Where have you been? I had to wait for that bloody woman to turn up just to have a cup of tea.'

Edie rolls her eyes. 'Sorry,' she says. 'I'll make one now, shall I?'

Her mum takes a pack of cigarettes from her dressing-gown pocket and lights one. 'Don't put yourself out.' With difficulty, she lowers herself on to the couch and, picking up the remote, turns on the TV, staring sulkily at the screen.

'Fine,' Edie mutters. 'Come on, Heather.'

I murmur a quick goodbye before hurrying after her.

Her bedroom is tiny, barely large enough for the single bed that she's lying face down on. Half-unpacked

57

cardboard boxes cover almost every inch of the worn pink carpet and I gingerly step over them until I'm standing by her feet. 'Are you all right?' I ask.

Her voice is muffled by her pillow. 'She does my head in. I wish my dad was still around.'

'Where is he?' I ask, sitting down.

'God knows. Buggered off years ago. They were only young when they had me. She drove him away, always on at him about something. Nag nag nag, the way she does with me. Tells me I wouldn't understand, like I'm a bloody kid. But I know it's *her* fault he left, that's for sure.' There's a pause before she adds, 'And I've not seen him since. Not even a phone call.' She sits up and gnaws at her fingernails, her eyes dark and brooding. Tentatively I move closer to her and, after a few seconds' hesitation, put my arm around her. She sinks against me, resting her head upon my shoulder as though she were a little girl and my heart thumps loudly as I stroke her hair. After a silence she murmurs, 'God, it's shit not having any brothers or sisters, isn't it? Someone else to deal with all their crap. Don't you ever wish you weren't an only, Heather?' When I don't reply she glances up at me and her face falls. 'Christ, what's the matter? What have I said?'

And so I tell her about Lydia. Not everything, of course, but still, it's more than I've ever spoken about her to anyone else before.

'Oh, Heather, that's awful,' she says when I've finished. 'I'm so sorry.'

We sit in silence for a while and I wipe my eyes, listening to the sound of some kids playing outside in the street. In the quiet I notice a drawing pinned to the wall above her bed. 'Did you do that?' I ask, nodding at it.

'Yeah,' she says, and jumping up, stands on her bed to take it down. 'It's a bit crap really.'

She passes it to me and I stare at it. It's a self-portrait, a close-up of her face, pouting and narrow-eyed like a model on the cover of a magazine. It's amazing. 'Wow,' I say, 'it's great.'

'Nah,' she ducks her head. 'Do you honestly think so? You can have it if you want.' She goes and pulls out a folder from underneath her wardrobe, takes out a pile of drawings and puts them on my lap, watching my face as I look through them.

My tears, Lydia, Edie's dad, everything is forgotten as I examine them one by one. A child holding a balloon, a couple kissing, a handsome boy holding some flowers, moonlight shining on water. I think they're wonderful, romantic, a version of life where everyone's happy and in love and beautiful. 'Oh, Edie,' I say, 'they're fantastic. You're so talented, you really are!' I look at her in amazement.

She shakes her head, 'Oh leave off, they're pretty rubbish.' But she jumps up and pulls out a sketchpad, waiting eagerly for my reaction as I turn the pages. And as I heap praise on her I watch as her sadness begins to lift, receding with every compliment I pay her. She's smiling, I've made her happy again.

Suddenly she says, 'You're different from other girls our age, aren't you?'

My heart sinks. 'What do you mean?' My classmates' voices come hissing back to me: *Weirdo, fucking freak.*

She yawns and stretches like a cat, her top riding up to reveal her midriff. 'Don't know. You don't go on about clothes and who felt you up last night, and what a bitch so-and-so is. It's good.' She hesitates, glancing away before adding very softly, 'Even with my friends back in Manchester, I used to feel lonely sometimes. None of them seemed to have the same crap going on at home that I did. Do you know what I mean?'

'Yeah.' I nod. 'I do.' And we smile at each other in the silence.

'He's asked me to meet him on Saturday,' she tells me a few moments later.

'Who?'

She grins. 'Connor, of course! Will you come with me? In case he doesn't show.'

'Oh, I don't—'

'Please,' she says. 'Oh go on, be a pal.'

I hesitate, and she makes a daft face, fluttering her eyelashes until I laugh, and say OK.

It's Saturday lunchtime and we're sitting on the bench by the statue in the town square. Edie can't sit still, tugging at her dress, reapplying lip gloss and spraying herself with the White Musk her Uncle Geoff sent her last Christmas. A couple of girls from school walk past

60

us and look Edie up and down before turning to each other and sniggering. 'Skank,' they whisper, but I don't think Edie hears.

'Where is he? We've been here half an hour now.'

'I'm sure he's on his way,' I tell her, secretly hoping that he's not. I think about how I'll comfort her when he doesn't show, how maybe we can go to the café instead. Perhaps I'll buy her a milkshake and listen sympathetically as she confides in me about how disappointed she is. I'll tell her it's probably for the best after all, that he wasn't worth it and she can do a whole lot better – all the things I've heard you're supposed to say in this situation. But when I next look up, there he is.

The market's on today and the square is full of people, huddled beneath umbrellas or caught unawares by the first rainy day we've had in weeks, but Connor cuts through the crowds as though there's no one there at all and I see him through Edie's eyes: his handsome face, his confident swagger, something bold and focused against the smudgy grey blur of the square.

He stops in front of us. 'All right,' he says. I'm surprised by how nice his smile is and I find myself momentarily dazzled by it.

'Hiya!' Edie jumps up as if he'd pulled her by a string.

He looks her over. 'You got dressed up.' His eyes are a little mocking now, and she shrugs, her own smile flickering uncertainly. Then, reaching out a finger, he traces the low neckline of her dress, not taking his eyes from hers. Edie flushes, opens her mouth as if to speak

61

but seems hypnotized by the slow sweep of his finger. Her flesh goose-pimples beneath his gaze and the rain. Something passes between them, thick and private, containing them, wrapping them together, leaving me outside.

At that moment a passing dog rears back on its lead, barking and snarling, baring its teeth at me and I jump back, giving a little cry as its owner pulls it on. My heart pounds with shock. They both stare at me. 'This is Heather,' Edie tells him.

He nods then lights a cigarette. 'You coming?' he says to her.

'Where're we going?' she asks.

'Back to mine.'

She hesitates. 'Aren't we going out?'

He takes a drag on his cigarette and looks away. 'Where to, the Ritz?'

She flicks her hair again and bites her lip, weighing it up. 'Can Heather come?'

He glances at me and shrugs. 'If she wants.'

The look she shoots me is so beseeching that I nod and we set off, the two of them walking ahead, both so slim and good-looking as though made for each other, me trailing along behind.

I've never been to the Pembroke Estate before and I pause in its centre, staring up at the three high towers, looming black against the grey sky. The motorway is very close here; you can hear the traffic as it roars past somewhere just out of sight. There's a kids' play park with broken swings and a sandpit filled with bottles and dog mess and a group of teenage boys sitting around on its climbing frame. They fall silent, eyeing me blankly as I pass, and I hurry to catch up with Edie and Connor.

The lift that takes us to the sixth floor has bumpy metal walls and smells of cigarettes and urine. Connor ignores us as we climb higher and higher, taking out a phone and turning it on, his brow furrowed as his fingers tap away at the buttons. I watch him with curiosity: no one I know has a mobile phone and it looks flashy and expensive. When I glance over at Edie I see that she's eyeing it too and I wonder if that's why he got it out now, so that we would notice it and be impressed.

The door to Connor's flat is at the end of a long row of identical blue ones and we have to traipse along an outdoor walkway to get to it. Above us light bulbs fizz and flicker in little wire cages. If you lean over the metal barrier you can see right across Fremton and down to the roofs of the cars whizzing past below. We stop outside his flat and hear the thud of music from within, which blasts out at us when he opens the door. He leads us through to the lounge, past an empty bedroom with mattresses on the floor, a kitchen with a sink full of beer cans and a bathroom with a broken toilet. I imagine my mum's face if she knew I was in a place like this and glance over at Edie but she's looking around herself with bright, excited eyes as if it is in fact the Ritz he's brought us to.

In the lounge a very thin ginger boy is stretched out on the sofa wearing only his boxer shorts. He's asleep, despite the music. Connor kicks his foot and he sits up, dazedly rubbing his face, his ribs protruding beneath white, freckled skin. 'All right, Rabbit?' Connor says, and he nods sleepily, yawning widely and running both hands over his bristly carrot-coloured hair.

Edie sits on the sofa and I perch on its edge, as far away from the ginger boy as I can. The beige corduroy fabric is covered in stains, and by my feet a large plate that's been used as an ashtray spills cigarette ends on to the carpet. There's a smell in the air of old food and stale beer.

'You want a drink?' Connor asks, then has to repeat himself over the noise. 'Got some vodka if you want?'

Edie nods and flashes him a smile.

He looks at me but I shake my head, and he shrugs and leaves the room.

'All right, girls?' the ginger lad says, grinning now, and I suddenly notice the size of his front teeth. He's got the same thick local accent as Connor, which makes them both, in my opinion, sound a bit stupid, and he's rolling some tobacco into a cigarette paper. It's only when he lights it and the putrid stink fills the air that I realize what it is. He passes it to Edie and I'm shocked when she takes it from him. I know about marijuana from a talk they gave at school. Perhaps she doesn't realize. Perhaps I should warn her. I watch her closely in case she passes out or collapses or something and I need to call an ambulance. I wish we'd never come.

When Connor returns he sits next to Edie, passing her a half-full bottle of vodka. Rabbit wanders off and I get up and look out of the window, at the fields stretching out beyond the motorway. The rain has passed and the sky is a brilliant blue again, the sun bouncing off the roofs of the cars. I perch on an armchair and watch as, across the room, Edie laughs and twirls her hair then leans into Connor, putting her head on his shoulder. I can tell she's a bit drunk. They're talking and laughing but I can't hear what about because the music's too loud. Suddenly they both stand up, Connor pulling Edie after him towards the door. She looks at me and holds up a hand, fingers splayed. 'Five minutes,' she mouths, giggling. The door closes behind them and I'm left sitting on my own, the music thumping on around me.

A minute slowly passes, then another and another. Restlessly I go to the window again and look out, biting my thumbnail and hoping Rabbit doesn't come back. When ten minutes have gone by I turn the stereo down, craning my ears to listen for Edie's voice. Nothing. I don't know what to do. My stomach twists anxiously. Is she all right? What if he's locked her in somewhere and she needs my help? At last I creep to the door and stand out in the hallway until I hear the low murmur of voices.

One of the bedroom doors is ajar and I tiptoe over to it and look through. I see Edie lying on the mattress with Connor. As I watch, he slips a hand under her dress, pulling down her knickers. Shock reverberates through me. I hold my breath, feeling my skin burn as he reaches up and begins to touch her there. She gives a low moan, her eyes closed, her face flushed. I can't move, a painful lump in my throat making it hard to breathe.

And then a sound behind me makes me jump and turn around. Standing a few feet away is Rabbit, his eyes fastened on me, a slow smirk of realization spreading across his face as his gaze flicks away from my face to where Edie's lying on the bed. I stumble backwards, heat coursing through me, and go back to the lounge, and though I don't know why, hot tears prickle my eyes as I sit down again to wait.

After

I'm about to go to bed when the first contraction comes. I stand clutching the bathroom sink while the sudden, searing pain almost knocks me from my feet. The baby is on its way. And though I've prepared for this for weeks, and know exactly what steps I'm supposed to follow, I can only stand motionless, frozen in disbelief, light-headed with fear. At last the pain passes and I stare at my reflection in the mirror, hollow-eyed with panic.

Get a grip, Edie, come on. I know that it could be hours before the next one comes. I pace restlessly around my flat, my chest tight with anxiety, then for something to do, double-check the bag that's been packed and ready in the hallway for several days. I read through my midwife's notes, though I already know them mostly by heart. I am not to call the hospital until the contractions are ten minutes apart. Until then I am to monitor them:

how frequent, how long they last, how intense the pain, and in the meantime I must try to relax and keep calm. I make myself get into bed and turn the TV on, forcing myself to focus on the screen.

It's nearly two hours later when the next one comes. I lie doubled up in bed, gritting my teeth through the pain. I have never felt so horribly alone. For a desperate moment I think about calling Heri, but even before the thought has properly formed I know that I never could, that it's far too late for that – besides, I'd deleted his number months ago. I suddenly long to hear my mother's voice and get up to search frantically through old shoe-boxes and drawers for the little folded piece of paper with her number on that I know I have tucked away somewhere. Eventually I sink to the floor without it, sobbing into my hands, remembering the disgust on her face the last time we saw each other, knowing I'll never call.

I thought I'd be able to do this. I'd told myself it would be OK. But as I look at the empty, waiting cot, the packets of nappies and the second-hand car seat in the corner, the world seems to shrink away and I'm overwhelmed by the enormity of getting through it all alone. I have no one. And yet how can this be? I'd had friends in Manchester, a gang of girls from school I'd been devastated to leave behind when my mum moved us to Fremton. But once I'd met Connor, nothing else had mattered. After it was all over and I had moved to London the memory of Heather and what had happened between us had meant I'd kept my distance from other people, turning my back on any friendships that came my way. And now here I am. I feel as though I'm on the edge of a cliff, about to leap, and there's no one to catch me as I fall.

It's an endless, sleepless night. For a long time I stand at the window looking out at the street, watching as it gradually clears of life, the darkness thickening, only the occasional sweep of a car's headlights or the odd solitary figure to show me that anyone else exists in the world but me. I think of my Uncle Geoff, but the thought of his panic if he was summoned now almost makes me smile.

When the next contraction comes in the early hours of the morning it's so painful and frightening that I call the hospital, too desperate to wait any longer. When I finally get through to the duty midwife, her voice with its strong London accent is calm and kind. 'Is there anyone with you? The baby's father?'

I gulp back a sob. 'No,' I say. 'He's not involved.'

'I see. Well not to worry. Can you call a friend, a relative perhaps? Someone to wait with you, help you time the—'

'No, there's no one.'

There's a pause. 'OK. Well that's fine, my love. You'll be fine,' and the sympathy in her voice brings fresh tears to my eyes.

'Yes,' I whisper.

'I'm sorry, sweetheart, I know it's hard. But you need

to wait just a little longer. We're full to bursting here and we're asking our ladies to come in when the contractions are five minutes apart and are lasting for at least one minute. We'll be waiting for you, though, I've marked you down for admittance today, so there's no need to worry.'

'OK.' I grip the phone, desperate not to let her go. In the background I hear telephones ringing, the noises of a busy ward.

'That's great. You're doing really well. You call right back if you need to, OK? And as soon as those contractions start to speed up, you call a taxi and come straight here.'

'OK,' I say. 'Yes. OK. Thank you.' Reluctantly I hang up and begin to wait. It's nearly noon by the time I call the cab and begin the journey to the hospital.

Her name is Maya and her skin is a pale, rose-tinted brown. Her hair is thick and black and her father's large dark eyes gaze back at me from beneath long black lashes. She's perfect. And from the moment I meet her, from the moment the nurse hands her to me, I know that I can't love her.

It seemed, in the delivery room, as if the panic and confusion had come from nowhere. I remember sudden shouts for backup, being wheeled at speed down corridors, the midwife's urgent explanations about the cord wrapped around the baby's throat. And then an operating theatre, people in masks, a large Scottish woman shouting that it was all going to be OK, to try to relax, to breathe deeply, that there was nothing at all to worry about, nothing at all, but that I must stay perfectly still.

A strange dislocation had beset me, as though I was entirely divorced from whatever was happening to me in the lower half of my body, which was numb by then and shielded from me by a blue screen. A calm, dream-like state engulfed me, half hypnotized by the bleeping machines, the doctors' tense exchanges, the air of urgent concentration. When one of the masked figures held aloft, like a rabbit from a hat, the bloodied, blue-tinged creature, when I heard its weak, scratchy cry, I felt with complete certainty: that is not mine, that did not come from me. 'A girl!' the Scottish voice announced. 'Look, hen: a lovely wee baby girl!'

The ward I'm on is busy, with several other new mothers squashed in here beside me. When my baby is brought to me I smile, I hold her to me, I nod and listen to the nurse when she shows me how to put her to my breast. And then she is left by my bed, sleeping, while the horror washes over me in icy waves: this is not my child. She did not come from me.

I wake an hour later to feel hot burning pain spreading from my pelvis. I watch the other mothers, their exhausted triumph, their loving smiles, the congratu-lating visitors gathered around their beds. My baby lies in its clear plastic crib, staring back at me, mewling helplessly.

Uncle Geoff visits the following day and sits by my bed on a plastic chair, too big and too male amidst all the nightgowned women with their smells of milk and babies, averting his eyes in horror when my neighbour unfastens herself to offer her child her breast. He holds Maya in his large, tobacco-stained fingers, her head lolling awkwardly against his old leather coat, and tries to think of something to say. 'Tiny ears,' he offers eventually, and we both nod. When she begins to cry he thrusts her back to me. 'What's wrong?' he asks anxiously.

'She wants feeding, I think.'

His eyes fall to my chest and he jumps up in alarm. 'Well, then, I'd best leave you to it, shall I?'

I take Maya from him and try to smile. He pauses and says, 'I'll tell your mother, shall I?' His eyes meet mine and he adds gently, 'I mean, she'd like to know, I expect, that you've had her.'

Mutely I nod. He takes my hand and gives it a squeeze. 'Well done, love, she's a little belter, you've done me proud.' He leans down and gives me a hug, my face crushed against his chest, breathing in his aftershave and leather smell, and the lump in my throat threatens to choke me.

'See you soon,' I say.

'Aye, see you soon,' he smiles, and I manage to make it until he's left the ward before I begin to cry.

When I'm finally discharged the cab drives me through the London streets, Maya asleep in the seat next to me. Peckham and Nunhead slide past, the sun shines, people and traffic go about their business and yet nothing seems real, substantial, trustworthy. The cab stops at the lights and I have to fight every instinct in my body not to open the door and run. And when the two of us are alone in the flat for the first time, fear – shocking, overwhelming, gutting fear – almost knocks me off my feet.

I look at her beginning to stir in her car seat on the kitchen table and I'm paralysed by indecision, unable to remember what I'm supposed to do with her, how I am to begin. In the hospital, because of her difficult birth, she was regularly taken away and monitored, only given back to me when it was time to feed. It seems incredible, mind-boggling that they have entrusted me with her, that they deem me capable of keeping this creature alive and free from harm.

But the minutes pass, and then the hours and the days. We fall into a sort of nightmarish routine, she and I, tinged by lack of sleep and the feeling that I'm only seconds away from losing my mind. Through the constant, exhausting panic I manage somehow to change her and feed her when I need to; I sleep, fitfully, when she does, but when she's fed and changed and still she cries, wanting something else, something that I can't give, I can only lie and listen to her, waiting for it to stop.

I try hard to breastfeed her at first, but with every passing day it seems to get more difficult. She roots endlessly, painfully at me and when at last she latches on it seems to take an age before she's satisfied. Afterwards she sleeps fitfully, waking far too soon, demanding food again. I cradle her small head, horribly fragile and alien in my hands, while her neck lolls uncomfortably, and she cries and cries and cries.

The health visitor, a small, very pale girl named Lucy, comes the following Tuesday. I don't tell her that I fantasize about running away and never coming back, that every day the feeling of dread gets worse and worse, that most days I don't get dressed or washed. Instead, Lucy sits on my sofa and drinks my tea and weighs and measures Maya and checks my scar and talks about how the traffic's bad today and where she's going on holiday and insists on calling me 'Mum'. I listen to her in a kind of stupor, watching her efficient white hands as they dart to and fro like mice.

'How's the feeding going, Mum?' she asks. 'Any problems there?'

I look away, it already having been drummed into me on the maternity ward how dimly I'd be viewed if I didn't feed her myself.

'OK,' I mumble, though clearly not very convincingly, because her eyes narrow and she immediately pounces on my words.

'Would you like to feed her now, Mum, so I can check her latch?'

I shake my head. 'She's fast asleep and I don't want to wake her. It's fine, honestly.' The truth is I don't want her to see how bad I am at this. The softly smiling, dreamy-eyed women in the breastfeeding leaflets pressed on me at the hospital, those loving mothers with their contented, suckling infants who seem to be everywhere suddenly, are such a far cry from my reality that I can't bear for her to see it. I don't tell her about the tin of formula I bought in desperation only this morning, the blessed relief of feeding Maya from a bottle, not having to have her gnawing at me or listen to her ear-splitting frustration.

Little by little I slide, deeper and deeper each day. 'I'm going to go and stay at my mum's for a while,' I tell Lucy the next time she comes. Harassed and overworked, she gratefully signs me off, with a vague promise to phone in a few weeks' time. When Uncle Geoff next visits I see that he has no idea that when he leaves I'll sink exhausted to the floor, my face a mess of snot and tears, while Maya wails alone from across the room. Gradually I stop replying to his texts, or answering his calls.

I'm so tired that I have begun to see things that aren't there: from the corner of my eye black spiders scuttle across the ceiling; objects roll silently along the floor. Exhaustion has left me with a permanent sense of seasickness, of the ground being always unsteady beneath my feet. It isn't often that I leave the flat, but it's on a day that I'm forced out to the corner shop to buy more nappies that I see my new neighbours again. As I queue

I spy the two lads from the window, walking across the street, their heads bent, their hoods all but obscuring their faces, their dog strutting leadless and collarless in front of them.

Maya, who had slept peacefully the entire way there and back, waits until we've returned to my building and I'm standing in the communal entrance, trying to muster the energy to carry both her and the buggy back up the four flights of stairs, when she wakes and begins to cry, loudly and unceasingly.

It's like a thousand crows are cawing in my head, scratching and pecking to get out. I lean against the banister and close my eyes, summoning every ounce of strength I have not to leave again by the front door, to walk away without her and never come back. I don't know how long I stand like this before I realize that I'm being watched and I look up to see the woman staring at me from her open doorway. I start guiltily, but before I can say anything she comes over to Maya's buggy and, without looking at me, takes the handles. 'Grab the other end,' she tells me.

I do as she says and, at her nod, begin the climb. On the way up I steal glances at her, the small face with its hard bright eyes and fine lines, the red hair and map of tattoos on her scrawny arms, the thick gold rings on her knuckles, but we don't speak – even Maya has lapsed into vague half-hearted grumblings now – and it's not until we reach the top that I thank her. She has started back down the stairs when I hurriedly say,

'I'm Edie, by the way,' and at first I think she's not going to respond, but at the last moment she turns and smiles briefly. 'Monica,' she replies, then disappears from view. I stand and stare after her and, though I can't explain why, I'm oddly comforted by the thought of this tough-looking stranger living her life only a few floors below, a glimpse of shore lights from the midst of a dark and choppy sea.

A few weeks later, passing a church hall in the pouring rain I notice a sign for a mother and baby group. I pause, glancing down at Maya who, for once, is lying quietly beneath her rain cover. I'm soaked, yet I can't quite bear to return to my cramped, messy flat. On impulse I open the door and peer in. The hall is large and packed with women sitting around drinking tea and eating biscuits, while in the centre what seems like hundreds of toddlers stampede through a sea of brightly coloured plastic toys. The noise is overwhelming. I'm about to back away when a woman in her sixties, wearing a vicar's collar, strides towards me. 'Are you coming in?' she says briskly. 'That's right, in you come. Close the door behind you, we don't want any escapees, do we?' Dazedly I do as she says. 'Pushchairs over there, that's the way, well done.'

Obediently I lift Maya from her buggy and park it with all the others then edge into the hall, looking around myself uncertainly. I notice a small group of women in the corner, balancing babies on their knees. I make my way over to them and, finding a seat, shift Maya in my arms, hoping desperately that she'll keep quiet for a while longer. Out of the corner of my eye I watch the other mothers, noticing enviously how relaxed they seem, their children slung casually over their shoulders or being jiggled on knees, the women paying little attention to them as they chat amongst themselves.

Eventually one of them turns to me and smiles. 'Hi,' she says and nods at Maya. 'Oh, isn't she lovely. How old?'

'Six weeks,' I tell her. 'Yours?'

'Eight months now.'

I hesitate, then blurt, 'Does it get easier? It's just, she just . . . she never stops crying. Do you know what I mean? I don't know. I suppose they're all like that, are they? Is yours? Does yours cry all the time too?'

The woman tilts her head sympathetically and blinks. 'No, he's a cheery little thing, this one. So easy! Always smiling.' She pauses then says, 'I think it's because my husband and I are such laid-back people, you know?' She gives a self-congratulatory smirk, and adds, 'Maybe you need to try and chill out a bit? Babies sense it if you're stressed. Have you tried yoga?'

I shake my head and murmur faintly that I'll give it a go, and she turns back to her friend just as Maya opens her mouth and lets out a piercing shriek. As quickly as I can I gather up my things and leave.

The sky clears as I reach the park at the top of my road and I sink gratefully on to a wet bench, Maya asleep now in her buggy next to me. The park has a panoramic view of London but I close my eyes to it, exhaustion carrying me to the edges of consciousness. I don't know how long I doze before I wake with a start, sensing a shadow fall in front of me, another presence near. I shield my eyes and look into a face that takes me a couple of moments to recognize as the man who sold me the cot before. I notice his peroxide tufts have gone, his black hair now closely cropped.

'Hi,' he says. 'Edie, right?' He stands by Maya's pram, smiling down at me. 'James. I sold you the cot. I thought it was you!' His son is a few feet away, poking at the grass with a stick.

I nod, conscious suddenly of my hair sticking greasily to my face, and the fact that I'd picked up the nearest clothes from the floor before braving what seemed like this monumental expedition. I realize I can't remember the last time I washed. 'All right?' I say.

'She's a beauty.' He's looking into the pram now, and I do my best to arrange my features into the expected smile. 'Thanks,' I say.

'How're you doing?' he asks. 'Everything going all right, is it?' and I'm horrified when my eyes fill with tears. I look down, willing myself to stop.

A silence falls while he tactfully glances away. 'It's hard, isn't it, doing it by yourself,' he says after a while, then adds, 'Me and Stan's mum split not long after he was born.'

I nod, staring at my hands.

'It gets easier,' he says. 'It sounds like bullshit, but it's true, it really does.'

I'm too embarrassed to meet his gaze; using every ounce of strength I have to keep the tidal wave of hopelessness at bay. At last to my relief he takes his son's hand, and begins to move off. 'Well, better go,' he says, 'lunch and so on.' I nod, swallowing hard. 'Take care,' he adds, and, with a final sympathetic smile, he goes.

It's at this moment that Maya wakes and starts to cry again. Any willpower I had managed to muster until that point entirely deserts me, and burying my head in my hands I give in to the tears. It's the endlessness of it all I can't stand: the awful knowledge that this is going to go on and on and on, except every day I will be that little bit more tired, that little bit less able to bear it. Maya continues to scream and yet the thought of picking her up is entirely beyond me; I am too exhausted to even lift my head.

And then, my face still buried in my hands, I feel the bench beside me sag with a sudden weight, the warmth from the sun that had been shining on my right side vanishes and a familiar, oniony smell fills my nostrils. A thick arm rests upon my shoulders. I look up to find Heather sitting beside me. 'There, there,' she says gently. 'Shush now.'

I don't think about how or why she found me, or what this means. Something inside me breaks at the sight of the old, familiar face, and I drop my head on to her shoulder and feel myself sink into her large, soft body. After a long time, she pats me on the back, gets up and, taking the handle of the buggy, holds a hand out to me as if I were a small child. 'Let's get you both home, shall we?' she says. 'And have a nice cup of tea.'

This is how Heather comes back into my life. This is how it begins.

PART TWO

Before

Sometimes when I'm feeling sad there's this thing I do to make myself feel better. I choose a memory from a time when I was really happy and I dive into it, leaving the world far behind; all its sights and sounds dissolving until the memory is all around me, more real and warm and colourful than the life I'd just been living.

Because it's Sunday we have all been to church, Mum, Dad and I. We were late so the pews were almost full and I had to sit across the aisle from my parents. The service went the same as usual with the same old prayers and hymns. But then, during the Lord's Prayer, as I bent my head with everyone else and began to say the words, I felt the strangest sensation, like a cold pressure on the back of my neck. I continued on with the prayer . . . *as we forgive those that trespass against us, and lead us not into temptation, but deliver us from evil* . . . the feeling grew stronger until at last I turned and there, amongst all the bowed, murmuring heads, was my mother, sitting bolt upright, her lips silent, her eyes fastened on me. And the expression on her face made my heart stop, actually stop for a long, dizzying moment.

A second later she looked away and I went back to my prayer. My heartbeat returned, hammering against my ribs, my body trembled. The prayer ended and in its place was the rustling, shuffling throat-clearing sound of the congregation preparing to sing the next hymn. But I wasn't amongst them any longer. I had left the sick, sad, desperate feeling far behind and the next thing I knew I was five and Lydia was two and we were playing together in our old room back in Wales.

My mother had gone out and my father was in another room. I was absorbed in my dolls so it was some time before I looked up to discover that Lydia was surrounded by the empty pots of poster paint I'd been playing with before. Her face and hands, her clothes, the carpet surrounding her was covered in multicolour streaks. I gasped as she grinned back at me, pleased with herself. Mum would be home any minute and she'd be furious: it was my fault the paints were left where Lydia could get to them. But just at that moment Lydia threw her head back and began to laugh and I realized suddenly I didn't really care. I went to her and put my arms round her and squeezed her tightly and laughed and laughed too, and love, I felt such love.

After

I can't seem to get myself started. I think about getting up, getting on with it, but the hours and days pass and still I don't move. Between waking and sleeping, memories gather and retreat. Sometimes Maya's cry pierces the murky sadness that's seeped into every part of me, leaving me listless and bedridden, without energy or purpose. Occasionally I'll surface long enough to hear Heather's soothing response, before I sink once again, pulled back deeper and deeper by the cold, dead fingers of the past.

I drift.

I'm in the street where I used to live with Mum. Above our row of pebble-dashed semis the sky is heavy with unshed rain yet somewhere behind it the sun still shines, infusing the world with a strange metallic light, the trees copper against an iron sky. A rainbow arches over the string of front yards with their washing lines and wheelie bins and abandoned toys and bits of junk, and somewhere out of sight the motorway roars on, like the blood rushing in your ears.

I walk on towards the Pembroke Estate and I marvel that before we met I never knew that Connor was there; all the time existing in the world, up there breathing, sleeping, feeling, being, without me knowing it, with no idea the world contained him. I feel a brief, sharp thrill of terror at the thought that I could easily never have met him at all, that my life might somehow have continued without him in it.

I awake to darkness. For some moments I'm lost between past and present, unable to anchor myself in either. I hear a car passing far below, voices drifting from the pavement to my window. And then the sound of snoring coming from the corner of the room. Heather. She is here, in my flat, bringing with her the past, and as I begin to remember, make sense of it, another sound infiltrates the midnight peace; a scratchy squawking that builds quickly to a full-throated wail coming from somewhere in the shadows. I hold my breath, anxiety giving way to relief when Heather stirs and reaches for the baby, staggering away with her to the kitchen. Soon there is the sound of bottles, a boiling kettle, low murmuring, Maya quietens and I drift.

I don't know how long ago it was that she found us in the park. I remember begging her to stay, telling her I had no one else to help me, and her promising that she would. The days seep into one another; Heather brings sandwiches or soup to my bed, occasionally she'll run me a bath and lead me gently to it, but mainly she leaves me to sleep, and stare, and remember. The hours slide by, light and shadows creeping across the ceiling, and I hear her leaving and returning again with Maya.

Sometimes during the endless hours I think about the two of us back then, how lonely and lost I'd felt when I first moved to Fremton. How with Heather it was as if, for the first time in my life, I could be myself, could tell her anything and she would still think I was great. It had been the most comforting friendship I had ever had. And then I think about how, slowly, everything had changed, and the horror of that final night comes rushing towards me like an express train and I curl up into a ball, my eyes tight shut, my hands over my ears trying desperately to block the memories out. I don't know why she has come to help me now, after all this time, after all that happened then, and I don't really care. I only know that I'm unfit to look after my daughter, that I'm no good for her, and that Heather is all I have.

Only once during these long, dark weeks do I leave the flat. I wake early, damp with sweat, my heart racing and my skin burning. Maya and Heather sleep soundly on the other side of the room while my chest tightens and tightens as though held in a vice, the sound of their breathing growing louder and louder until I think I might go mad from it. Ten minutes pass, then another and another. The ceiling seems to be getting steadily lower, the walls closer, and panic courses through me until I can bear it no longer. I need to get out, get out, and I scrabble about for my clothes, pull them on and leave at a run.

But the relief to be away from my flat is replaced by a terror of the wide-open sky and the buildings that seem to loom and leer over me. A motorbike's sudden roar makes me cry out in fright. I look wildly around me and on impulse set off in the direction of my GP, not knowing what I want from her, only that this horror is unbearable, that I need to make it stop.

The receptionist eyes me suspiciously when she opens up the surgery and I ask her for an appointment. 'Is it an emergency?' she asks.

'Yes, I mean – I think so, I don't know.' Tears fill my eyes as she sighs and peers at her computer.

'We have a cancellation in forty-five minutes,' she tells me grudgingly.

I nod gratefully and, after giving her my details, sit down to wait. Slowly the room fills up around me. An old man with a loud, hacking cough, a woman with two young children, a couple of gossiping schoolgirls. Little by little I feel my lungs empty of air. The sounds of the other waiting patients seem to grow louder and louder – the old man's cough, the schoolgirls' laughter, the children's whining. One of the boys begins repetitively banging together two toy cars and the noise echoes around my head like gunshots.

'Excuse me, are you all right?' I look up to find the receptionist standing over me. When I try to speak I hear myself gasping for air, feel the sweat coursing down my face and look round at the other patients to find that they too are staring at me with curiosity. I get to my feet and stagger out into the street and though my chest feels as though it might burst I set off for home at a run, not stopping until I'm unlocking my flat's door, stumbling past an astonished-looking Heather and finally sinking into my bed, pulling the duvet up over my head, still wearing my coat and shoes. I must stay here, I tell myself desperately, where I am safe, where I am looked after, where Heather is.

I awake in the early evening to the sound of my mobile ringing. I wait, my anxiety building, praying for Heather to answer it, and at last she picks it up. 'Yes?' she says, her voice reassuringly guarded. She listens for a moment or two. 'Geoff?' she says doubt-fully. 'Geoff – oh. Uncle Geoff. Right. No, I'm afraid she's not up to visitors, she's not very well.' She pauses. 'Who am I? Her best friend Heather – no, no, from Fremton. I've come to look after Edie and the baby for a while. Yes, she'll be fine, uh-huh, absolutely, of course I will. No, I don't think that would be a good idea, but as soon as she's better . . . yep, OK, will do. Bye, then. OK, bye bye.' She ends the call and our eyes meet, her usual, cheerful smile unwavering. 'Why don't I hold on to this,' she says, pocketing my mobile. 'You don't want people bothering you all the time, do you?' And I nod, and turn away, pulling the duvet tight around me.

Later, I hear Heather in the kitchen humming gently to Maya and listen for a while, trying to gather the energy to get up. When I do, I find the tiny passageway is littered with her stuff: boxes and plastic bags trailing dirty-heeled tights, a bottle of shampoo, a torn magazine, piles of clothes, and I wonder when she brought it here, how long it has been gathering without my noticing. In the bathroom I find her underwear – large greying knickers and bras – drying on the shower rail. A hairbrush loaded with dusty yellow hair is by the sink, and on top of the loo a box of sanitary towels sits.

I hesitate outside the kitchen door, listening to the two of them on the other side, trying to make myself go in. And when I push open the door they don't notice me at first, Heather smiling down at the baby as she feeds her from a bottle, Maya's eyes fixed contentedly on her face. When Heather finally looks up we stare in silence at each other for a beat or two until she says gently, 'Why don't you go back to bed and rest, Edie? I can manage here.'

Sleep lies waiting for me, thick and dark and warm. I step off the edge and it's there, ready to catch me as I fall, the memories pulling me, pulling me . . .

I lie with Connor on his bed, a shaft of sunlight streaking across our naked bodies. 'You're not like other girls, not like the ones I've been with before.' I'm tracing my finger along the tattoo that spikes and curls greenish black beneath his belly button. Celtic, he says it is, and I think about something my nan used to say when I was a little girl. She would hug me tightly and tell me that she loved the bones of me, and I think how I understand now what that means, how in these few short weeks I know how it feels to love every inch of someone; their eyelashes, their earlobes, their toenails, the skin and flesh and muscles and veins and bones of them, every one. He wraps my hair around one of his hands and gently pushes my head down from where it lies on his chest, pushes it down until my lips brush his tattoo then further down until he's in my mouth.

The days pass. I listen to Heather come and go with Maya, to the sounds of her taking care of me, of the mess I've made. There she is, boiling the kettle for the baby's milk. Now she's loading and turning on the washing machine, next tidying the kitchen, changing a nappy, running Maya's bath. I do everything I can to avoid looking at my daughter, the sight of her triggering such an overwhelming onslaught of guilt and fear that I can scarcely breathe.

My intercom buzzes loudly one afternoon while Heather and I are watching television, and the two of us stare at each other in blank surprise until Heather gets up and strides purposefully over to it. 'Yes?' she says, into the handset.

The receiver crackles. 'Edie?' Recognizing my uncle's

voice I instinctively jump to my feet but before I can say anything Heather speaks.

'Edie's not in,' she says.

There's a pause, and in the silence I hear traffic passing on the street. 'I'd like to come up and leave her a note then,' says Uncle Geoff, firmly. I'm about to speak when Heather turns and shoots me a look that silences me, my mouth immediately snapping shut.

'Hold on, please,' she says and putting down the receiver doesn't look at me as she murmurs, 'I'll deal with this.'

'But perhaps . . .' I begin hesitantly. 'I should, I mean, he's come all this way, and I think maybe I'd like to see if he's OK . . .'

'No!' Heather's voice is loud enough to make me jump and I stare at her in shock. A split second later her smile has returned. 'I don't think that's a very good idea, do you, Edie?' she adds softly. She drops her gaze and I feel her eyes sliding over me and I shrink away, covering myself with my arms. 'I mean, look at you,' she goes on in the same slow, gentle voice. 'You've got yourself into a bit of a state, haven't you?'

I gaze down at myself, at the dirty clothes I've worn for days now, feeling the grime on my skin, the grease in my hair, and I nod. 'Yes,' I whisper.

'Yes,' she says, and our eyes lock for a second before she turns, opens the door, and is gone.

As I listen to her steps descending the stairs, I know that I should go after her, should speak to my uncle

94

myself, but the thought of him seeing me like this fills me with shame. Instead I move to the window and wait, exhaustion sweeping through me until I see him walking away across the street. When he reaches the other side he stops in his tracks and turns to look up to where I'm standing by the window. Quickly I jump back out of sight, my heart thumping in the silence, until Heather returns and gently leads me back to bed.

And the longer Heather stays, the harder it is to imagine life without her.

Before

I stand on the bridge over the canal, dropping pebbles in one by one. I'm thinking about Lydia. Clouds pass overhead and the shadows they cast are dark, misshapen creatures swimming below the water's surface. When I was a little girl I used to think I was adopted. A foundling like a child from a fairy tale. It was the only way to explain why I always felt so different from the rest of my family. Sometimes I used to daydream about my real relatives living somewhere far away, looking and acting exactly like me. One day I would find them and I would know at last I was where I was supposed to have been all along.

It wasn't just my stupid yellow frizzy hair or the fact I'm so big and clumsy. I was different from my family on the inside, too. I never worked out how they kept everything within themselves, how they stopped it from bursting out of them the way it always did with me. I couldn't help it: if I felt happy or excited or whatever, it would build up and up until I couldn't contain it any more. Sometimes I'd get so cross that the rage would explode from me.

I remember the morning they brought Lydia home – how perfect she was right away. I loved her – everybody did – she was so pretty and good and sweet. She used to call me Hebba and she followed me everywhere. I'd pick her up from her cot and carry her off to the Wendy house or tuck her into my doll's pushchair and wheel her up and down the garden path. 'No, Heather! You're too rough with her,' my mother would say. 'Put her down! Put her down this instant!'

And then one day, when Mum was cooking tea, I took Lydia from her playpen and put her on the garden swing. When she fell and I saw the trickle of blood on her face, I'd been gripped by cold terror. At her screams, Mum had rushed from the house and scooped her up, her face furious. 'For Heaven's sake, Heather! What's the matter with you? Why can't you ever do as you're told?' And I had stood there, watching the way she looked at Lydia, how she covered her soft, silky hair in kisses and held on to her so tightly, and the sudden realization had come, like a stone dropping right through the centre of me, that my mother felt about Lydia in a way that she had never felt about me, and never would.

I throw the last of the pebbles into the water. Above me the sky has begun to darken with rain clouds, and

I shiver. Lydia still lingers somewhere in the damp breeze that trails its fingers around my neck, and in the darkly moving shadows of the water, and with effort I force her from my mind and look at my watch. Two o'clock. I will be seeing Edie in one hour exactly. Excitement flares inside me, Lydia pushed from my thoughts at last. I button up my cardigan and hurry off towards home.

It's half past three before she knocks on the door. 'Dad's at work, and Mum's gone to the supermarket,' I tell her. 'So we've got the house to ourselves.'

'Yeah?' she says, yawning, and I notice how tired she looks, her face drawn and wan. But she brightens. 'Hey, come on then, give us the grand tour.'

I feel a bit giddy as I show her around. 'This is our living room,' I say, and watch her face as she takes in the shelves of books, the plain, uncomfortable furniture, the dark green walls. A grandfather clock strikes the half-hour behind her and she jumps in surprise and laughs. As we wander around the house and I point out various things, I get the feeling she's only half listening, her replies dreamy and vague. I realize suddenly that she's thinking about him, about Connor. She told me before that she sees him all the time now, that she sneaks out late at night after her mum's gone to sleep. She mentions other names too. There's a Tully, and a Jonny and a Niall I think. A sad, sour feeling rises inside me. I don't think he can love her the way I do. I don't think he could notice all the little things about her that I see.

How her neck flushes when she laughs, or how, beneath her mauve nail varnish, her nails are bitten down to the quick.

When we come to my dad's study, I pause outside the door. 'What's in there?' she asks.

I hesitate, knowing I'm not allowed to go inside, then on impulse push it open. His desk is bare but for a pile of papers and a jar of pens. 'Bit boring really,' I shrug, but stop as I notice that Edie is gazing at a photograph in her hand.

'Is this you?' she asks, showing it to me.

I suddenly find it hard to breathe. 'Where did you find that?' I ask.

She nods to the bookshelf. 'There, sort of sticking out from between the books.'

'It's my sister,' I tell her, 'Lydia.' For a moment I'm too stunned to speak. I'm so used to my parents acting as though she never existed, never mentioning her name, that the fact my father has a secret photo that he might perhaps look at from time to time, leaves me speechless.

Edie nods. 'She's lovely,' she says softly.

And I see with a start of surprise that her eyes are swimming, that she feels sad for me. I want to tell her that Lydia had shoes with blue bows on them, that she liked me to sing her to sleep at night, that she couldn't pronounce her Ls. I want to tell her that I miss my sister more than anything, that my heart hurts from it still. But the silence stretches and I find I can't say any of these things, because if I start I might never stop crying.

100

Instead I take the photo from her and put it in my pocket and walk wordlessly from the room.

We're in the kitchen when my mother comes home. She frowns when she sees Edie leaning against the fridge, a glass of lemon squash in her hand. 'Hiya,' Edie says, and I'm struck by how carelessly she says it, how unafraid she seems in Mum's presence. I rush to help with the shopping, quickly unloading it on to the kitchen table. I can't seem to stop talking, and I'm telling them that it's two weeks until school starts again, when Mum interrupts me.

'Heather,' she says. 'Go and fetch a jumper from upstairs, will you, please? I'm a little cold.'

I hesitate, not wanting to leave the two of them together, but she glances at me sharply and says, 'Well, hurry up.'

Reluctantly I put down the potatoes I'd been holding and run up to my parents' room. I grab a jumper as quickly as I can and on my return take the steps two at a time. But at the bottom I pause when I hear Mum's voice.

'We're not used to Heather having friends call for her,' I hear her say.

'No?' Edie replies.

There's the sound of drawers and cupboard doors opening and closing, before Mum continues, 'No. She's never been the sort that other girls take much interest in.'

I feel the heat rise in my cheeks. Edie doesn't answer,

101

but I can almost see her frown and shrug, in that bored way she has.

'Especially girls like you,' my mother adds.

There's a short silence. 'Like me?' Edie asks, her voice suddenly very different.

Mum gives a little laugh. 'Well, she's never shown much interest in the sort of things I imagine appeal to you. Clothes and boys, for example. She's a quiet, hard-working girl. A bit . . . naive, I suppose.'

'Is that right?'

Another cupboard door opens and closes. 'It's just that I can't imagine you'd have much in common. We're hoping she'll study medicine one day, and I'm sure she will, if she's not allowed to become . . . too distracted.'

There's a long pause, and then Edie says, 'I'm friends with Heather because I think she's great. Because she's funny and kind. Perhaps that's all that matters, even to "someone like me". Excuse me, I think I'll go and find her.'

I hear her marching to the door and I stand there, clutching on to the banister, happiness coursing through me.

When Edie comes out and sees me she shakes her head. 'Christ,' she mutters darkly. 'I thought *my* mum was a bitch.'

It's a week later, a few days before school starts again, when Edie and I catch the bus to Walsall together. I have told Mum that I need to buy some books for the new term, though that's a lie, and I don't mention that Edie's coming too.

I used to think telling lies would make God angry and send me straight to Hell. I used to think He punished people who were bad. But lately I've been thinking that perhaps a lie here and there doesn't matter so much after all. Since the day Edie came to my house and spoke to my mother the way she did, it's as if there's an unspoken understanding between us; the realization that however bad things are at home for either of us, it doesn't matter, because we have each other now. We sit on the back seat of the bus, Edie and I, each of us with a headphone bud in one ear, listening to her mini disc player, and I don't think I've ever felt so happy. I used to hear the girls from school arranging to go shopping in Walsall together at the weekends, and now, for the first time, I'm going too.

The mall on Bridge Street has marble floors and arched glass ceilings and shop after shop like Aladdin's caves of colour and light, bursting with expensive, shiny new things, music pumping from each one. I glance at Edie, bouncing along in front of me, her hair flying behind her, and at that moment she looks around and grins, stopping outside a clothes shop. 'I love this one,' she says. 'Come on!' And she takes my arm and pulls me after her.

I follow her through the rails of clothes as she weaves confidently in and out, pulling out various things and holding them against me. I would never in a million years, come to a place like this on my own. 'This would look cool on you,' she says, 'and this.' I smile as she grabs an armful of clothes then drags me off to the changing rooms where we squeeze into a cubicle together, a red curtain shielding us from the bored assistant's gaze.

'Go on,' she says, handing me a pair of black jeans and a tight green top. 'Get these on.' She turns away from me and unselfconsciously begins to pull her own clothes off, until she's standing in her underwear. Red-faced, I do as she says, awkwardly trying to cover myself with my discarded skirt as I wriggle out of my top. Out of the corner of my eye I notice small red bruises flowering over her neck and chest. I know what they are because I remember when Sheridan Alsop had one on her neck and she and Aisha Robinson had made a big fuss about putting toothpaste on it in the loos.

When we're both dressed she looks me up and down. 'Wow, Heather. You look amazing!'

I turn to the mirror. I do look better. The neckline of the top she picked out for me is low, the fabric tight over my breasts before flaring out around my middle, the black jeans somehow making my legs less like trunks. I look older, sleeker. I almost look nice, I realize with surprise.

Edie is staring at my reflection too. 'You really do look ace, you know,' she says. 'Are you going to get them?'

'I'm not sure.' For some reason this new version of

myself makes me feel a bit afraid, though I don't know why.

Edie rolls her eyes, 'You've got to stop dressing like your mum buys your clothes for you.'

I'm about to reply when I notice the dress she's tried on. She looks beautiful, the petrol blue fabric clinging to her, the colour so lovely against her skin it's like she glows. She reaches behind herself, pulls out the price tag and grimaces when she sees how much it costs. 'They're having a laugh, aren't they?' Reluctantly she peels the dress off. 'Oh well, no chance of that, then.'

Later, when we're dressed and have handed the clothes to the assistant, she says, 'Hey, I know, let's go to McDonald's. I'm bloody starving.'

'I've never been before,' I tell her.

She stops. 'You're kidding me, right?' She shakes her head in wonder as she looks at me, then smiles and takes my arm, 'Come on. Let's gorge on cheeseburgers.'

We're still laughing as we leave the shop. When the alarms go off, the sudden, shrill racket makes us both stop guiltily and look around us in confusion. It's only when the security guard bears down on us and puts his hand on my shoulder that the cold horror hits me. As other shoppers stop and stare he takes my bag and begins searching through it. Waves of fear wash over me, my mouth filling with water as though I'm about to be sick. When he eventually, triumphantly, pulls out Edie's blue dress I watch as the realization dawns on her face. Her jaw drops. 'Oh, Heather, you didn't.' She shuts her eyes. 'Christ. You bloody idiot!'

We're taken to a small room at the back of the shop, where we wait in silence until a man with a badge that says 'Keith Liddle, Manager' comes in, followed by the girl who'd collected our clothes in the changing room before. I feel myself begin to shake. He's short and bald with pockmarked skin and he draws himself up and thrusts his face forward until it's an inch from mine. 'You make a habit of taking things that don't belong to you?' he asks, then glances back at the assistant, who smirks and twirls her hair. Tears fill my eyes. I look at my feet and shake my head. 'Oi!' he bellows. 'I'm talking to you!' and I jump and begin to cry. I'm too scared to meet his gaze so instead I focus on a faint brown stain on his pink tie. I can smell cheese-and-onion crisps on his breath. He folds his arms. 'Let's see what the police have to say about it, shall we?'

'Stop your mithering and get on with it then,' Edie mutters.

He eyes her with a level of dislike that I sense is somehow connected to how pretty she is, and how short and bald he is. 'You won't be so lippy when your mate ends up in prison, will you?' he says to her nastily.

Edie rolls her eyes. 'She's sixteen. She's not going to prison for nicking a crappy fucking dress. Heather, stop crying, for God's sake. You're not going to prison.'

The following hour has the sickening unreality of a nightmare. I hadn't thought I could be more frightened than I already was, but when the two policemen turn up, tall and brutal in their dark uniforms and with their hard, unforgiving stares, I feel my panic deepen. They lead us back out through the mall, amidst the watching crowds, to a door marked 'Security' next to the car park lifts. Even Edie is silent now, her mouth set grimly as we're shown into a low-lit office with a bank of TV screens on the wall. We're left on our own in the corner while the police are joined by Keith and the security guard, and together they watch the screens. Through a gap between their heads I see grainy black-and-white film showing the shop we'd just left, the footage spooling rapidly between different angles and perspectives, while the men confer between themselves.

I'm barely listening, my mind too full of panic to grasp what they're saying, and when I hear the words 'black spot' I can't take it in until Edie nudges me in the ribs and whispers, 'Did you hear that? It means they didn't film it, they haven't got you on tape,' and she smiles triumphantly.

A desperate hope begins to swell within me until the manager turns and snaps, 'We still found the dress in your bag though, didn't we, so don't get too cocky.'

And through it all, the knowledge that we are coming closer and closer to the thing I dread most of all: the moment when my mother finds out what I've done. Soon it's the only thing I can think of, and I feel almost that I would prefer to go to prison than have to face her. By the time one of the policemen asks me to write down

107

my address and phone number, I'm shaking so much it's all I can do to hold the pen. I listen in a sort of daze as he picks up the phone and dials the number. 'Mrs Wilcox?' he says, and the world seems to stop.

Edie touches my hand. 'Are you OK?' But I don't answer, just listen to the flatly authoritative voice explaining to my mother what I've done. I imagine her on the other end of the line, the disgust on her face. At last he puts the phone down and, glancing at his colleague, says, 'On her way.'

The manager, one of the policemen and the security guard have all left again before, forty endless minutes later, she arrives. In the seconds before she looks at me, I have the peculiar sensation of seeing her through a stranger's eyes and I'm shocked at how ordinary she looks, like anyone's mum, her expression a little fearful, a little vulnerable and I feel a sad, desperate flare of love. And then her gaze finds mine and in that second before she has time to alter it, the look in her eyes transports me back instantly to a moment ten summers ago. I feel a crushing pressure in the centre of my chest and a second later she turns away.

'What exactly is this about?' she asks the policeman.

'Your daughter was found trying to leave a shop with an item of clothing she hadn't paid for,' he tells her.

Mum presses her lips together. 'Well, there must be some mistake.'

'It appears that the item was put into her bag in an area not covered by CCTV,' he goes on. 'But security personnel were alerted by the alarm system and the item was found on your daughter's person.'

I'm so dizzy with fear that I don't hear properly at first when Edie begins to speak. And then I notice that everyone has turned to look at her. She sniffs and folds her arms, levelling her eyes at the policeman. 'It was me,' she says. 'I put it in her bag when she wasn't looking.'

I shake my head. 'N—' but the look Edie shoots me stops me in my tracks. Her voice is very clear and sure. 'I did it,' she says.

My mum snorts. 'There!' she says triumphantly. 'You see? My daughter is not a thief.' She gathers up my bag and coat. 'I don't think you need to keep us any longer, do you? Come on, Heather. We're going home.'

The officer considers her, then shrugs and nods. 'As long as you're aware of the seriousness of the situation she can go, but we will need to speak to her at a later date. We'll be in touch.'

Mum pulls me by the arm but I don't move. I look at Edie, sitting there in the office all alone with the policeman, and I want to stay and shout that it's not true, that it wasn't her, that it was me. But my mother yanks my arm so hard that we are back in the busy mall with the door swinging shut behind us before I can even draw breath. 'No!' I say, shaking my head frantically. 'No.'

She narrows her eyes at me, her icy fury instantly silencing me. 'Don't, Heather,' she hisses. 'Just don't.'

On the drive home she doesn't say a word, except once, through gritted teeth, as we pull out of the car park, 'You are never seeing that girl again. Do you hear me?' I lean my head against the window and I drift away inside myself, thinking about Edie all alone in that horrible room with no one to come for her, and of how she'd rescued me.

After

It's slow, the rising out of the blackness, but it's steady and it's sure. I awake one bright, cold morning to a gust of rain scattering against the window and for a while I stare out at the empty white sky and struggle to remember what time of year it is, or how many days or weeks have passed since I've been lying here, unable to get up. Could it be autumn, or even winter now?

A piercing cry slices through the silence. Maya. I stay where I am, waiting anxiously for Heather to come, but still she cries and cries. I put my hands over my ears and close my eyes, feeling the familiar panic rising in my chest. Thirty seconds pass, then another, and Maya's screams become more and more urgent, edging ever nearer towards hysteria. Has Heather gone out? Has she left me? At last I pull myself up from under my duvet, and I force myself to go to the cot.

Maya stops mid-wail when she sees me and we watch each other silently, warily, for a long moment or two. I take in her angry red face, her thick black hair, her pursed little mouth, her balled fists and furrowed brow and then, without any warning, she smiles. It spreads across her face like sunlight and I'm barely aware of what I'm doing as I slowly reach out my hand. I hold my breath as she curls her fingers around my thumb. Time stops, the world waits. Silently I lift her from her bed and hold her to me, her head tucked beneath my chin, her breath warm against my neck. We stay like that for a long moment, and I breathe in the sweet, warm scent of her, as the realization hits me that this is the first time I have touched her for many, many weeks. She stirs gently in my arms as the tears roll down my cheeks, and she sighs, softly, against my chest.

'Maya!' Heather's voice makes us both jump and the baby's face instantly crumples. Guiltily, I begin to lower her back to her cot while Heather, wrapped in my dressing gown, wet hair plastered across her face, crosses the room and snatches her from me so roughly that I stumble backwards in alarm. I watch, my heart pounding in shock as she takes her away with her to the window. 'Did you have a fright?' Heather is cooing softly, 'Poor little girl, I'm here, don't you worry, I'm here now.'

And so I go, leaving them alone, closing the door behind me. But something, something has changed.

*　　*　　*

I'm aware of myself and my surroundings for the first time in weeks – of my grimy skin and hair, the stale, thick taste in my mouth, the airlessness of the flat. And finally I wake one morning and know that I can't lie here any longer, here on this dirty sheet in my own stink with my memories and my nightmares, for one moment more. I listen to the flat for a while until I'm sure that Heather and Maya are out before I haul myself from my bed and stumble towards the bathroom.

It's only when I'm standing under the shower that I realize how much weight I've lost; my ribs jut out beneath grey skin, my arms and legs are puny, stick-like. I close my eyes against the scorching water, letting it wash over me while I stand motionless, trying not to think. When I emerge, smelling of soap and wearing clean clothes, I feel oddly raw and frail, as though the dirt and grease had been protective armour against a too-bright, too-cold world. My mind feels foggy and slow. I stand at the window for a while, looking out at the rainy streets below, the roofs and cars and lampposts, the dogs and people and pigeons pecking in the gutters.

Heather has made us beans on toast and for the first time since she moved in we sit together in the kitchen to eat. I feel almost as though I'm sleeping, dreaming still, my mind unable to fully process the reality of the two of us sitting here together like this, after all this time.

'Are your mum and dad doing all right?' I ask and the words hang in the air, absurdly polite.

113

She nods. 'Yes thanks,' she says. 'They're OK.'

A silence. 'What is it they do in Birmingham again?'

She shrugs. 'Dad teaches there,' she says vaguely.

I remember that she had told me, when she first turned up on my doorstep all those weeks ago, that she worked in a newsagent's, and I leap on this eagerly. 'And you work in a . . .'

'Library,' she finishes for me, brightly. 'Yes. That's right.'

'But—' I stare at her in confusion. However there's something about her unblinking gaze that makes any further questions die on my lips, and we continue to eat in silence for a while.

I can only hear the sound of myself chewing and swallowing, the food sticking to the roof of my mouth. I sneak glances at her, trying to gauge what she's thinking, but her face once again has the same mild, cheerful expression I remember so well, apparently entirely content not to speak, oblivious to the strangeness of the situation we have found ourselves in.

Suddenly, a fly that had been buzzing sluggishly around the room lands on the table between us. Heather considers it for a moment or two before calmly raising her hand and squashing the insect beneath her palm. She wipes her hand absent-mindedly on her jumper, before continuing with her meal.

I put down my knife and fork. 'I'm so sorry, Heather, to have lumbered you with all this.' She looks up at me, still chewing, her expression unchanged. 'I got a bit overwhelmed by it all, I suppose. I felt so . . .' I shake my head, trying to put into words how desperate I'd felt, how little I'd cared about Maya or whether I'd lived or died, how total the darkness had been. And how frightened I am that this small reprieve is only temporary; that whatever it was is waiting to claim me again, and that there's nothing I'll be able to do to stop it. 'I'm so grateful for all your help, especially as we haven't been in touch for . . . such a long time.'

At this Heather blinks and smiles. 'Don't be silly, Edie,' she says. 'I'm your best friend. I'm glad we found each other again, glad I could help. Don't worry, I won't go anywhere, I won't leave you.' She reaches across the table and takes my hand in hers. 'We'll be all right, the three of us, you'll see.'

I stare down at the large white fingers clasping mine. I'm about to ask her *why* she came to find me now, after all these years, when I notice that her sleeve has pulled back to reveal the skin on her forearm. The underside is covered in scars, some so old that they are silver, faint; but most darker, more recent, a mess of raised bumpy redness that covers her lower arm up to her elbow. A second later her eyes follow mine and she pulls her hand away, the scars disappearing once more beneath her sleeve while shock pulses through me.

At that moment Maya begins to cry in the next room, and I half stand. 'What does she want . . . ?' I ask anxiously. 'Should I . . . ?'

But Heather smiles and gets to her feet. 'She wants her bottle, that's all,' she says. 'Don't worry, I'll get it.'

And so I find myself in this most bizarre of predicaments, living here with Heather, someone I'd once hoped I'd never see again for the rest of my life. I make myself get up each morning, forcing myself to wash and dress and eat breakfast with her in the kitchen. I find that I can keep the waves of anxiety at bay if I try not to think further than the next hour ahead. Heather and I squeeze past each other in the cramped flat as she tends to Maya; washing and changing and feeding her with such assurance that my tentative, fearful attempts to help are useless almost before I've begun. 'It's OK,' she says, each time I reach for a nappy or a bottle, 'I can do it.'

'You're good at this,' I tell her.

She beams at me. 'I like looking after you both,' she says. 'You and Maya. She's so beautiful, I love her so much.' Heather reaches over and pats my hand, her fleshy fingers surprisingly hot. I try my best to smile back at her, and silently count to four before I pull my hand from hers.

'You do so much for us,' I say later, gazing at the fridge full of food, the bags of nappies and wipes and tins of formula. I dimly remember handing her my debit card at some point during those dark and desperate early weeks, so she could access my child benefit. 'I'll do the next big shop, I promise.' But even as I say it, the thought of leaving this flat is terrifying.

Instead I spend my days sitting in front of the TV, or staring out of the window or watching Heather as she moves busily about, taking in the familiar size and shape and feel of her, the frizzy yellow hair that has strands of grey in it now, the wide, round face that's exactly as it was but for the fine lines around her mouth and eyes. And as I watch her, I wonder what life has been like for her since leaving Fremton, where she has been and what she has done in the years between then and now.

I try to imagine what somebody who'd never met her before would think of her, what sort of person they'd see. A plain, heavyset woman, entirely ordinary; the kind you'd see anywhere, on any day. And yet there is something – has always been something – off-kilter about Heather, something you only notice after you've known her for a while. An indefinable thing missing somehow. It's there, in the too-eager smile that never falters, in that fixed, hazel stare. The way she is so large and clumsy yet can creep up behind you so silently that you don't realize she's there until you turn and find her right behind you, just inches away.

I think about our early friendship, how lost and lonely I'd been when Mum had first moved us to Fremton. Heather had been so sweet to me, so loving, so endlessly supportive. She'd listen to me complain about my mother and I knew she understood; it was something we had in common after all, the feeling that our parents didn't care. And I suppose I even liked that she was a bit out of step with the world, because it meant she looked up to me and gave me her endless attention. I liked the person I was in her eyes – so much more impressive than the person I felt I actually was. But before long, I'd become wrapped up in Connor and his world. Perhaps she'd felt abandoned, then. Perhaps that's why, later, she betrayed me the way she did.

In the evenings, when Maya sleeps, we sit side by side on the narrow sofa, eating our dinners off our laps. She likes to watch reruns of *Friends*, four or five episodes back to back, and she sits in the flickering darkness with her microwaved ready meal wobbling on her lap, chuckling along with the canned laughter, entirely absorbed, her thigh or her arm rubbing against mine as she eats.

Finally I wake one morning with another long, empty day stretching ahead and realize that if I stay inside these three cramped rooms for very much longer, I will go back to bed and stay there for ever, not moving until I have disappeared entirely, until there's nothing left of me. And though the desire to give into that is almost impossible to resist, nonetheless there is something that stops me, something that began to stir within me the day Maya smiled and I held her to me. A quiet little voice that won't go away telling me to pull myself together, to take care of my daughter, to at least try.

I wait until Heather has gone to the bathroom and I hear the shower running and then, my hands shaking, not quite believing what I'm about to do, I make up a bottle of formula, gather Maya's outdoor clothes and blanket together, lift her from her cot, and ignoring the banging in my chest, the tightness in my throat, slip out of the door.

The outside world feels too big, too bright, the everyday noise and rush too loud and frantic after the stuffy, reassuring prison of my flat. I hurry along the street without any real idea of where I'm going or what I'm doing. At first it's as though I'm walking in a dream, my legs not seeming to work properly, the sycamore trees, traffic, lamp-posts and paving stones swimming behind a haze of light autumnal rain. I walk with my face turned away from passers-by, expecting them to stop me, to ask me what I think I'm doing; a kidnapper, a criminal. A bus pulls in at a stop ahead of me, letting a stream of jostling passengers on and off, and after hesitating for just a moment I jump through the doors a second before they close.

Inside it's warm and crowded. When someone stands to give me their seat I sink into it gratefully, holding Maya tightly, wrapped inside her blanket still asleep. Early-morning commuters press against me, smelling of damp coats. Rain begins to pelt hard upon the windows, the bus sighs and shudders its way through the school-run traffic towards Lewisham and I feel myself begin to relax for the first time in months. I look down at my sleeping daughter and feel her warm, solid weight in my arms and I realize with a sense of wonder that for once there is no accompanying rush of panic. I shift her in my arms, guarding her from the swaying press of steaming, warm bodies.

119

My attention wanders to a crowd of schoolgirls by the door, a damp huddle of Ugg boots and navy uniforms beneath a cloud of clashing perfumes. They giggle behind their braces, their nervy, excited eyes flitting to each other beneath mascara-clogged lashes. But when at the next stop another girl gets on, her skirt short, her legs long, the breathless giggling and chatter vanishes as they silently watch her climb the stairs and disappear. Their young faces instantly sour.

'Thinks she's fucking lush.'

'Thinks she's gorgeous.'

'He'll dump her, then she'll be all like, trying to be our mate again.'

'Knew I liked him.'

'Bitch. Fucking two-faced bitch.'

The bus has climbed the hill from Lewisham to Blackheath now and beyond the wet windows I see the wobbly green expanse of heath stretching out on either side. On impulse I ring the bell and when I get off I see that the rain has stopped and small patches of blue have begun to appear amidst the grey. I take a path that cuts through the middle of the heath, away from the road and traffic. The sky seems vast here with no buildings to clutter it. I breathe in the scent of wet grass and feel as though a dark pressure has lifted from my chest. I find a bench to sit on, the church and shops and streets of Blackheath behind me, and watch a couple in the distance walk their dog towards Greenwich Park. A gentle breeze picks up, the sky has paled to a light, hazy blue. Far away to my right, three children chase an orange kite. The dark, cluttered flat and Heather seem very far away.

I feel Maya stir in my arms and watch as she begins to wake, her large brown eyes fixed upon my face. I hold my breath, afraid of her reaction when she realizes it's me and not Heather who holds her, but she merely yawns and looks about her, apparently unfazed to find herself here, outside, in the middle of the heath with me. She turns back to consider me again and I feel a strange, fleeting lightness, a momentary sense of weightlessness as our eyes meet. Something inside me at that moment seems to unlock, and we look and we look at each other and I feel such shock as I think: How did I not see? How did I not see before how beautiful, how lovely you are?

It's less than a couple of hours later when another bus returns us to the bottom of my road, but it's as if some of the wide-open space and fresh air I'd left behind has seeped into me, lifting my spirits, lightening my step. As I walk, Maya rests against me, trusting and peaceful in my arms. The feeling of calm stays with me as I make my way to my building, but as I fish my key from my pocket I look up to the top floor and stop in my tracks to see Heather there, a faceless silhouette against the glass. My forehead tenses with a sudden ache as I look doubtfully down at Maya. She will be hungry soon and needs to be changed, but though my chest begins to

121

tighten with anxiety, the thought of returning to the flat fills me with despair. I remain on the step, frozen.

'Are you all right?'

Monica is on the pavement behind me, laden with shopping bags.

I feel myself redden, aware of how strange I must look. 'Yes,' I say, but I'm unable to continue, or make myself do anything else but stare back at her, my door key in my hand.

Her eyes are a pale greyish blue, like cool, still water, and they assess me silently for a moment, before she steps past me and, unlocking the door, lets us both in.

'Haven't seen you about much,' she says, when we're standing in the hall. She has a nice voice, low and husky with a strong London accent. I hold Maya closer to me. 'No,' I say, and I look at the floor. 'I haven't been very well.'

She nods, and I feel her thoughtful gaze linger before she goes to her own front door. 'Well, mind how you go,' she says, and I know this is my cue to leave, to return upstairs, but I still can't seem to move.

I watch her turn her key in first one lock, then another and at the third one she hesitates. 'You can come in for a cuppa, if you want,' she says and I find myself nodding and following her into her flat, looking about myself as she bolts the door behind us again.

Before

Dad stands behind his desk with his back to me, looking down at the garden below. Finally he clears his throat. 'Corinthians tells us, Heather, that bad company ruins good morals.' He turns and peers at me, as though checking whether I've taken it in, and dutifully I nod. For as long as I can remember, Dad has spoken to me in Bible passages, it's like he finds it easier somehow. At any rate, I'm glad it's him doing this and not Mum, who hasn't spoken to me since we returned from Walsall two days ago.

'Your mother is – well, your mother and I are – extremely concerned about what happened last Tuesday.'

'Dad,' I begin, but he holds up a finger to silence me.

'Now, I'm aware that it was the, er, the other girl who was responsible, but it is nevertheless troubling that you allowed yourself to become caught up in it all.'

I look at my feet.

'You have your future to consider,' he continues. 'What about your education? Your medical career?'

I'm not sure whether he wants an answer; it seems not because he hurries on: 'I think it's best if you avoid this . . . Ellie person from now on.'

Instead of replying I clench my fists so hard the nails dig into my palms. After a pause he comes over to me and puts his hands upon my shoulders. 'Heather, trust in the Lord with all your heart, and do not lean on your own understanding. In all your ways acknowledge Him, and He will make straight your paths.'

I nod, wondering how on earth he manages to remember this stuff, and I murmur a vague response until finally I'm dismissed. I go to my room and sit down on my bed to think about Edie. I haven't spoken to her since Tuesday and sometimes I can't sleep for worrying. What if the police arrested her? What if she's in huge trouble? It would all be my fault. Twice I've sneaked out to the phone box on the corner to call her. The first time it rang and rang, the next it was snatched up almost immediately, only for my hopes to be dashed as soon as I heard her mother's voice on the other end. 'She's not in,' she'd said snappishly. 'Haven't seen her for hours. If you do find her, tell her to come home, I need her to go to the shops for me.' At least it didn't sound as though Edie had been thrown in prison. I sit and gnaw at my thumbnail. Where is she? Is she all right? Does she hate me?

I hear my father's door open and the sound of his footsteps retreating down the stairs. A little later there's the muffled rise and fall of voices. Even from here I can tell they're arguing. The sharp staccato of my mother's voice against the low, unyielding rumble of Dad's, like pebbles clattering against a brick wall. I cover my ears with my hands and then on impulse jump to my feet. My heart racing with a sudden daring I pause at my door and listen. Then I dart across the hall to Dad's study. I stand staring at the phone on his desk before snatching it up and dialling the number I've learnt by heart. *Please please please*, I think. And on the fifth ring she picks up. 'Edie!' I hiss. 'It's me!'

'Oh, hiya,' she says, and it sounds as though she's eating something, the words muffled by a crunching, chewing noise. I imagine her biting into a piece of toast, her fingers sticky with butter or jam, her lips covered in crumbs. Relief and joy floods me.

'Are you OK?' I ask. 'I've been so worried.'

'What?' she says distractedly. 'Oh, yeah, the police and that. What a fucking drag.' I'm so happy to hear her voice my face aches with smiling. 'What were you thinking, you doughnut?' she says.

'I know,' I whisper. 'I'm really, really sorry. What happened? Are you all right, did they . . . did they, charge you?'

'Give over. Course not. Sent me home and phoned my mum. Who didn't give a shit, obviously. More worried that she'd run out of fags.' She takes another

125

bite of whatever she's eating, and I hear her chew then swallow. 'They wanted her to go to the station but course she can't. So they're sending someone over, or so they reckon. Though they haven't. Obviously.'

'I don't know how to thank you,' I tell her, 'for taking the blame like that, I mean. No one's ever done anything like that for me before. It was amazing, Edie, it was . . .'

'Yeah, well. Your mum looked like she was going to kill you, so—'

I hear the kitchen door open downstairs. 'I've got to go, I've got to go!' I tell her frantically. 'I'll see you at school, shall I? You'll be there, won't you?'

'Yeah,' she says. 'I'll—'

But hearing my father's step on the stairs I quickly replace the handset and shoot back across the hall to my room.

That night as I'm getting ready for bed I think about how great it had been to hear her voice. Three days until school starts, until I see her again. And best of all, I'll have her all to myself because Connor won't be there. I picture the two of us, gossiping and laughing together in the corridors between lessons, lending each other make-up and sharing secrets in the loos. I think about how she'd saved me in the shop and my heart almost bursts with happiness.

Later, when the house is quiet and the night is thick and dark outside and I'm in bed beneath my duvet, my mind wanders as it often does to the memory of when

126

Edie and I went to Connor's flat, of how I'd seen them lying together on the bed. I wonder how Edie had felt, to have Connor's hands on her like that, and I think about how her dress had been undone, its skirt pulled up, her skin flushed and trembling beneath his fingers.

On Saturday I sneak out early to the market and manage to find a couple of tops like the one Edie had picked out for me in Walsall. On Sunday I go to church with Dad, expecting Mum to join us, and I'm surprised when we set off without her. I glance at Dad and consider asking him where she is, but think better of it. It occurs to me that Mum hadn't gone to church last Sunday either – she'd said she'd not felt well and Dad had left without her. Puzzled, I try to cast my mind back to previous weekends; had this happened before? I'd been so caught up with Edie I'd not noticed.

On Monday I wake early and shoot worried glances at Mum over breakfast, wondering if she'll say anything about my new clothes and the make-up I'm wearing, but she barely looks at me. I feel a little shocked, so accustomed am I to her watchful, critical gaze. In fact, the only time she speaks is to say to Dad, 'I won't be here when you get back, I'm spending the afternoon over at Wrexham. A fundraiser I'm helping with.' He nods, but they don't look at each other, and I ponder this for a moment or two before my attention returns to Edie, and to wondering what time she'll be in school.

The sixth-form block is already full of people, the

corridors buzzing with students when I arrive. I search the crowds for Edie's face, waiting until the last bell has gone and the corridors have completely cleared before I reluctantly make my way to my Maths class without having seen her. Sick with disappointment, I find a seat and try to concentrate on the lesson. Mr Shepherd's voice drones endlessly on while I stare unseeingly at my textbook and the hot, early autumn sun pours through the window, making my eyelids heavy and my head ache. As soon as it's over I scramble from my seat and head for the canteen. I take my place in the queue and, full of hope, buy myself and Edie a Coke, then quickly add an orange juice and a cup of tea too, just in case she'd like that more, before finding a table for two at the window and settling down to wait.

I hear her before I see her, her loud laugh ringing out across the canteen's hubbub, and I jump to my feet, craning my neck until at last I see her, flanked on either side by Alice Walsh and Vicky Morris, two girls who had been in my form last year. I hesitate, my heart sinking. As I watch, they queue and buy their food together before taking their trays over, still laughing, to the far end of the canteen and finding a table. She doesn't even look for me.

Slowly I pick up my tray and make my way over. 'Edie?' I say, and I have to cough and repeat myself before the three of them look up.

'Oh, hiya,' she says, smiling. 'Was wondering where you'd got to.'

I feel Vicky and Alice's eyes on me and the heat rises in my cheeks. Why, of all people, did it have to be these two who Edie chose to sit with? I clear my throat. 'I thought we . . . well, I saved us a table over there,' I mumble.

'Oh, right,' she says. 'Sorry, didn't realize.'

I continue to stand there, holding the tray, wishing that she'd get up. 'Well, why don't you sit down here?' she asks, with a puzzled laugh.

And so I do. I notice that she's already got herself a Coke and I look at the four drinks on my tray, not wanting any of them now. 'All right, Heather?' Vicky says, and I mutter a 'hello'.

'You all know each other, right?' Edie is glancing from one to another of us.

'Yeah, we all know Heather,' Alice says, and the tone of her voice is unmistakable. 'How are you?' she adds in a phony grown-up voice, but I don't reply. She turns back to Edie, ignoring me again. 'Yeah, so why don't you come along some time?'

I don't know what they're talking about and I don't care. As I sip my Coke I shoot glances at the three of them: Vicky with her flat, blonde hair and peach lipstick and sly blue eyes, Alice a slightly less pretty carbon copy of her. The school's A-listers. Five years' worth of their taunts and ridicule echo around my head. I bite the inside of my cheek until I taste blood and realize that Edie is looking at me. 'They're talking about this club they go to in Walsall,' she explains. 'You fancy it?'

129

Before I can answer, Vicky says with a little laugh, 'I don't think it's really your thing, is it, Heather?'

I stare down at my plate.

'Wouldn't want you having one of your funny turns, would we?' says Alice, and she and Vicky both titter.

I feel myself flush a hot crimson. They're talking about the daydreams I have, the ones I can't seem to snap out of. Sometimes in the middle of a lesson I'll sort of 'wake up' to find the whole class staring and sniggering at me and I'll look around me, blinking and ashamed. And then there are the other times, when I lose my temper or get upset. I don't want Edie to know about those, either. I don't want her to think I'm a freak too.

'What're you on about?' Edie's voice is sharp as she looks at Alice. 'Heather?' she turns to me but I get to my feet and run from the room.

I'm halfway across the playground by the time she catches up with me. 'Hey,' she says, grabbing my arm. 'What the hell's wrong with you?'

I stop, my breath thick in my throat. 'It's just. I thought . . .' My voice trails off weakly. 'I saved you a seat.'

'Oh, don't be mental. I can sit where I like, you know.' She stares at me in exasperation and when I don't say anything, she sighs. 'Those two were in my class earlier, that's all. I didn't ask them to follow me to lunch.'

I nod miserably and she gives me a nudge. I look up to see that she's smiling at me, and it's her lovely, warm, toothy smile, the one that makes me feel as though no one else exists in the world but the two of us; it beams down on me, warming me, as though I've been pulled from cold dark water into sunlight.

'Didn't want to hang out with them anyway,' she says. 'All they do is bitch bitch bitch, I can't stand it.' She mimics their local accent, 'Did you see so-and-so in that skirt, she looks well fat. So-and-so got off with what's his face, she's a right slapper.' She rolls her eyes. 'God! It's so bloody boring, don't you think?'

'Yes,' I say, starting to smile despite myself.

She takes my arm. 'Come on mardy-arse, I'm off to meet Connor in the square. You can come too, if you want. Love your top, by the way.'

He's already in the square when we get there, standing with a group of other lads by the statue, and when she goes to them I sit on a bench to wait. Maybe she'll want to do something later, I tell myself. Just the two of us – maybe this day will end up the way it was supposed to after all. I hug my school bag and watch them. They're the type you'd usually cross the road to avoid, Connor's friends. They stand around, hard-faced and shifty-eyed, shaven-headed and tattooed, sucking on roll-ups or from cans of lager, an edgy sort of boredom rising from them into the clear blue sky. My parents would call them lowlifes, would faint in shock at the thought of me near them.

Connor stands in the centre of them all, his good looks and quiet, watchful air setting him apart from the others, who glance back at him frequently, as if waiting for his approval. Edie stands next to him, her hand on his arm and talking animatedly, but he barely responds, as though he's not really listening, and as I watch, his eyes meet mine, his cool green stare resting on my face before it flicks away again and I shiver.

And then, suddenly, a commotion. A beer can sails through the air and hits a lad I hadn't noticed before standing on the edge of the group, the frothy spray exploding over his face and down his neck. 'Fuck's sake,' he says, as the others laugh and jeer. He walks away from them, towards me. He's younger than the others, probably about my age, his shoulders thin beneath the hoodie he's wearing, something childlike in the way he's pulled the sleeves right over his hands. He sits down at the other end of the bench and starts rolling a cigarette and after a while I take a breath and say, 'Hi, I'm Heather, Edie's friend.' He glances up and nods; 'Liam,' he says.

'Look at him, daft cunt,' the jeering voice carries over to us, 'chatting up the fat lass!'

I feel myself flush. 'Shut up, that's my mate,' Edie says, and though her tone's indignant, for a moment I think I detect a hint of laughter there too. I look back at her sharply but she's turned away now and I can't be sure.

Suddenly Connor mutters something and a loud laugh erupts. Heat courses through me as I realize they're staring at my chest. I look down and see that my new

132

top has started to gape at the neckline, exposing a large chunk of cleavage. Mortified, I tug at it, trying to cover myself. When I look at Edie I see her smile has vanished, her eyes cold as she looks from me to Connor.

'Come on,' she says to him sullenly. 'Thought we were going to the rec for a smoke?'

He nods and they start to move away. At the last moment Edie looks back at me, 'You coming, Heather?' she says, not quite meeting my gaze.

I shake my head. 'No, it's OK, I better—' But she's already turned away.

Liam gets to his feet and glances down at me. 'Later,' he mumbles, before hurrying after them.

I remain where I am, watching them move off across the square, a dull sort of misery rising inside me as the crowd parts to let them through. Finally I get up and start to walk home, dragging my feet slowly. But as I'm crossing the bridge that goes over the canal, I glance down and see a figure hurrying along the towpath away from me, wearing a familiar coat. It's my mother. I stop in my tracks and watch, astonished, as she walks off in the direction of Langley. What on earth is she doing? She'd told Dad she was spending the day in Wrexham, but that's miles in the other direction – and besides, the canal is the last place I'd expect her to walk by herself. Baffled, I watch until she disappears from view before continuing on my way home.

After

Monica's flat is very different from mine; much bigger, and, despite the security bars at the windows and the closely drawn net curtains, it's light and warm and uncluttered. The kitchen she leads me to is clean and freshly painted with colourful prints on the walls and photos of her smiling sons stuck to the fridge. The dog I'd seen before lies peacefully in the corner of the room, merely thumping its tail when we enter. I take the seat Monica offers me and, with Maya on my lap, watch her as she puts the kettle on and begins to unpack her shopping.

She is, I guess, in her early forties, her small face lined beneath the red, scraped-back hair that's peppered with strands of grey. Although she's very small she has a wiry sort of strength, a toughness in the way she moves and holds herself. When she pauses to remove her jacket I study the colourful, intricate patterns and pictures tattooed over almost every inch of her slender arms and shoulders. She turns and catches me staring and I feel myself redden as I look away. As she finishes making the tea and takes the seat across from me I shift Maya in my arms and mentally grasp about for something to say.

I wish I hadn't come. I'm astonished that I have, so unlike me is it to barge my way into a stranger's flat like this, and now that I'm here I feel painfully aware that she must already be regretting having asked me, that she probably has a hundred better things to do.

'Bug, was it?' she asks, her eyes suddenly fastened on me. 'You said you've been ill.'

'No,' I say. 'Not a bug.' To my dismay I feel a lump in my throat and have to stare hard at the table until it goes away. I look at Monica's hands cupped around her mug of tea, her slender fingers heavy with gold rings. I notice that her tattoos stop a few inches before her wrists and I feel myself oddly touched by this small, private segment of un-inked flesh. I shake my head. 'I don't know,' I say. 'I guess I—'

'Been a bit low, have you?' she asks, and when I nod she considers this before telling me, 'I had that, with my first – Ryan. Couldn't hardly get out of bed for weeks. My sister had to look after the baby for me, dragged me to the doctor's in the end.' She doesn't look at me while she talks, apart from brief, penetrating moments when her eyes land upon my face, cool and warm at the same time, very different from Heather's unblinking stare.

'What was wrong with you?' I ask her hesitantly.

She shrugs. 'PND. Baby blues, whatever you want to call it. Doctor gave me some pills and I was all right after a while.'

Was that what it had been? I roll the thought around my head. PND. This deadening, dragging weight. 'It's been weeks, though,' I tell her. 'I haven't . . . I couldn't take care of her, of my baby.' I feel a rush of shame, and my eyes fill with tears.

I'm grateful that, in response, she merely reaches for a pack of cigarettes and lights herself one while I pull myself together. She exhales a long line of smoke before asking, thoughtfully, 'This the first time you've been out for a while, is it?' I swallow hard and nod. 'Well, then,' she says, 'maybe you're starting to feel a bit better.' She smiles at me, and despite my tears I'm struck by how it transforms her face, making her look in that instant like a much younger, prettier woman. 'Sometimes it just passes, goes of its own accord,' she continues. 'Hormones and that.' She nods at Maya. 'How old is she?'

And I realize with something close to panic that I have absolutely no idea. 'Um, what's the date again today?' I ask as casually as I can.

'First of October.'

Quickly I do the calculations. 'Six months,' I say quietly at last, 'she's six months old.' *But how could that be?* How could I possibly have lost so many weeks?

137

That would mean Heather had been living with us for over four months! I feel disorientated and afraid and at that moment Maya begins to cry. I try to quieten her, stroking her back like I'd seen Heather do, but she howls even harder, her face screwed into an angry red ball, her wail quickly gathering strength. 'Shush,' I say desperately, feeling a knot of anxiety in my chest. 'Come on, Maya, please stop.' But she only screams louder.

Monica, nonplussed, watches me for a while. 'Here, let me try.' She puts her cigarette in the corner of her mouth and takes Maya from me, moving around the room with her, shushing and jiggling her until she quietens, before handing her back to me. I take her nervously, certain that she'll only begin to cry again as soon as I touch her. 'Rock her,' Monica tells me encouragingly. 'Walk her around a bit and hold her close to you.' I do as she says and am amazed when Maya settles contentedly once more in my arms. Monica smiles. 'See?' she says. 'You're doing fine.' I look down at my daughter and wonder if it can be true.

We sit and drink our tea in silence, both of us watching Maya as she sleeps again in my lap, and I find myself wondering about Monica, about the scar on her back, about the locks and chains on her door, the security bars at the windows. After a while she lights another cigarette and says, 'See you've got your friend here. Seen her going in and out with the little one.' She blows out another stream of smoke. 'Been looking after you, has she?' And there's something in the way she looks at me,

138

something in her tone that suggests more than idle curiosity.

I nod. I had forgotten about Heather for a few minutes and I'm aware of the sudden sinking feeling her name brings.

'Good friend of yours, is she?' Monica persists and I think about how to answer this.

'It's only that I thought it was a bit odd,' she continues when I don't reply.

'Odd?'

'Because I recognized her, from before. I was a bit surprised to see her again, to be honest.'

'Recognized her? From where?'

But we are interrupted by a barrage of knocks on the door. The dog wakes and begins to bark ferociously, baring two huge rows of gleaming teeth. Heather's face flashes into my mind and I feel a stab of alarm, which disappears as soon as I look at Monica and realize with shock that she is almost white with fear. 'Who is it?' she asks, her voice low and tense. The hammering continues, and when a male voice calls, 'Mum. It's us. You've locked us out again,' I see, when she goes to the door, the relief that floods her face.

The tall, deep-voiced young men look amazed to find me sitting at their kitchen table. But they smile politely when their mother introduces us and I'm struck by how different they appear close to, compared to the picture I'd formed of them from afar. The eldest, Ryan, towers over Monica, an arm wrapped protectively around her shoulders, while his younger brother Billy kneels down to the dog, cooing lovingly at her as he strokes her ears. They fill the room, it seems to me, with their energy and their youth and their maleness, looking back at me with their mother's sensitive, shrewd blue eyes.

'You been all right, Mum?' asks Ryan, watching her carefully. 'Had a good day?'

She smiles. 'Not bad. Did the shopping earlier.'

Billy looks up from the dog, his eyebrows raised. 'By yourself?' When Monica nods, he looks pleased. 'Cool.'

Reluctantly I get to my feet, shifting Maya to my hip. 'I suppose I better get back,' I say. 'Thanks, though, for the tea.'

Monica smiles. 'You come back down if you need anything.'

It's only when I reach the door to my own flat that I remember she hadn't answered my question. What had she meant when she said she'd recognized Heather? Still puzzling it over, I take my key from my pocket and let myself in.

Standing on the threshold of my flat I gaze in with fresh eyes at the cluttered hall, its threadbare carpet covered in the sea of half-full plastic bags and cardboard boxes that contain Heather's belongings. It's begun to rain again and the gloom of the outside world has permeated the three small rooms, the only light coming from the flicker of the TV in the living room, its pale, fuzzy blue glow seeping weakly across the passageway and carrying on its tide a babble of chirpy American voices, applause and canned laughter.

When I switch the overhead light on Heather jumps from the sofa and crosses the room to where I stand so quickly that I take a step back and knock my shoulder against the door frame. She stares at me, her eyes bright, her hands opening and closing by her sides in agitation, and the thought occurs to me that she's going to hit me, until I realize it's Maya she's desperate for and I hand my daughter over wordlessly.

'Where have you been?' she asks, already moving away towards a bottle of milk perched in its warmer on the arm of the sofa, and I wonder how long it has been there, waiting for us.

'Out for a walk.'

'I was worried about you,' she says sullenly, as she settles herself with Maya and the bottle.

I sit down on the arm of the sofa. 'I know,' I say. 'I'm sorry. I should have told you or left a note or something.' She doesn't look up from Maya, who's drinking hungrily now. 'I thought it was about time I tried to pull myself together,' I tell her, 'and that maybe a walk alone with Maya would do me good.'

'I saw you come back ages ago, though,' she says. 'I watched you from the window.'

'I bumped into a neighbour,' I tell her, and when Heather's eyes shoot to my face I falter before continuing: 'Monica, who lives on the ground floor. She invited me in for a cup of tea.' I shrug, aware of my defensive tone. 'Maya was happy so I ended up staying for a while.' But as I talk I'm conscious of Heather's eyes on me, travelling over the surface of my face, her pupils twitching intently as though watching me speak rather than listening to what I say, and this lack of reaction is strangely unnerving, the way it is when you talk to someone whose eyes are hidden behind dark glasses. Eventually my voice trails away and we sit without speaking, the TV blaring.

Later, when Heather has bathed Maya and put her to bed, I go into the kitchen and begin to clear up. When I've finished I close the door and sit at the table and think about Monica and what she'd said today, and I think about how I'd felt when I'd held Maya on the heath and looked into her eyes, and I hold the memory of it close.

I half wake, sleep clinging to me; my dreams reluctant to release me as my eyes stare into the blackness. I had been dreaming about Connor, and his scent, his taste, his touch is still with me, as though he could reach out across time and distance, through the silent, dark night and pull me back until I'm there with him again. I feel myself slipping, slipping, his fingers strengthening their grip, pulling me closer as I drift back to him. And then, all at once, I'm wide awake and alert, my heart pounding. Something had woken me. What was that? A sound, a movement close by, very close. I reach out to push myself up from the mattress and my fingers suddenly, shockingly connect with flesh. I cry out in fright, launching myself backwards so quickly that I almost fall to the floor. As I look wildly about me my eyes adjust to the milky moonlight and see that it's Heather, sitting on my bed, staring back at me.

Confusion and fear twists in my gut. Is she awake? Sleepwalking? She doesn't move, only continues to watch me intently. It's so strange, so eerie. How long has she been sitting there? My voice when I manage to speak is a whisper. 'Heather?'

She moves suddenly, leaning towards me a fraction, and at last she speaks, 'You will help me, won't you, Edie?' she says. I stare at her. 'You will, won't you?' she persists.

My heart stiffens, almost stops, and in the darkness I nod. 'Yes,' I whisper. Her eyes remain fastened upon me, and then, as if satisfied, she nods once and gets up, the mattress shifting beneath the absence of weight. I watch as she makes her way back to her bed, hear her grunt as she lowers herself on to it then zips herself back into her sleeping bag. Moments later, her breath deepens into a snore.

When I wake again bright sunlight is streaming through the windows, Heather is moving back and forth humming softly to herself, Maya slung across her chest. Nothing has changed. She glances over and smiles brightly when she sees me watching her. 'I'll make some tea, shall I?' is all she says. Had it really happened? My dreams are so

143

vivid lately. Uncertainty washes through me. It makes no sense, after all; what could she possibly have meant? A dream, that was all. Just another one of my dreams.

Today is one of those perfect golden autumnal days when the sky sparkles over London, cloudless and blue. But Heather stands with her back to the window watching me in silence as I get Maya ready to go out. I've noticed recently that with every passing day, the stronger and more capable I feel, the more despondent Heather seems to become. Today she hasn't even bothered to have a shower or get dressed; instead she picks miserably at a piece of peanut butter on toast, wiping her sticky fingers on her dressing gown as she follows my movements around the room.

When she sees me grappling with the poppers on Maya's jacket she darts over to help. 'Let me do that,' she says eagerly, 'this one's a bit tricky.'

I'm surprised at the rush of irritation I feel. 'It's fine,' I say, resisting the urge to smack her fingers away. 'I can do it.'

Later, when Maya and I are ready, I pause at the door, feeling the customary pang of guilt. 'What are you going to do today?' I ask her. 'It looks really nice out there.'

She shrugs. 'I could come with you,' she suggests.

I nod, frowning as if thinking it over. 'Yeah, you could, but look, we're ready now and we won't be very long anyway, so we might as well just nip out quickly.' When she doesn't reply I can't help adding, 'Besides, do us good to have a breather from each other, don't you think? Cooped up together the way we are. This flat's so tiny . . .'

'But I like spending time with you,' Heather replies, and I smile, and I nod, and I mumble something in agreement, and finally I open the door. But before I leave I pause. 'Heather?' I say.

She looks up eagerly, 'Yes?'

'Do you have my phone?' Her eyes immediately flick away and she doesn't reply. 'Only, I was wondering where it was.'

She shrugs. 'Don't know,' she says vaguely. 'I put it somewhere . . .'

A flash of annoyance. 'I'd quite like it back, please. I need to phone my uncle.'

She nods again, and still doesn't meet my eyes, but I see something flicker across her face that makes me pause. 'Heather?' I say.

She looks at me sullenly. 'Yes, OK, I'll find it.'

And then finally, in the strange, thick silence, I leave.

I haven't seen Monica since the day I went to Blackheath so I'm pleased when I bump into her outside her front door. 'How are you?' she asks.

'I'm OK,' I tell her. 'Actually I'm a lot better.'

She gives me one of her quick, shrewd appraisals. 'Good,' she says. 'Where're you off to?'

I shrug. 'Just going for a walk.' I make a face. 'Had to get out.'

'I'll walk with you,' she says, and I feel a ripple of pleasure. It's been so long since I had friends that I'm not sure how it's done any more – how you make that leap, show someone that you want to spend time with them. We walk in silence for a while, Maya babbling happily in her buggy, the soft October sun on our faces. 'Why'd you have to get out of the flat?' Monica asks.

I hesitate, thinking of how to answer, but in the end I say, 'There's not much room with the three of us there.'

She nods. 'Yeah,' she says. 'I'll bet.'

And there's something in her voice that reminds me of what she'd said before about Heather. 'What did you mean,' I ask her, 'the other week, when you said you'd recognized my friend? Where had you seen her before?'

'Months ago,' she says, lighting a cigarette. 'I used to see her hanging around outside.'

I laugh nervously. 'Hanging around?' I ask. 'What do you mean? When?'

'Soon after I moved in.' We've reached the park gates now and we walk to the furthest side, to a bench beneath a horse chestnut tree. 'I have a problem with my ex,' Monica continues, staring straight ahead. 'We moved here to get away from him. I try not to let him get to me, but I spend a lot of time looking out of the window to check he's not out there, especially at night when I can't sleep.' She glances at me. 'There she'd be, your friend, sitting on the wall opposite our building, sometimes at two or three o'clock in the morning.' She shakes her head, frowning. 'I even went out to talk to her once, see if I could find her a hostel or at least give her some food, but she ran off. Went on for weeks, it did. Couldn't believe it when I saw her coming in and out of our building a few months later with your buggy.'

As Monica talks an icy chill creeps up my spine. When had this been? I cast my mind back to when Heather had first knocked on my door. Was it after that she'd started to – to what? Watch me? *Stalk* me? Or had it been going on for longer? Unease and confusion twist in my gut. I think about how, sometimes, when I turn to catch Heather staring at me, there's this moment, gone almost before it's there, when I see a coldness in her eyes. And then the usual fixed smile returns, her gaze darts away again like a mouse into its hole, and everything is normal once more. I realize Monica is watching me, waiting for a response, but I have absolutely no idea what to tell her.

After a few moments she tactfully looks away. 'Well anyway, it's none of my business. I'm sure there's an explanation for it all.'

In the park we sit on the bench in the sunshine for a while. I take Maya out of her pram and put her on the grass next to a pile of conkers some other child must have left. Red and orange leaves drift down to us, a smell of bonfires floats over from the allotments a few streets away, and a faint hum of traffic, of idling buses and car horns and sirens rises from the mass of city streets stretched out far below. Maya reaches for a conker, holds it up to examine it and lets out a peal of laughter.

It's as we're leaving the park again that we bump into the man who I'd bought the cot from all those months ago. 'Hi!' he says, so enthusiastically that I have to check over my shoulder that he isn't talking to somebody else. 'James,' he says, a wide smile on his face. 'I sold you the, um . . .'

'I remember.' I nod, trying not to think about the state I'd been in the last time we'd met. 'How's it going?'

I turn to Monica. 'James sold me Maya's cot.' There's a flicker of amusement in her eyes as she says hello.

A short, awkward silence follows. 'Well, nice to see you again,' I say.

'I was just heading to work, actually,' he tells me as we're about to move off.

'Oh,' I say, and, because I've no idea what else to do I stand and nod for a while, aware of Monica's eyes on me, and for no reason I can think of, feel myself redden. 'OK, have a good day then.'

But he doesn't move. 'I teach evening classes at Goldsmiths. Fine art, actually.' When I don't reply his eyes flicker over Monica and he adds, 'It's the, um the university down the road.'

'Yeah,' I say. 'We know what it is.' From the corner of my eye I see Monica's mouth twitch.

'My students have a show of their work next week,' he goes on hurriedly. 'You could come, if you want.'

'Me?'

148

He laughs. 'It's usually a good night – a few glasses of shit wine while you look at the art, then there's a bit of a party in the pub afterwards.'

'I could babysit,' says Monica, and smirks when I narrow my eyes at her over James's shoulder.

'Well anyway,' James is searching in his bag for a pen, and begins scribbling something on a piece of paper. 'Here's my number. If you fancy it, next Tuesday, give me a ring.'

I take it. 'Right. OK. Thanks.'

Monica barely manages to wait until he's out of earshot before she starts to laugh. 'Bless him. He could hardly pick his tongue up off the floor.'

I shake my head, embarrassed. 'What, him? Don't be silly.'

She nudges me with her elbow, 'Don't give me that.' She has a nice laugh, and I find myself smiling back at her.

'Well, anyway, he's really not my type,' I say.

She glances at me in surprise. 'He was all right. Thought he was a bit of a sort, actually.'

'A *sort*?' I say, laughing too.

We walk on a little further before she asks mildly, 'So what is your type?'

I shrug. Heri's face pops into my mind, followed by the handful of men I'd been careful not to get involved with over the years. In fact there has been nobody really since Connor, and the moment I think of him, of his green eyes, his mouth, I see him so clearly, recall exactly

149

the way he smelled, the way it felt to kiss him, the overwhelming, all-consuming attraction I'd felt for him, that I shudder. I never want to feel like that about anyone again. 'No one,' I say quietly. 'I don't have one.' I'm aware of Monica looking at me but I avoid her eye and the jokey atmosphere between us dies. We walk on in silence.

When we reach the top of our road she says gently, 'Why don't you go to that art thing? You never know, it might be a laugh. Do you good to get out, even if it is for' – she imitates James's slightly posh accent – 'a glass of shit wine.'

I smile. 'Maybe,' I say.

'I really could babysit.'

'Well, but there's Heather,' I reply.

'Oh yeah,' she says, looking away. 'That's true, there's Heather.'

We say goodbye and I pause outside her flat, staring at the closed door and mulling over what she'd said before about seeing Heather outside our building all those months ago. It makes no sense, and as I start up the stairs to my flat, unease shifts in my gut.

Before

I stare down at my maths homework, unable to concentrate, my mind returning repeatedly to the strange sight of Mum hurrying along the towpath an hour before. The house is still and silent; my dad won't be back for hours yet. I suck my Biro and turn another page, trying to concentrate. Had there been something furtive in the way she moved – her quick stride, her head bowed as though she hadn't wanted to be seen – or had I imagined that? My mother never did anything she wasn't supposed to. She did everything properly and correctly – my mum was never wrong. Fractions and statistical tables swim before my eyes and at last I put aside my textbook and go downstairs to watch TV.

I'm making myself a snack in the kitchen a couple of hours later when the front door opens and Mum appears. Instinctively I shove the jar of peanut butter to one side, but too late, her eyes pounce upon it and she frowns. 'Heather, you do realize how fattening that is, don't you?' She puts her bag down and fills the kettle. 'How was school?' she asks briskly.

'All right,' I say, grateful that she's at least talking to me again.

'I hope you stayed away from Edie?'

Mutely I nod.

'Good.' She busies herself making a cup of tea. 'I expect you have some homework or reading to do.'

I watch her turn away to the fridge and a sudden anger flares inside me. *I'm sixteen. I can see whoever I bloody well like!* When I don't move she looks round at me, eyebrows raised. 'Well?'

I nod and head towards the door, but at the last second I turn. 'Mum?' I say.

'Yes?'

I keep my voice level. 'How was it at Wrexham today? With the fundraising thing?'

Her eyes flicker and she pauses before replying, 'It was fine, Heather. Thank you for asking. We achieved a lot, I think.' Our eyes meet, but she looks away first. She's lying to me, and the realization is astonishing. After a moment longer I turn and go up to my room.

I don't see Edie for a few days after that, except once, in the distance, walking with Alice and Vicky towards the art department. I think about running after her but in the end I stay where I am, watching them until they're out of sight, the lower school's bell ringing out across the playground before I make a move myself. It's Thursday before I see her again, standing outside the gates and smoking a cigarette as I'm leaving. She squints distractedly at me before her face clears and she smiles. 'Oh, hi,' she says. She looks awful: her skin pale and greasy, her clothes creased as though she'd slept in them. 'Where are you going?'

'Home, I guess.'

She flicks away her cigarette. 'I'll walk with you.'

'Don't you have a class?'

'Yeah, but . . .' she shrugs, 'you know, fuck it.'

When we get to the empty field behind the old dairy at Tyner's Cross we stop and sit on one of the crumbling walls of the outbuildings. Neither of us speaks at first. A damp autumn breeze trails its fingers through the long grass and the sky's as thick and grey as spat-out chewing gum. Somewhere behind us the motorway drones on. I look around myself, at the graffiti covering the bricks, the trails of rubbish on the broken cement floor. I notice a dirty syringe by my foot and hurriedly I kick it away. 'Are you OK?' I ask.

She nods, running a hand over her face. 'Yeah. Just tired.' She looks off in the direction of the Pembroke Estate, and I feel something brooding and troubled in her silence. I wonder if she's still annoyed about what happened in the square. And then, unexpectedly, she turns back to me and smiles. 'What've you been up to anyway?' she asks.

I think about telling her about the atmosphere at home, how Mum and Dad seem to go through entire days without talking to each other. How I went to the bathroom at 2 a.m. this morning and saw the light shining through the crack of Dad's study's door, heard the creaking of his chair. But before I can speak she puts her hand to her throat. 'I've lost my necklace,' she says. 'My little gold locket one.'

'Oh no!' I remember how she'd been wearing it the first time we met, how pretty it was.

'Yeah. It was my nan's, she gave it to me. I've looked everywhere but it's vanished.' She sighs, and chews despondently at her thumbnail, then brightens. 'That Vicky's having a party on Saturday,' she tells me. 'Her parents are on holiday so she's got the house to herself.'

I nod. 'Oh, right.'

'Well, do you fancy it?'

I stare at her. 'They won't want me there.'

'Who cares? I'm bringing Connor and some of his mates. Not a lot she can do about it once we're there. Go on, it'll be a laugh.'

'I don't know. My parents . . .'

She exhales sharply. 'Oh for God's sake, Heather! Don't you get fed up with it? They treat you like you're six!'

I'm taken aback by the strength of her irritation. I think about Mum, Dad and me, about all the things unspoken, all the secrets between us. And I realize that Edie's right. For all the clocks in our house, time never moves on for any of us; we're all held fast in that day ten summers ago, unable or unwilling to leave it behind. To my parents and maybe even to myself, I am, as Edie says, still the child I was the day we lost Lydia. I try to speak, but my throat is constricted by a rush of grief.

She gathers up her things. 'Anyway, it's up to you. Me and Connor are meeting some of his mates in the square first if you want to come. Otherwise, I guess I'll see you around.'

And I watch her go, striding away through the long grass, a sinking, desperate feeling in my chest.

The necklace I find in the jeweller's shop in Wrexham on Saturday morning is not as pretty as the one Edie lost, but still I feel pleased with myself as I hand the money over. I leave with it tucked away in its tiny velvet bag and begin the long cycle home. I hope she'll like it. I think about when I'll give it to her, and picture her face when I do, how surprised she'll be, how pleased.

Later that day, at lunchtime, when the three of us are sitting around the kitchen table – Mum talking only to me, Dad in one of his vague, distracted moods, squinting down at his newspaper – I take a deep breath and say, 'I was thinking of going out tonight.' Then I put my fork down, and hold my breath.

My mother looks up, frowning. 'Where to?'

I hesitate, avoiding her eyes. 'To a party.'

She shakes her head. 'I don't think so.'

I begin to reply but Dad rouses himself. 'I think, after what happened at the shopping centre—'

'It wasn't even me who took the bloody dress!'

A short silence follows my outburst. My mother glares at me, her face flushed an angry red. 'And it's not Edie's party anyway,' I add sulkily, stabbing my fork at a potato. 'It's someone else's. Someone from school.' But I know I'm defeated. My mother gets up and begins to clear the lunch things away.

It's almost ten before I sneak out of the house that night. I wait until Dad's upstairs in his study and Mum's watching *Midsomer Murders* before I shout goodnight, walk noisily up to my bedroom then turn off the light and wait. Ten minutes later I tiptoe back downstairs, carefully lift the back door's latch and creep out into the night. My heart pounds, but more with exhilaration than fear – it strikes me that I don't care whether my parents find me out or not – and I hurry on, away from them, to Edie, to where she'll be.

The night is cold and bright and I pull my coat close as I pass through empty, silent streets, past darkened front rooms where strangers sit motionless on their sofas, faces flickering in the ghostly blue light from their television sets. Even the high street is deadly still and quiet. I have never been out so late alone before and I feel giddy, and free, and full of daring. I reach into my pocket and find the necklace nestling there, my fingers stroking the shiny gold paper I'd wrapped it in so carefully.

And then, magically, when I turn the corner into the square, the world is full of people again. I hang back, surprised by the unexpected life and activity. In the centre by the statue little groups stand huddled together or sit on benches, their faces dipping in and out of the dim light from the street lamps, clouds of cigarette smoke caught in their yellow glow. A girl's laugh rings out harshly against the cold night and from somewhere behind me a bottle smashes, a lad's voice shouts, 'Oh, you wanker!' to a chorus of shouts and jeers. From a parked car comes the fast thud thud thud of music. Uncertainly I edge closer, scanning the faces for Edie's.

'Heather!' There she is, emerging from a group of people standing outside a pub on the corner. I smile and wave, relief flooding me as she runs over. 'You came!' When she reaches me she wraps her arms around me, stumbling so we both nearly topple over. She laughs and kisses me, turning her face at the last moment so that her mouth touches mine, sticky with lip gloss. She's very drunk, and when she passes me the bottle of Bacardi she's holding I take a long swig, and then another, ignoring how the taste of it makes me want to gag. 'Whoa!' she says, in a sing-song voice. 'Heather's getting piiiiii-ssed!'

'Edie! You coming or what?' Connor's voice, rough and hostile, calls over to us from across the square and for the first time I notice him amongst the group she'd run from. She takes my hand and pulls me after her, and nothing else matters, suddenly, nothing else in the world but being here with her. When we reach him she releases my fingers and they tingle at the loss of warmth as I stand there, in the midst of them all, these rough-looking strangers who glance briefly over and away again. I think of my quiet, warm room, my unsuspecting parents sleeping soundly next door, and feel a flicker of doubt. At that moment Connor shouts something and instinctively I shrink back as he lunges at a boy just behind me and grabs him round the throat, so aggressively that fear pulses within me until I see that they're both laughing – that it's a joke, after all. I notice Liam, suddenly, the boy I'd met before, standing a little further off, but he's talking to Rabbit, Connor's flatmate, and I quickly look away.

Edie weaves in between them now, taking hold of Connor's arm, 'Hey, I'm back – did you miss me?' It strikes me that there's something forced, a little desperate in her too-loud laugh, and I stare at her in surprise. He glances down at her and almost imperceptibly shrugs her off, and I see her bright smile slip, just for a second, something bereft and bleak left in its place before she slicks it back on and turns to me. 'Heather! Heather!' she calls. 'Come here!' Reluctantly I go to them. 'Hey, this is Heather!' she says to the others. 'This is my friend Heather! You better be nice to her, OK?' She puts her head next to mine and as they all turn and look at us I'm aware of how plain my face must appear next to hers, how beautiful she must look beside me, and the idea, gone almost before it's there, strikes me that maybe that was her intention – but I dismiss the idea immediately.

'Are we going now or what?' Connor says.

She puts her arm around me and we move off down the street, the lads following behind as she staggers along next to me, her body bumping against mine. 'Fuck, I'm so wasted,' she says. 'I'm so fucking wasted.'

'I sneaked out tonight,' I tell her proudly. 'My mum and dad don't even know where I am! They think I'm in bed asleep!' I grin at her expectantly, but it's like she's barely heard and we walk in silence for a while.

'Do you think he loves me, Heather?' she says suddenly. 'Connor? Do you think he does?'

I glance at her in surprise, trying to think of the right thing to say. 'Of course I do,' I offer at last. 'I mean, yeah, I'm sure he does.'

'Because I love him so much, I love him so fucking much,' she says with sudden intensity.

'I—' I begin.

But a second later she's laughing again, and, grabbing my hand, shouts, 'Come on!' as she sets off at a run, pulling me after her.

Vicky's house is at the end of a quiet cul-de-sac and we hang around outside for a while, listening to the thud of music and shouts of laughter coming from within, while Edie peers through the window. When Alice comes to the door she squeals in an excitable, over the top sort of way to see Edie there, before her eyes drift to me and the seven lads standing behind her, and her smile falters.

'This is my boyfriend, Connor,' Edie tells her quickly, pulling him in front of her. 'You said it'd be all right, didn't you, if I brought him.'

Alice goes a bit pink as she gazes up at him. 'Yeah, yeah, of course,' she says dazedly, and stands aside to let us in.

We traipse down the narrow hallway, past the packed-out living room and into the kitchen, and I realize I feel very drunk, the rum I'd gulped on the way over combining queasily with the stuffy heat of the house. In the kitchen we find Vicky giggling at a group of boys who are downing shots of vodka, slamming each one on to the table and cheering each other on. Her smile freezes as we all pile in, and I see her exchange a glance with Alice, who stands uncertainly in the doorway behind us. In that moment they seem very young, their vodka-drinking friends like fresh-faced kids compared to Connor and his mates.

No one speaks until Connor, going over and slapping one of the boys on the back so hard he stumbles, says, 'You got some of that for me have you, mate?' before taking the bottle of vodka from his hands and carrying it away with him. The boy shrugs and ducks his head, his eyes flitting nervously to his friends. At that moment Rabbit opens the fridge and pulls out a four-pack of beer. I see Vicky open her mouth to say something, before glancing over at Alice and shutting it again. I watch the two of them, so uncertain and flustered for once, in fascination.

Edie tugs at my arm. 'Come on,' she says, 'let's go and dance.'

I follow her along the hallway, as more people arrive at the front door, surging into the house on a wave of cold air and raised voices. Edie takes my hand and pulls me after her into the crowded lounge full of people jumping around to the music that thumps from the speakers, the air thick with cigarette smoke. She picks up an almost-full bottle of wine from a bookshelf and, holding it aloft, grins then downs some of it and passes it to me before she fights her way into the throng.

I stand and watch her dance for a while and I'm filled with admiration. I could never move like that: I wouldn't know how to begin. I clutch the wine bottle self-consciously, too hot in my coat that I don't want to take off in case I lose Edie's present, and I'm pushed this way and that as more people try to get past me and into the room. Eventually I stumble towards a sofa, sinking down into it gratefully, taking swig after swig of the wine for something to do. Time blurs and lurches past, song follows song and still Edie dances. I have begun to feel horribly drunk, my eyelids heavy, my head spinning, my belly slopping with nausea. Suddenly a very drunk boy sits down next to me and begins shouting something in my ear. I try to focus on his words but the music's too loud and I feel as though I'm going to be sick. Stumbling to my feet I try to catch sight of Edie, but she's vanished.

In the hallway I grab hold of the banister and begin to haul myself up the stairs, fighting my way past the people sitting or standing on almost every step, wanting only to find Edie, to make the horrible churning sickness stop. When at last I reach the bathroom and find it locked, I push at one of the bedroom doors instead, hoping for somewhere quiet to sit and clear my head. But the scene that greets me there makes me stop in confusion. Edie is sitting on the bed, her head bowed over the bedside table, Connor and Rabbit standing behind her, watching in silence. They look up sharply when I come in. 'Edie?' I say, in confusion. And then, taking a step nearer, I see the three thin lines of white powder. I watch in astonishment as Edie puts a rolled-up note to her nose and gives a long, hard sniff before she straightens up and looks at me, eyes wide and bright, her face flushed. 'Hiya, Heather,' she says.

I can only stare at her, shock reverberating through me. 'See you later, babe,' she says to Connor, passing him the note and getting to her feet, before walking past me and out into the hall. After a stunned moment, I follow.

'Edie!' I hiss, grabbing hold of her arm. 'Was that . . . are you . . . on *drugs*?!' I gape at her incredulously.

She laughs. 'Chill out, Heather. It's only a bit of coke. Everybody does it.' She shrugs and begins to make her way down the stairs, while I trail after her.

At the bottom I put my hand out to stop her. 'Edie!'

But she pulls away, 'Jesus, Heather, you've really got to lighten up. It's a party, for Christ's sake.'

162

I watch as she disappears into the lounge. I want to go home. Dazedly I wander into the kitchen, inching my way through the noisy crowd until I reach the sink. Amongst the dirty glasses filled with beer and cigarette butts I find an empty tumbler and fill it with cold water before gulping it back and holding the cool glass to my forehead. Dully I pull the gift-wrapped package from my pocket. The paper's creased and tired-looking now. I hadn't even had a chance to give it to her. Disappointment swells inside of me. It's only then that I notice Vicky and Alice talking intensely to each other a few feet away.

'What the hell am I going to do?' Vicky is saying. 'My parents are going to fucking kill me! The neighbours are going to call the police in a minute. I've asked people to leave but they won't listen.' Alice puts her arms round her as Vicky sinks against her shoulder. 'This is a nightmare,' she wails. 'What am I going to do?'

Suddenly Alice looks up and sees me watching. 'What the fuck do you want?' she snaps.

Vicky turns, wiping away her tears. 'Yeah, Heather. What are you even doing here, anyway?'

'Edie invited me,' I mumble.

Her face twists into a sneer. 'Yeah, well I'm uninviting you, so why don't you fuck off?'

I stare back at her, drunken exhaustion beginning to overwhelm me. And at that moment she looks down at my hand, still holding Edie's gift-wrapped necklace. 'Aaaah,' she says mockingly. 'Have you brought me a present? Look, Alice, Heather's brought me a present!'

163

Before I have a chance to react she snatches it from my hand, and laughing now, says, 'Come on then, let's see!'

A dull anger rises in me. 'Give it back,' I say.

But people are starting to look and Vicky is enjoying the attention. 'Nope!'

I make a lunge for it but stumble, knocking into the table.

'Watch it,' Vicky says, 'fucking 'tard.' Everybody's staring now and there's a smattering of laughter.

'Give it back!' I shout, diving for it again but she throws it to Alice, who catches it and holds it above her head, with a high peal of laughter. 'Come and get it!'

The rage comes from nowhere, it engulfs me, emptying my mind of everything but the need to get Edie's present back. With a lunge I grab hold of Alice's wrist and prise her fingers away from the parcel. I don't know what I'm doing or how much force I'm using until she screams. The room goes silent. She's cradling her hand, her face a mask of shock. 'Jesus, my finger!' she shouts. 'My fucking finger!'

I gape at her. 'I . . . I didn't . . .'

'You've fucking broken it! What's wrong with you?' Her face has drained of colour.

Vicky, who has been staring at us both open-mouthed, jolts into action. 'Right, you!' she says, grabbing my arm. 'Get the fuck out of my house!'

I stare dumbly back at Alice. 'I'm sorry,' I say. 'I'm so sorry – I just, I didn't . . .'

But Vicky is pulling me out of the room. 'Get lost. Go on.' She marches me down the hallway, her fingers digging into my arm before opening the door and shoving me out into the street, slamming the door behind me.

After

When I get back from the park I'm surprised to find that the flat's empty. I stand in the hallway for a moment or two, listening to the silence. I'm so used to Heather's constant presence that at first I can't quite believe it, expecting at any moment to hear her familiar tread on the stairs. But when the minutes pass and still she doesn't return, I sit down with Maya and give her a bottle, a pressure I'd barely been conscious of lifting instantly from my shoulders.

Maya watches me as she drinks, her small fingers wrapped around my wrist. I gaze down at her, taking in the mass of thick black hair that has grown into shiny curls, the enormous dark eyes – Heri's eyes. I have so much time to make up, I feel as though I've wasted so many hours and days and weeks of her life, and now I can barely tear my eyes from her. In my darkest moments over the previous months what had scared me most was the thought that Maya was somehow just a version of me, an extension of all that's wrong with me. But I see now that she's entirely herself, her own, separate person, and it's this realization that has finally unlocked something in me.

Later, when the morning has seeped into afternoon and I've put Maya in her cot to nap and still Heather hasn't returned, I watch the TV idly for a while until I find my thoughts turning to Uncle Geoff. Guilt gnaws at me: I had barely thought of him in the weeks since Heather turned him away, my head too full of my own misery and confusion to allow room for anything else. And yet, he had not made contact with me since either, and that strikes me suddenly as a little strange – no phone calls, no more visits or texts. It was not like him to take offence or sulk, so why hadn't he been in touch?

I get to my feet and begin to search for my mobile. I look through every drawer and shelf, bag and pocket, but find nothing. Next, with increasing exasperation, I begin to rummage through Heather's things. At last, wrapped in a jumper and shoved down to the bottom of one of her bags beneath her puzzle books and DVDs, I find it, switched off.

When I turn it back on I find countless missed calls and text after text from my uncle, sent over the previous six weeks: 'Are you OK?' and, 'Look, love, I'm worried about you', and, 'Please drop me a line to tell me you're all right.' Some of them Heather had replied to. 'Hi, I'm fine. Just busy, Edie.' Or, 'Sorry I missed your call, will be in touch, E.' My jaw drops in shock.

Next I listen to my voicemail, my heart twisting when I hear the hurt in my uncle's voice. 'I know your friend said you don't want visitors, but I'm worried about you. Everything OK, is it?' He pauses before adding, 'You know if you need help you can always count on me, don't you, Edie love?' And another, more recent, his voice guarded and tight: 'Did you get my letter, love? Look, I won't bother you again, but I just wanted to check that you . . .' his voice trails off and he sighs resignedly. 'Anyway. Be nice to have a chat.' There's another pause and then he puts the phone down. I feel his baffled hurt keenly.

What letter? My mind spins. Why didn't Heather tell me? Why did she text him, pretending to be me? Anger flares inside me and I remember how, back in Fremton, she had lied and deceived me once before. How bloody *dare* she? Immediately I try Geoff's number, but though it rings and rings, he doesn't pick up. I pace around my flat. Where *is* Heather anyway? Monica's words from this morning come back to me: *I used to see her hanging around outside, at two, three in the morning . . .*

I look at the boxes of Heather's junk, her clothes hanging over the backs of chairs, the smell of fried onions suddenly thick in the air. I look down and find several strands of thick yellow hair clinging to my jumper and feel a little sick – no matter how many I pick off these days there always seems to be another. My head

169

starts to ache and I feel my neck and shoulders tense. Glancing at Maya, sleeping soundly, I sigh and go to the bathroom and run myself a bath.

It was something I used to enjoy, before Maya, before Heather, having a long soak in the middle of the day when I didn't have a shift at the restaurant. I turn the radio on and sink into the water, closing my eyes against the clouds of steam, letting my mind drift to the music, forcing Heather and my uncle from my mind for a while. Instead I think of Monica, of her smile as she'd teased me in the park today. Idly I daydream about getting to know her better, picturing myself asking her casually round for a coffee, knowing I probably never will. And then James's face unexpectedly appears to me, his large, warm eyes, the way he'd looked at me in the park, and I feel a gentle creep of heat. 'Jesus,' I say out loud, laughing at myself, before I lie back and submerge myself in the water.

It's only fifteen minutes or so later when I leave the bathroom wrapped in a towel. I think about making myself a sandwich and as I pass the living room I glance in at Maya's cot to check that she's still sleeping. And then I stop in confusion. 'Heather?' I call. I go to the kitchen and, irrationally, the bathroom I'd only just left, but the flat, including Maya's cot, is empty. A cold, sharp fear grips me. Hurriedly, panic beginning to course through me, I dress and leave the flat, running down the stairs to the ground floor two at a time. Out on the doorstep I look frantically to left and right but the street

170

is deserted. I freeze in indecision before impulsively turning left, setting off at a run.

Calm down, I tell myself as I hurry along the street. After all, Heather has taken Maya countless times while I've barely noticed or cared where they were or when they'd be back. But what Monica had told me about Heather had frightened me – and why would she take Maya without saying anything? Why sneak around while I'm in the bath, quietly appearing from wherever she'd been to grab her and then vanish again? What the *fuck* was she playing at? A feeling of dread grows inside me and, running now, I retrace my steps towards the park.

When I find it empty I hurry back to the flat, hoping that Heather might have returned without me seeing her, but there's no one there. The fridge ticks noisily in the silence. I sink into a chair, my heart pounding as I try to think of a rational explanation for where they could be. I feel Maya's absence like a physical pain. They've gone for a walk, that's all, I tell myself. They'll be back any minute! And yet the nagging unease I'd felt since my conversation with Monica has sharpened into panic. What had I been thinking, letting Heather move in, entrusting Maya to her care? I think about the cuts on Heather's arms, and that long, awful summer before I left. A memory of a long-ago party returns to me. Hadn't something happened between Heather and another girl there? Alison, Alice maybe – a broken finger or something? Heather had caused it. I can't quite remember why. Probably too wasted, I think with a rush of self-hatred. Shame engulfs me. The fact was, I had been so desperate when Maya was born that I couldn't have cared less who I'd allowed to help me – or what their motives might be. But surely Heather wouldn't hurt Maya? My eyes fill with tears and at last I get to my feet, unable to wait a minute longer, and I run down the stairs to Monica's flat and pound on her door.

A few seconds later I hear a hesitant male voice say, 'Hello?'

'It's me,' I say, 'Edie, from upstairs,' and tap my foot impatiently while the bolts are drawn and the locks unturned. When Billy finally opens the door he takes one look at me and calls for his mother.

'Edie? What's the matter? What's happened?' She pulls me into the kitchen.

'It's Heather,' I tell her, trying to catch my breath. 'She's taken Maya and I don't know where she's gone.'

'What do you mean, "taken"? How long have they been gone?'

'I don't know! Half an hour, maybe? Have you seen them?'

'No,' she says, shaking her head, and I groan in despair.

She shoots me a confused, searching look before leading me to a chair. 'Well, they can't have gone far, can they?' She sits me down. 'Why don't I ask the boys to have a quick drive around on the bike and look for them?' When I nod she gives me a reassuring smile. 'They'll find them, Edie. Maya will be fine.'

After she's gone I try to pull myself together. I go to the sink and rinse my face and stand there for a while, forcing myself to take long, deep breaths. After a minute or two I hear the front door close and Monica returns. We sit together at the kitchen table.

'What's going on, Edie?' Monica asks levelly. 'I thought you and Heather were friends?' She shakes her head. 'Why this panic?'

And it's then that, to both of our surprise, I begin to cry. Huge, uncontrollable sobs that seem to come from nowhere shudder through me, and within seconds my face and hands are a mess of snot and tears. And now that I've started, I can't seem to stop. I cry for myself, for how fucked up I'd been when I met Connor; I cry for Heather and what happened back then. And finally I cry for Maya, for how I'd done nothing but fail her since the moment she was born. Monica doesn't say a word, but I feel her hand on my arm and I lean against her, sobbing on to her shoulder.

'God. I'm so sorry,' I say, when I'm able to speak. 'I'm just so frightened.' I take the handful of tissues she passes me and hide my face in them.

After a few moments Monica says gently, 'They'll find her, Edie. She won't have gone far.'

I nod, and we sit in silence for a while, waiting for Billy and Ryan to return. I'm grateful when Monica asks no more questions. My phone lies on the table in front of me and I watch the minutes tick away. She gets up to make some coffee and we sit and drink and wait until at last I hear her sons' key in the door and I spring from my seat. But Ryan and Billy are alone. They shake their heads. 'No sign of them,' says Ryan.

I pick up my phone. 'I'm calling the police.'

But Monica restrains me with a hand on my arm and, after her sons have left the room again, asks calmly, 'OK, but what are you going to tell them? Why do you think Heather's taken her? As far as the police will be concerned, your flatmate has taken your little girl out for a walk – so what? They've hardly been gone an hour. They'll ask you why you're so worried.' She pauses and says, 'Why are you so worried, Edie?'

I stare at her, then at the mobile in my hand, and in a brief moment of madness it occurs to me that it would be a relief to tell her everything, right from the beginning. But of course I don't. I only have to remember my mother's face to know that I'll never tell anyone again. Instead I put my head in my hands as a wave of hope-lessness crashes over me. 'I just want my baby back,' I tell her.

The minutes drag interminably and with every passing one my fear deepens. Where is she? What has Heather done with her? I get up and pace around the room. I think about Heather, and I think about what happened that night at the quarry and my panic grows. *What if she hurts Maya?* Suddenly I can bear to wait no longer. I reach for my phone and, my hand shaking, begin to dial 999. It's at that moment that I hear the door to the building slam closed. I take one look at Monica before

174

rushing from her flat. There, in the hall, is Heather, with Maya in her arms.

'Where the fuck have you been?' I shout.

Her mouth falls open in shock as I pull my daughter from her. 'Out for a walk,' she stammers.

I glare back at her, too incensed to speak.

'Why?' she asks. 'What . . . what's the matter?'

'You didn't tell me you were taking her! I got out of the bath and she was just . . . gone. What the fuck is wrong with you?'

Her eyes fill with tears. 'I didn't think you'd mind. I've taken Maya out lots of times!'

'But why didn't you say something?'

Heather shakes her head and her voice is pleading, 'I don't know. I didn't want to disturb you!'

Monica has tactfully closed her door and the two of us stand alone in the hall staring at each other. 'I found my phone,' I tell her, and watch as her eyes dart guiltily away. 'I saw the texts you sent Uncle Geoff. What the hell were you playing at?' I hear my voice rising in anger again. 'Well?'

'I was only looking after you! I didn't want anyone to bother you. We don't need anyone else, do we?' Tentatively she reaches over and touches my arm and I flinch. She stares at me imploringly, 'Hasn't it been lovely, just the three of us? You and me and Maya, we've been so happy together.'

I back away from her. 'Heather . . .' I begin, but I have no idea what to say. The silence stretches until

175

finally I shake my head in disgust and set off up the stairs, Heather trailing after me. Once we're home I shut the kitchen door in her face and try to calm down. As my heart begins to return to normal I look down at my daughter and feel such an intense rush of love and relief it takes my breath away. 'I will never let you out of my sight again,' I promise her. Outside, dusk has begun to fall. I stand at the window looking out for a while, thinking about Heather.

Why had she come to London to find me? It didn't make sense. After what had happened in Fremton, why would she even want to? To be constantly reminded of what happened back then. We had agreed never to speak about that night. It was our secret, long buried. I look down at my baby and realize that what happened today had changed everything. My life and the person I'd once been are not important any more, it's only Maya that matters now. It's time to draw a line under the past and move on. By the time I leave the kitchen I have convinced myself. My mind is made up.

I find Heather sitting on the sofa, still wearing her coat, staring at the TV's blank screen. I put Maya in her cot and sit down next to her. The room has darkened, outside, angry clouds spit needles of rain at the windowpanes. I take a deep breath and begin. 'Look, Heather,' I say gently, 'I think it's time you moved out.'

She doesn't reply at first, just continues to stare fixedly at the switched-off TV, and for a moment I wonder if she's even heard me. 'I'm so grateful to you for helping me look after Maya the way you did,' I plough on. 'But this place is so small, there's just not enough room.'

At this Heather finally turns to look at me. Her eyes are dull. 'You want me to leave?' she asks, her voice flat.

'Yes,' I say firmly, determined not to back down. 'Yes, I do. I'm sorry.'

In the same, expressionless tone she says, 'I'm sorry about taking Maya. I'll never do it again, I promise.'

My heart sinks. 'It's not that, Heather,' I say. 'I just think Maya and I need to try to get on with things by ourselves now.'

'But how will you manage?' she asks. 'All by yourself, with no one to help?'

'I need to try to do this alone,' I tell her. 'Besides, if I need help, there's always Uncle Geoff, or Monica, she's only downstairs.'

At this, a shadow passes across her face. She gets up and stands in front of me and she's so close, so tall and broad, towering over me, that I lean away from her, a little afraid. 'I can't leave,' she says, her eyes blank. 'Don't make me. I've nowhere else to go.'

'What do you mean?' I ask. 'Can't you go back to Birmingham? To your parents?'

She looks away. 'I haven't lived with my parents for years.'

I gape at her. 'But you said—'

She goes to Maya's cot and gazes down at my sleeping daughter. 'I don't have anything but you and Maya,' she says. And before I can stop her she reaches down and picks her up, crushing her tightly against her chest. Maya gives a cry of alarm at being woken but Heather doesn't seem to hear.

'You can come and see her whenever you like!' I promise desperately, wishing she'd put Maya down. 'We could even come to Birmingham for a visit.'

When Maya begins to scream I jump to my feet. 'Heather, please give her to me.'

But she doesn't move or reply. And now she stares dully down at my screaming daughter. 'Don't make me go,' she repeats.

I prise Maya from her and move away to the window and it's only then that Heather looks at me again, her face entirely expressionless.

'Heather,' I say. 'Why did you come looking for me?'

Her eyes drop, and after a long silence she whispers, 'My mother . . .'

I shake my head in bewilderment, 'What? What about your mother?'

'She . . .' Her face is desperate, but her voice stalls.

'What, Heather? What do you mean?'

She continues to stare back at me, the same tortured expression in her eyes, and suddenly she opens her mouth and begins to wail, one high, awful, endless note so loud and surprising and eerie it makes my blood run cold. All at once she crosses the room towards me, her eyes bright with rage, her movements so fast and aggressive that instinctively I cower, crying out in fear and shielding

Maya from her, my arm held up to fend off the attack I know is coming. But it never comes. Instead I hear the sound of smashing glass and look up to see that the thin Victorian pane of my window has completely shattered and Heather is staring down at her fist that's dripping now with blood.

'Heather!' I shout. 'Jesus Christ, Heather!' Adrenalin surges through me. But her eyes are dull and confused as she looks from me to her hand, and, a moment later, she turns and runs from the flat. Stunned, I listen to her footsteps as they retreat down the stairs. After a minute or two I hear the front door slam far below and from my window see her emerge from the building and run away down the street, the rain pelting at her back. My breath comes in ragged gasps of shock. I should go after her, I tell myself: what will she do now, where will she go? But I don't move. Instead I watch until she disappears from sight, and the relief is overwhelming.

PART THREE

Before

I walk home from the party half blinded by tears, retracing the dark, silent streets I'd walked so full of hope and excitement only a few hours before. What have I done? What on earth have I done? I remember Alice's cry of pain as I'd wrenched her fingers from Edie's present. It had been an accident, I tell myself desperately – just an awful, terrible accident! But then, against my will, memories of a day four years ago come rushing back to me; the day I broke my mother's arm.

I had been about twelve when it happened. An argument about homework blowing up between Mum and me one night in our kitchen. 'You'll never get anywhere in life if you're lazy,' she had said. And the injustice of this, the sheer unfairness of it after all the studying I did night after night to make her and Dad happy, had suddenly been too much for me.

I'd stood up and screamed at her, the rage instant and uncontrollable, 'I'm not lazy! I'm not!' Over and over I had screamed it, 'I'm not, I'm not, I'm not!' And when I'd turned to run out of the room my mother had followed me. 'Come back here, young lady,' she'd said. 'Come back here this instant!' I was already as big as her by then. When she'd tried to follow me through the door I'd turned and with all my might pushed it back on her, slamming it over and over when I met resistance, too enraged to see that her arm was trapped inside it, making too much noise myself to hear her scream. It was only when my father came running down the stairs and dragged me away that I returned to my senses and realized what I'd done.

Her arm was broken in two places. It hadn't just been the cast she'd had to wear for weeks that served as a constant reminder of my guilt, the expression in my mother's eyes whenever they met mine would forever confirm it. There was a sort of triumph there that seemed to say, *I knew it*.

After

The garden of the Hope and Anchor is busy tonight. Despite the late-October chill the crowded bar spits out a constant stream of people, come to huddle under patio heaters or sit beneath strings of brightly coloured lanterns, raising their voices above the music thudding from the outdoor speakers. I stand on the edge of a small circle of drinkers and sip my beer, not quite a part of their conversation, and watch James's students celebrate their end-of-year show.

I don't know, exactly, why I came tonight, except I'd wanted I suppose to do something to mark Heather's leaving. Phoning James was something the old me would never have done but that solitary, fearful person left when Heather did, following her along the dark and rainy street three nights ago. And when I'd shut the door behind her I had made myself turn a lock on the past too, on Fremton and everything that had happened there. Later, I had sat with Maya in my arms and felt stronger and more determined than I had in years. The future – Maya's future – was all that mattered now.

It had been Monica who had persuaded me to phone James last night. 'So what if you don't fancy him?' she'd said as we'd sat together in her kitchen. 'Go and have a few beers anyway. Might be a laugh. I'll look after Maya for you.'

'No,' I'd said. 'Thanks, but there's no way I'm leaving Maya.'

But gradually, bit by bit, she'd persuaded me. 'It'll be absolutely fine, you'll see.' She'd smiled. 'You've got nothing to worry about, I promise.' And so, in the end, I'd agreed.

I spy James by the door, talking to an older man I recognize from the exhibition earlier. I watch as he throws his head back and laughs at something so loudly that people near him turn and smile too. At that moment a tall, blonde woman in her twenties appears by his side. They kiss on both cheeks and I notice how her hand lingers on his waist, and I find myself wondering about her, about who she is to him.

I'd been nervous as I'd arrived at the university earlier, following the signs and arrows to the exhibition hall, unsure about what I'd find there. But the place had been buzzing with people, their voices bouncing off the walls, sudden eruptions of laughter rising to the high ceiling like flocks of startled birds. I'd spotted James in the centre, surrounded by his students, and, unsure what else to do, had begun to make my way around alone.

At first I'd felt self-conscious, afraid that people would be able to tell I've not been to a gallery since school. I'd stood in front of each painting and worried about how long I should pause for, what sort of expression my face ought to wear, but within minutes I'd entirely forgotten myself. I know nothing about art, not really, and yet soon a series of landscapes had held me transfixed. They were of the Thames at Greenwich, the paint applied in thick, angry whorls, the colours in jarring, clashing greens and reds, the water bleeding into the shore and sky.

I'd looked at them for a long time and afterwards had moved around the rest of the exhibition entirely absorbed. Occasionally I'd paused and glanced around the hall, trying to match each set of images with its creator. I'd felt envious as I'd watched them all – their proud, happy faces as they'd celebrated with family and friends. How must it feel, I wondered, to have achieved something like this?

At last I'd stopped in front of a series of drawings of various deserted buildings: a dilapidated church, a house with its windows boarded up, a derelict pub. It was only after closer inspection that you noticed in each the ghostly trace of human presence. A featureless face at a window, a disappearing figure, a shadow of someone standing just out of view. I had been admiring them when James appeared.

187

'You came!' he'd said, and we'd looked at each other for an awkward moment or two, each of us wondering, I suppose, what my being there meant. 'It's good to see you,' he'd said at last. 'I'm really glad you came.' And he'd smiled at me then the way men do who fancy you and are trying to work out what their chances are and I'd turned away and said too quickly, 'I like these.'

'Yeah, they're pretty great, aren't they?' He'd come and looked at them with me. 'Do you want to meet the artist?' And before I could reply he'd shouted across the busy hall and waved over a very fat Welsh man with a booming voice and grinning face so at odds with the eerie, melancholic images I'd been looking at that at first I'd been too stunned to speak.

'This is Tony,' James had said and I'd shaken hands with the man and then his wife and after that the following hour had seemed to pass in a flash as more of James's students drifted over to join us. I had become caught up in the celebratory atmosphere and the artists' discussions of their work and while I'd stood there and listened and smiled and sipped my wine I'd watched him, James; noticed his enthusiasm and his warmth as he'd talked to his students, saw how liked he was in return. When people began to move towards the pub next door I'd let myself drift with them.

The crisp, clear evening turns to rain and one by one we leave the pub garden and squeeze our way into the crowded bar instead. James finds me by the door saying goodbye to Tony and his wife. 'I'm so sorry,' he says when they've gone, raising his voice above the music and drunken laughter, 'I've barely had a chance to talk to you since we got here.' He looks at my coat. 'You're not leaving too?'

'I should, really. Monica's babysitting and I'd better get back.'

'At least let me buy you another beer?'

I see now that he's a little drunk, his dark eyes a shade bolder as they rest upon my face. And this time I don't look away or make a hurried remark, instead I return his smile until someone pushes roughly past us and on impulse we clutch at each other to steady ourselves, then laugh. James pulls me to the end of the bar, away from the thudding speakers.

'I had a good time tonight,' I say, when he's ordered us some drinks.

He laughs, 'You sound surprised.'

'It's not the sort of thing I'd go to normally, but yeah, I enjoyed it. How about you? You must have felt proud of them, your students?'

He grins. 'They did all right, didn't they?'

'Must be a nice job.'

'It is, I love it.' He takes a sip of beer. 'But you're an artist too, aren't you? I remember the drawings you had in your flat. I thought they were very good.'

I look away, embarrassed. 'Thanks. It's . . . I don't know, I did them a while ago. It's not something I'm serious about or anything.'

189

'Why not? You should keep it up, I thought they showed real promise.'

I remember how much I'd loved art at school before I'd moved to Fremton, how my teacher would let me stay behind after class and work away at something while she carried on with her marking. I recall the smells of the art department, how completely involved I'd be, caught up in the pleasure of being entirely focused on what I was doing, how ambitious I'd been for the future. I feel a flicker of sadness and I shrug, 'Maybe. I – it's just something I used to do in my spare time.'

'What do you do? For work, I mean.'

'Nothing right now, I had some savings and help from my uncle when Maya was born, but usually I'm a waitress. I suppose I'll go back to that soon.'

He nods. 'Do you like it?' he asks.

I laugh. 'God no, but it pays the bills.'

'I guess that's the great thing about painting, or whatever – a chance to escape all that, forget the everyday shit for a while.'

As he talks I take in little glances, the way he does of me; covert, quick appraisals. It's the openness of his face that's so attractive, I realize: how easily he smiles, the way his eyes flash light and dark as he talks, the obvious pleasure he takes from life. Like I used to be, I think, a very long time ago. I take another gulp of beer.

'You can come to the studio if you like, some time,' he says now. 'Use our materials, if you ever fancy getting back into it.' And then he asks, 'Would you like another beer?' and the air between us flexes and waits as his eyes hold mine.

I shake my head. 'I should go. Better get back to Maya', and I see the disappointment that flickers across his face.

As we say our goodbyes he gives me a brief hug and I breathe in the clean, lemon scent of his neck. We linger for a touch longer than necessary and I have to fight a sudden impulse to sink against him, because I sense that it would be OK to do that, that he would take my weight and wouldn't mind. 'I'd better go . . .' I draw away.

'Hey, Edie?' he touches my arm. 'How about a drink some time? Shall I give you a ring?'

And I find myself saying, 'Yeah, OK. I'd like that.'

I walk home hugging myself, my arms wrapped around my body to keep the cold out, and something else in; something I haven't felt for a long time. Police cars and buses and drunks and gangs of teenagers pass me in the damp, orange-black night, the street lights casting a hazy glow upon the thin mist that hangs now in the air, and I turn down a narrower side street and think of the paintings I'd seen and the people I'd talked to, and the calm, steady warmth of James's eyes as they'd looked back at me in the bright boom and clamour of the pub.

When I get home I find Maya asleep in her cot, Monica

watching TV with the sound down low. We tiptoe into the kitchen. 'How was she?' I ask.

'Yeah, good as gold. Drank her milk and out like a light.' She smiles. 'How about you? Did you have a good time?'

I take my coat off, avoiding the pale blue searchlight of her gaze, and say casually, 'It was all right.'

'Yeah?' She grins at me. 'And how was James? Will you see him again?'

'Maybe.' I shrug. 'He said something about going for a drink some time.'

'Nice one!' She nudges me in the ribs and despite myself I laugh.

We stand by the window and look out at the sea of lights in silence.

'Wow,' Monica says.

'Yeah, you kind of forget what a shithole this place is when you look out at that.'

We turn and consider the poky, cluttered space, at Heather's things still piled up in the hall. 'It's not so bad,' she lies.

'I suppose I'll get it sorted one day.' I turn to her and smile. 'Thanks for looking after Maya tonight.'

She shrugs. 'Nothing else to do – the boys were both out and I don't like staying in on my own.'

I hesitate, before putting an awkward hand on her arm. 'I mean it though,' I say. 'Thanks for being so good to me over the past few weeks.'

She smiles again and we stand there for a while, the

two of us, up here in my tiny kitchen, looking out at the city far below.

Later, after Monica has gone home and Maya begins to stir, I take her to the sofa with me and idly watch the muted TV screen while she drinks her milk. I hold her to me, her head tucked neatly beneath my chin, her body warm against mine, and in the midnight peace I think about my mother. A memory comes to me from when I was six, the day my dad left home. I'm sobbing, holding on to his arm, begging him to stay as he packs his bags in angry silence. 'Mum!' I scream, turning to where she stands in the doorway, watching him with a pale, pinched face. 'Don't make him go! Please don't make him go.' But she turns away into the kitchen and shuts the door behind her. A few minutes later my father leaves and I scream at the closed kitchen door with all the fury I can muster, 'I hate you! I hate you! I hate you!'

But then another memory comes to me, a recollection of being held myself when I was very small in the same way I'm holding Maya now: the sensation of my face against my mother's chest; the smell and warmth of her skin, the feeling of being wholly and completely safe. I look down at Maya. I didn't know what love was all about, I think, until I had you.

I'm about to go to bed when I hear the noise outside my flat. I freeze in the passageway, straining my ears. There it is again. A creak on the stairs that lead directly to my door. Perhaps it's Monica – maybe she's forgotten something. I wait and a few moments later hear the sound again, but louder this time – footsteps retreating back down the stairs to the landing below. Fear prickles my scalp. Who on earth? One of the other tenants? I creep to my door and, after listening for a while longer, hesitantly open it and look out. Nothing. The stairwell is silent now. I step out on to the landing but no one's there. Someone *had* been outside my door, though. Hadn't they? I suddenly notice that the door to the communal store cupboard on the floor below is slightly open. It's a large space – big enough for my neighbour to keep his bike in. Big enough to hide in. I stare at it. Hadn't it been closed when I'd passed earlier? I wait for a few moments more, before eventually going back inside my flat, and, feeling a little ridiculous, double-lock the door behind me.

Before

On Monday I stay off school, telling Mum I'm ill and resolving not to return till the end of the week. Each time I think about the party I'm gripped by cold horror. But though I'm thankful not to have to face anyone for a while, the empty hours and days seem to stretch out endlessly before me. At first I lie on the sofa in my pyjamas, watching my *Friends* videos and eating whatever I can sneak from the kitchen, deciding to get dressed as soon as Mum starts getting annoyed with me. But the strange thing is, she never does. In fact she barely seems to notice me as I lie amongst my empty wrappers and crumb-covered plates. 'I have to go out now,' she calls from the hallway as she's halfway out the door each morning, and I wonder why she's suddenly so busy, an unsettled sort of feeling rising in me, before I fast-forward to the next episode of *Friends*, and open another bag of crisps, and think about what Edie might be up to today.

And as the days pass, the more I think about Edie and about what happened that night, the more I think that perhaps I'd been wrong to be so cross with her. Maybe she hadn't really wanted to take those drugs at all. Maybe Connor had made her do it. A picture pops into my head of him standing over her with a syringe in his hand as she cowers in fear, and my anger is replaced by anxiety. What a terrible friend I'd been! Instead of helping her I'd judged her and told her off. I should have been taking care of her! On impulse I turn off the telly and run to the hall phone, my heart beating fast as I dial her number. But it rings and rings and nobody picks up. I put down the phone, promising myself that I'll try again later, that I won't give up until I've made sure she's OK.

But later that day, something happens to push Edie from my mind completely. I'm back on the sofa watching TV when Mum and Dad come into the room. I can tell straight away there's something wrong. I sit up, hastily running a hand through my greasy hair, pushing a Mars Bar wrapper behind my back. 'Hi,' I say quickly, muting the telly. 'Sorry, I was about to . . .' But the strange way Mum's looking at me stops me in my tracks. 'What?' I say. 'What's the matter?'

'We need to talk, Heather,' she says.

I look from her to Dad, who's turned to the window

and is staring out at the street. My heart thuds. 'Why? What's happened?'

She sits, and then, not quite meeting my gaze, clears her throat and says, 'I'm leaving, Heather.'

Nobody says anything for a long time, the silence seems to buckle beneath the weight of her words, my shock so profound I feel myself begin to shake. I laugh, a strange, unnatural sound in the quiet. 'What?' I say. 'What do you mean?' Because if I pretend not to understand, perhaps it will prevent it from being true. She doesn't answer at first and my eyes swim with tears.

She purses her mouth. 'Your father and I have decided to separate,' she says, in the matter-of-fact, slightly exasperated voice she might have used to tell me my room's untidy. 'I'm very sorry, Heather,' she adds. For a while nobody speaks until at last something alters in her expression and we stare back at each other for a long moment before she says, softly, her voice catching, 'It has all been too difficult, you see.' And I feel myself nodding, because I know why this is happening, how this started, know exactly when our old life began to fray and unravel. I had caused this.

My father hasn't moved from his position by the window, his shoulders held tight, rigid, his head very still. 'But where will you go?' I whisper.

'I'll be staying in Langley, with a friend.'

'Who?' I ask. 'What friend?' My mother doesn't have any friends.

Dad makes a peculiar, strangled sort of sound from

197

the other end of the room and I look at him in surprise.

'Jonathan,' she says. 'Jonathan Pryce. From church.'

A mental snapshot of a man in a burgundy waterproof, glasses and a beard, who had dropped Mum home a few times after some fundraiser or other. I shake my head, 'But . . . but . . .' *What?* Was she . . . having an . . . was that where she'd been going when I saw her that time? To . . . *him?* The idea was utterly ridiculous. I watch her open-mouthed but she's looking away now, her face resuming its usual primness.

She gets up and begins to collect the dishes and sweet wrappers from where they lie scattered around me on the sofa. Painful tears sting my eyes. What will we do when she's no longer here? How will I cope? How will Dad cope? It's impossible. 'Mum,' I say, 'please don't go.'

She pauses at the door, and I'm shocked to notice that the plates in her hands are trembling. She glances at me and then away. 'I'll be in touch. When I'm settled, you can come round. I'll only be in Langley.' Her eyes dart to Dad's back as she says, 'We thought it best not to disrupt your studies . . .'

'But when are you going?'

'Today. Now. I'm sorry, I'm very sorry.' And with that she leaves.

Dad turns and we regard each other wordlessly for a second or two. He opens his mouth as if to speak, but closes it again as though he's thought better of it, before hurrying away too. On the TV, Ross and Rachel kiss for the first time in Central Park. I love this bit; it's one of my favourites. I turn the sound back on as the studio audience erupts into cheers and applause and I stare numbly at the screen until the end credits come up, the chirpy theme tune filling the stunned and empty room.

A week passes before I see Edie again. Seven days of Mum's absence, of my father and I mostly keeping to our own corners of the house, silent and shell-shocked. Though I still haven't returned to school I wait for Edie nearly every day as near to its gates as I dare, not wanting to risk running into Vicky or Alice. And finally I see her. The sight of her takes my breath away. She's wearing a short purple dress beneath her coat, a green scarf wrapped around her neck. Her hair is a golden chestnut in the sun, the cold turning her lips and cheeks rosy red. The sight fills my heart, the awfulness of the last week melting away, and it's all I can do not to run to her.

She rolls her eyes when she sees me. 'If you're going to lecture me again, Heather, seriously you can—'

'I'm not,' I say hastily, jogging to keep in step with her long stride.

'Good. Because I'm not in the mood.'

Bad temper crackles off her, and I wonder what has happened to make her so cross. She's walking even faster now, as though she's trying to lose me, and it hits me that she really doesn't want to talk to me, she doesn't want anything to do with me any more, because of what happened at Alice's party. Everything's ruined and it's all my fault. When I burst into tears she glances back at me and stops.

'Oh, Heather,' she says wearily. 'What on earth's the matter?'

We have reached the high street and I sit down on a bench by the bus stop. She sighs and sits next to me, and I tell her about Mum.

'You are *kidding* me?' She shakes her head in disbelief. 'Holy fuck. That's nuts.' She doesn't say anything for a while, then takes out a cigarette and lighting it says thoughtfully, 'Goes to show though, doesn't it?'

I find a tissue in my pocket and blow my nose. 'Show what?'

'Well, you know, that you never can tell about people.'

I lean my head on her shoulder and she puts an arm around me, and we sit like that in silence for a while. At last she says, 'What the hell did you do to Alice, by the way?'

I twist the tissue between my fingers. 'It was an accident,' I say.

'Well she's absolutely raging. She says the only reason she didn't call the police on you is because she didn't want her mum finding out about the party.'

'Is it . . . is it broken, her finger?'

'No, course not.' And she looks at me as though she's a little impressed. 'It's only sprained, but she's got a splint on it and everything. To be honest, I didn't know you had it in you.'

I look down at my feet and she nudges me in the arm. 'Come on, let's go and get a drink.'

The King's Arms is almost empty when we arrive, apart from a very drunk old woman sitting by herself and a couple of lads playing pool. Cigarette smoke hangs in thick yellow banks and a country and western song plays from the only unbroken speaker. My stomach flutters apprehensively as we approach the bar, but when Edie asks confidently for two vodka and Cokes, the middle-aged barman serves us without a murmur. 'You got any money?' she asks me, when he's put the drinks in front of us.

Once I've paid we take them over to a corner table and Edie lights a cigarette and smiles. I sip my drink and feel myself begin to relax for the first time since Mum left. It's nice here, just the two of us. 'Think my dad's going a bit loopy,' I tell her. 'He hasn't even wound his clocks all week. Hardly comes out of his study.'

She exhales a long stream of smoke. 'Seriously, Heather, you're best off out of it. Do your A-levels, get yourself to uni, you'll be well away. Do you good, if you ask me.'

And that's when I tell her my idea. I hadn't planned to, it was my secret that I turned to whenever I felt sad, pulling it down from a high shelf in my mind to stare wonderingly at it, occasionally adding a little detail, honing it and polishing it until it shone. It feels right though, somehow, to tell Edie all about it now. I lean forward and say in a rush, 'I'm going to apply to a

London uni. Mum and Dad think I want to go to Edinburgh, but I don't. That way when you go to Saint Martins we can see each other all the time. Maybe even be flatmates!' Eagerly I wait for her response.

But she only smiles, a distant, grown-up sort of smile, and flicks away some ash. 'Yeah, well, I don't know if I'll even bother with all that, to be honest.'

My mouth falls open in astonishment. 'But . . . why? You're so good. That's all you ever wanted!'

She frowns at me as though I'm being a bit dim. 'But I'm not going to leave Connor, am I? I mean, God, Heather, some people go their whole lives not finding love like this, you know? Never finding their soulmate? I know you don't really understand yet, but you will one day. When you've found it you don't just let it go.' She takes a sip of her drink and sits back.

I stare at her in dismay.

'Have you got any more money?' she asks, and I nod dully, reaching into my bag for my purse. Dad had given me enough cash to do a weekly shop. I was supposed to go to Co-op and get a cab back with it all, but it didn't seem that important any more.

She buys a round of drinks, and then another and then some more. I hand note after note to her until I've lost track of how much I've given her, and I don't care. The strange thing is, I don't even feel very drunk. It's like the alcohol just sits in the pit of my belly, its effect not spreading to the rest of me, like I'm too numb to feel anything. I watch Edie as she talks, her eyes alight as she tells me how wonderful Connor is, how good-looking, how clever, how sexy. It's only when she's on her sixth or seventh vodka – I'd started giving her mine to drink when I'd begun to feel sick – that something changes in her mood.

There's a darkness in her eyes as she fixes them on my face and murmurs, her words slurring a bit, 'I just wish . . . I don't know. I wish I could make him happy, you know?'

'What do you mean?'

She shakes her head and doesn't answer at first. And when she finally speaks, her voice is very quiet. 'I don't know. Sometimes I feel like I could love him and love him for ever and it would never be enough. Like there's this big hole right in the centre of him and nothing will ever fill it.' She stares down at her drink. 'When he gets in his moods, you know, his really bad ones, it's like nothing I say is right and I don't know what to do to make it better.' She looks at me and I reach over and take her hand. 'I don't know why he has to be so cruel to me.'

'Cruel?'

'I do everything he asks, Heather, everything, but it's never enough; never.'

I feel a ripple of unease. 'What sort of things? What do you mean?' Her eyes slide away, and she falls silent. 'How is he cruel to you, Edie?' I persist, my voice rising.

She begins to cry and I feel my heart might break. 'Does he hurt you?' Adrenalin pulses through me. She

203

doesn't reply and I hold her hand tightly and feel such an intense rush of anger and hatred for Connor that I think I could scream with it. How dare he be cruel to her? How could he? When she loves him so much, when she's so lovely and kind? I pick up one of the glasses and knock back the drink in one gulp. My words come out in a rush. 'You have to finish with him, Edie.'

The spell is broken. She jerks her head up and snorts as though I've understood nothing, as though I'm the most stupid person in the world. 'Don't be an idiot, Heather,' she snaps. 'I love him. Why would I finish with him? He's all I have. Don't you see that? I don't have anything else.'

You have me! I say silently, and I think about the drugs he makes her take and how unhappy she is, how he makes her do things she won't tell me about; awful, disgusting things, probably. How she's not going to art college any more, and before I know what I'm saying, the words are out of my mouth. They're out of my mouth and there's no way of taking them back again. 'You have to finish with him because he's cheating on you,' I blurt. 'He doesn't love you. He loves someone else.'

I don't even know where it came from, the lie. I hadn't known I was going to say it. When she doesn't reply I look up and see the meaning of my words break across her face. Her mouth hangs open in astonishment and she's gone very pale, but I notice with a tiny shock of revelation that despite her horror she isn't entirely surprised – not completely.

'What the fuck are you talking about?'

'I . . .'

'What do you mean?' she demands again. 'Why would you say that? You're lying, aren't you?'

I look at her angry face and feel myself waver. 'I'm not lying,' I tell her. 'I saw him! Down by the . . . um . . . the canal. He was holding hands with some girl, and then he . . . then he kissed her!'

'Why didn't you say something before?'

I feel a rush of sick regret. 'I didn't want to upset you.'

'Well . . . *when*? When the fuck is this supposed to have happened?'

'The other evening,' I stammer, frightened now by the way she's shouting at me.

There's a long, awful silence. The world seems to hold its breath. The pub and its music and the lads playing pool all melt away, and my heart thuds against my ribs. And then, all at once, her face crumples, all the fight and anger knocked out of her, and I realize that she believes me. She believes me completely. And I'm not sure if this is because she has so much faith in me, or so little in Connor, but I watch her, fascinated, as the devastation sweeps across her face: *I did that*.

She sinks her head into her hands and begins to cry again, great heaving sobs, her face soon a mess of tears and snot that she doesn't even bother to wipe away.

After a second or two I put my arms around her and hold her to me tightly, a strange excitement rising inside me as I stroke her hair and whisper, 'I'm so sorry, it'll be all right. It'll all be OK.'

Eventually she wipes her eyes and says in a bleak little voice, 'But what am I going to do? Oh, Heather, what am I going to do? How could he do this to me?' She bursts into tears again and says, 'I can't go home. I don't want to be on my own. I just don't know what I'm going to do.' She looks up at me so helplessly that my heart fills with love and happiness.

'You can come home with me,' I tell her. 'I'll look after you. Don't worry, I'll always look after you.'

I know that I will look back on this night forever. The single best night of my life so far. It's a shame that Edie has to be so upset, but she'll get over it, I know she will. And it's for the best, really. It's definitely for the best. When we get home I usher her up to my room, handing her a pair of my pyjamas to wear while I sneak back downstairs and find Mum's cooking brandy in the kitchen. When I return she looks so sweet, like a little girl in my too-big clothes.

We stay up most of the night, talking about Connor. It's funny, because after a while, it's almost as though it *did* happen. I can see the girl – who I've decided is blonde and slim but not nearly as pretty as Edie – walking with Connor by the canal, can see them stop and kiss each other so clearly that I find I can describe it in perfect detail. Edie wants me to go over it again and again, but I have to be firm with her eventually, and tell her that she needs to get some rest. She settles down under my duvet and says with a yawn, her eyes huge hollows in the lamplight, 'You're such a good friend, Heather. I mean it. No one has ever really given a shit before. Sometimes I think you're the only one who loves me.'

She falls asleep with me lying beside her, and I stay awake for ages, watching her. Beyond my bedroom door the clocks around the house strike eleven. A faint unease flutters around my heart. Edie will talk to Connor eventually, she's bound to. And he'll tell her that it isn't true. But after a few anxious moments I push the thought away: so what? Let him! It's me Edie loves, me she trusts now. She won't believe him over me, not any more. I feel my own eyelids begin to droop, but I stay awake and watch Edie sleep for a while longer. I don't want to move, I don't want to miss a thing.

And the following week is just as magical. She comes around most days, turning up on my doorstep at any time of day or night looking lost and desperate, needing me. I welcome her in and we order pizza and we talk. We talk so much, about lots of things. Connor mainly, of course. But that's OK, it's to be expected. Soon she'll get over him, move on, and we'll be happy again. I only have to be here for her, be a good friend. Sometimes I talk about our future, about how we'll be together in London one day, but I don't say too much, because it almost makes me too happy; it almost seems too wonderful to say out loud in case it's spoilt somehow.

Dad doesn't interfere at first. Just looks a bit puzzled every time he sees Edie, before retreating back to his study. Until one afternoon when he returns from work to find me singing to myself in the kitchen as I prepare a sandwich for her lunch. I feel his eyes on me as he hesitates by the door, then he clears his throat and speaks. 'Your mum, um, your mother thought it was best if you didn't see Edie, didn't she?' he says. 'I mean, after what happened . . .' he trails off, watching me uncertainly as I return the butter and ham to the fridge.

I glance back at him and smile. 'But Mum's not here, is she?' I say, holding his gaze.

After a second or two he looks away. 'No. I suppose she's not,' he murmurs. And then he leaves and a few moments later I hear him climbing the stairs, before shutting his study door firmly behind him.

After

Uncle Geoff lives in a narrow road of terraced houses off Erith's high street. While almost all the neighbouring properties have been smartened up or renovated, my uncle's stands defiantly unchanged since he moved in nearly three decades ago. Unlike his neighbours' homes the ugly brown pebble-dash hasn't been removed to reveal the original Victorian brick, the front path doesn't boast lovingly restored tiles, and the most attractive feature of his cemented-over front garden is his wheelie bin. Yet I usually love coming here – the familiar smells and warmth and comfort signalling to me refuge and safety, my uncle's home the place I feel most relaxed and cared for.

Today though my stomach tightens with nerves as I knock on the chipped front door. When he opens it we regard each other in silence before he stands aside and lets me in. In the kitchen he takes Maya from me, 'You've got so big,' he tells her with a sad smile. Maya takes hold of his little finger and grins back at him.

'Uncle Geoff,' I say, taking a deep breath. 'I'm so sorry I haven't been in touch.'

He turns away and puts the kettle on. 'Expect you've been busy,' he mutters.

'No, it wasn't that, I wasn't well, I—'

'Yes,' he nods, looking at me for the first time. 'So your friend said,' and I see how his expression sours at the mention of Heather.

There's a silence as I wonder how to explain. My uncle, warm and kind though he is, has never been one for discussing 'feelings'. A docker for thirty-five years, the closest I'd ever seen him come to showing emotion was over a pint on a Friday night, talking about snooker with his mates. I take in the tall, broad bulk of him, the craggy face with its deep lines and thick grey eyebrows, and at last I say in a rush, 'Heather's gone now and she won't be coming back. I thought I could trust her but, well . . . she turned out to be bad news. I never got your messages, or your letter, and for a long time I was too ill to get in touch.' I feel tears sting my eyes and say, 'I'm so sorry, Uncle Geoff, I really am.'

For a moment he doesn't respond and I hold my breath as he stares down at Maya. At last he comes over to me and puts a hand on my shoulder. 'OK,' he says gruffly. 'Don't upset yourself.' I'm overwhelmed with relief: he has forgiven me, because he loves me,

210

sees the best in me, and I can't speak for the lump in my throat.

Later, as we're drinking our tea he says with unexpected vehemence, 'I'm glad you got rid of that Heather woman. Not often I take a dislike to someone but there was something about her . . . I hated thinking of her up there with you and the baby.' He glances at me, before continuing hesitantly, 'In fact, I spoke to your mum about her.'

My eyes shoot to his face, and I feel a little sick. 'Yeah?' is all I can whisper.

'I thought she might remember her, what with Heather being a friend from Fremton and that.'

I nod, and though I can hardly bear to hear the answer, I ask with a kind of fascinated horror, 'What – what did she say?'

He frowns. 'Well, it was strange really, her reaction. She got quite agitated. Especially when I said she'd moved in to help with the baby, she was very upset about that – not that she'd say why. Clammed right up on me, she did.' He gives a wry smile, 'To be honest, I wished I hadn't phoned her – didn't exactly put my mind at rest.' He pauses and looks at me with sympathy, then says carefully, 'I got the idea Heather did something very nasty to you back in Fremton, love – that's the impression your mum gave, anyway. Is that right?' I don't reply, staring down at my hands as he goes on, 'That's why I wrote you the letter. Thought it might get through to you even if my texts and whatnot didn't. But you didn't reply – I know why now, of course,' he adds hastily. 'Edie? Edie love, are you all right?'

I nod, getting to my feet. 'I'm fine.' My heart still hammering in my throat, I force myself to smile, and take Maya from his arms. 'Think I need to change this one, that's all.' In the bathroom I lock the door behind us and take long, deep breaths as I hold Maya to me, trying to quell the nausea rising inside me. I stay up there for as long as possible, and when I finally go back down, my uncle thankfully, tactfully, changes the subject.

On the doorstep I hug him as I say goodbye, silently thanking God that Heather hadn't managed to come between us. But before I can open the door he clears his throat.

'Listen, Edie, don't you think it's time you and your mum buried the hatchet? Specially now you've got the little one. She obviously cares about you, to worry the way she did when I rang.'

For a moment I let myself imagine knocking on my mother's door with Maya, seeing her face again after so many years. But then the memories of that last night return and instantly I'm back there, in the kitchen of our house in Fremton. I see the revulsion in her eyes as I told her what had happened, and in my uncle's hall I begin to feel sick and shaken again. I force myself to smile. 'Maybe,' I say, before busying myself with Maya's buggy, then hurrying on my way.

*   *   *

I push the last box up into the loft and look down at my newly cleared hallway. It hadn't taken long to pack up Heather's things; those few sad piles of random belongings that had accumulated during the months she'd lived here. I had dithered for a while over whether to bin them or not and at last had hit on the idea of the loft – the one saving grace of this tiny, top-floor flat.

It had been depressing going through her stuff – the dust-clogged hairbrush, half-filled-in puzzle books, bitten Biros, old *Friends* DVDs and bags of clothes and underwear. As I'd packed it all away I'd brooded over the things she'd said the night she left, wondering where it was she'd gone to, whether it was true she never saw her parents any more – and whether she would ever return. As I slide the attic hatch back into place I think about how she'd been when we were younger. How manipulative she could be, how suffocating.

A sudden knock on the door makes me jump, my heart shooting instantly to my throat. I hadn't heard anyone on the stairs and I feel a brief stab of fear. *Heather?* I nearly cry out with relief when I hear Monica call my name. 'Are you OK?' she asks when I open the door. 'You're white as a sheet.'

'I'm fine. Sorry, it was—' I stop, and force myself to smile. 'Nothing.'

She nods. 'I was at a loose end, so I thought I'd come up.' She looks around at the newly cleared space. 'Wow. You've been busy. Looks great.'

I feel my heart slowly begin to return to normal. 'I

guess I'll have to look for a bigger place soon,' I tell her. 'Now I've got Maya.'

'You can't move,' she says, 'I'd miss you both too much.' She picks up Maya and brings her to the sofa with her, while I make some tea.

'Can't believe Christmas is almost here,' she says as I bring our drinks over. 'What're you doing for it? Do you have family back where you're from?'

The question takes me by surprise and I momentarily forget the stock answer I usually give. 'My mum lives there still,' I say slowly, handing her her tea. 'But we're not in touch any more.' There's a pause while I feel her eyes on me, and at last on impulse I admit, 'I haven't seen her for years, actually. Not since I was seventeen.'

'Really? How come?'

'Oh, usual teenage stuff, I guess. I got together with a lad and he was bad news. I started getting involved in . . . all sorts of shit. He messed with my head. I wasn't . . .' I shake my head and sigh, 'I wasn't in my right mind when I was with him. I was obsessed. Sixteen and completely obsessed. And then it went . . . everything just got really messed up.' A silence opens up between us and I can't quite believe I've said the words out loud. I've never spoken about Connor to anyone before.

'How so?' Monica asks gently.

I bite my lip, realizing I've said too much. 'Nothing. Teenage stuff, you know? My mum couldn't handle it, so I came to London to live with my uncle and the two of us . . . we just lost touch.'

214

I feel her puzzled eyes on me as I walk over to the window. I'm about to change the subject when she says, 'Must be hard.'

I stare out at the sky for a long time, caught up in a memory of my mum. When I was a kid she hadn't looked like other people's mothers. Her skirts were too short, she smoked in the playground and flirted with my friends' dads. I hated her for it, convinced she wished I wasn't around to spoil her fun. 'You're so embarrassing,' I'd shouted at her once when I'd caught her trying it on with our next-door neighbour. 'None of my friends' mums act like you!' and I'd been shocked when she'd sunk into a chair and burst into tears. 'I'm so lonely, Edie. I'm so bloody lonely,' she'd said.

I'd stood there, not knowing what to do, pity and resentment mingling and leaving me tongue-tied. A part of me wanted to comfort her, but instead I'd muttered, 'You made Dad go. You wouldn't be lonely if you'd let him stay.'

'Your precious father didn't want us!' Mum had spat. 'He put it about with anyone who'd have him. He didn't care about us, he only cared about getting his end away!'

It was as though she'd slapped me. 'I don't believe you. You're lying!' Tears of confusion had stung my eyes and I'd run to my room and locked myself in, refusing to come out again, no matter how much she begged me.

Here in my flat I turn to Monica and say, 'You don't know, do you, when you're a kid, how hard it is being a grown-up. All you want is to be a grown-up too. I

215

thought I'd be so much better at it than she was, and now I am one, I realize how stupid that was.'

After a silence, Monica asks, 'Do you miss her?'

A lump blocks my throat. 'Yeah,' I say quietly. 'I just wish . . . I wish things had been different.'

Monica comes and joins me at the window. 'Well, there's a lot of water under the bridge since then, love,' she says. 'You've got your own little one now. Maybe you should take her to see her nana one of these days – make a trip up there.' She smiles. 'I bet she'd be proud of you, your mum, to see what a lovely little girl you've got.'

I nod, swallowing hard. And it feels to me in the silence that follows that a warmth gathers in the space between us as we stand there, the two of us, at my window. After a while I ask her hesitantly, 'What happened with your ex, Monica? You don't have to tell me if you don't want to. I just . . . I know you're scared of him.'

Abruptly she turns away, returning to the sofa, and inwardly I kick myself. But after rummaging in her bag for a cigarette and lighting it, she sighs. 'Phil. He liked to kick the shit out of me.'

'Jesus.'

'I should have left years before I did. But it became . . . normal, you know? And at least he never touched the boys.' She smiles wryly. 'Just me he used as a punchbag. Whenever he was in a bad mood, or drank too much, he'd flip.' She exhales a long breath. 'Then

216

one day he went too far.' She stands up, raises her top and shows me the long, deep scar that runs almost the entire width of her body.

'He did that?' I whisper.

'He came back drunk one night. Started a fight because I hadn't answered my mobile earlier – didn't hear it ring. Picked up a knife and did this to me.' She lowers her top and shrugs. 'At least it was enough to make me see sense. He went to prison. I moved to a shelter with the boys, then to another, and another. He always found out where, though – had his spies, even from inside.' She sits back down. 'Only got a couple of years. He was released not long after we moved here. He came looking for me, didn't give a shit about the police. I know he won't give up.' She taps her head. 'He's sick. Twisted. He's biding his time.'

'What will you do if he does come back?' I ask.

'I don't know.' She seems to me in that moment very small and vulnerable sitting there, as though even the memory of Phil has diminished her. 'Every time my phone rings, I panic. Every time I go out by myself or someone knocks on the door, I think, that's it: he's come back for me.' She turns and looks at me. 'I haven't been able to work since it happened. I keep having these panic attacks. I think he'd kill me, Edie, I really do.'

I watch James as he peels and chops an onion. It's a nice room, his kitchen: light and airy with whitewashed brick walls covered in paintings, drawings and black-and-white photographs. Every surface, including the large pine table, is cluttered with books or CDs, pot plants or cooking things. A band I've never heard before plays on the stereo and the scent of the food James is cooking fills the air.

I'd been pleased when he'd phoned earlier and invited me over. I'd dug out a dress I'd bought years before and for the first time in ages made an effort with my hair and make-up. When Monica had come up to babysit she'd looked me up and down and whistled. 'Blimey, you scrub up all right, don't you?' and she'd surprised me by giving me a quick hug, 'Have a great time, love,' she'd said. 'Don't do anything I would do,' and I'd laughed.

But then something strange had happened on the walk over here. My mobile had rung and when I'd pulled it out and looked at it 'Caller ID Withheld' had flashed across the screen. I'd answered it and when no one had replied I'd stood beneath a lamppost, repeating, 'Hello? Hello?' into the silence. Except it hadn't been silent, not completely. I could hear whoever it was breathing on the other end, could feel them listening to me. After a long moment they had hung up.

I stand here now in my too-high heels trying to hide my stupid, too-short dress behind the coat I'm clutching, feeling ridiculous about being so dressed up and trying not to think about who it had been on the other end of my phone. James is stirring a pot on the stove wearing jeans and a pale blue T-shirt and I feel entirely unable to think of anything to say.

He looks up and smiles. 'Take a seat,' he says, and hurriedly I pull out one of the kitchen chairs. 'Would you like a glass of wine?'

My hand flies to my mouth. 'God, sorry. I should have brought a bottle. I didn't think.' I can hear the nervousness in my voice and he shoots me a surprised look.

'That's OK. I've got a couple in the fridge. Or I've red, if you prefer? Go on, sit down, I'll pour you one.'

Once he's passed me a large glass and turned back to his chopping, I take a big gulp, and then another. As he cooks he chats about this and that, but every question he asks I can only seem to answer with a 'yes' or a 'no', and as hard as I try, I can't seem to think of any conversation of my own. It'd been different in the pub, after the show; there'd been something between us, a connection. But here, now, I've no idea what I should say or do. And I can't quite shake the thought of Heather from my mind. Had it been her on the phone earlier? I feel the old, nagging unease.

'I'm making a lamb tagine,' James tells me. 'Do you like Moroccan?'

I shake my head. 'I don't know, sorry. I've never tried it.'

He laughs. 'Stop apologizing.' In the following silence I drink more wine and as my eyes follow him around the room I try not to think about how attractive I find him. At last, in desperation, I pick up a book from one of the piles lying near me and ask, 'This one any good, is it?'

He glances over. 'Haven't started it yet, but I love his other stuff so I hope so. How about you? Read any of his?'

I take another gulp of wine. 'No. I'm not much of a reader, I'm afraid.'

He nods and begins stirring something. 'Won't be a tick.'

I finish my glass and, while he's not looking, help myself to more. I realize that I've begun to feel quite drunk. When he brings the food over and sits down, he fills both of our plates, and raises his glass. 'Cheers,' he says. 'I hope you like it.' We eat in silence for a moment or two. 'This is really nice,' I tell him, taking a large bite to try and steady the fresh wave of nerves I feel.

He smiles. 'You look lovely, by the way. It's good to see you.' And there's something in the way he says it that makes me feel he means it, and I begin to relax a little. The low hanging light above the table illuminates the two of us, the rest of the room in darkness beyond its warm glow.

'Is your son asleep upstairs?' I ask.

He shakes his head. 'Stan's at his mum's. We split up not long after he was born and he stays with her half the week, me the rest.'

'Must be hard.'

'Nope. Not really. We parted on pretty good terms.' I nod, and wonder if anything has ever been very difficult for James.

'Were you with Maya's dad long?' he asks.

'No.'

'Ah, that's a shame. He's involved, though?'

'He doesn't know about her.'

He looks shocked, his fork poised in mid-air. 'Really?'

I shrug. 'He was someone I worked with. I didn't tell him I was pregnant.' James nods and looks away, but not before I've seen the disapproval in his eyes. I try to think of something else to talk about, but, glancing around at the books, the exotic food, the music and art, feel once again entirely at a loss. The silence lengthens.

In the end it's he who speaks first. 'I don't even know where you're from,' he says, his voice light again. 'Can't quite place your accent.'

'Manchester originally.'

He nods. 'So your family's still there?'

I take a swig of wine. 'We kind of lost touch.'

'Oh. I'm sorry.'

This time the pause stretches and stretches and I know that I should fill it, should say something else, anything at all, but the fact is I'm no good at this: I don't know how it's done, what I should say. I should give him something of myself, I realize: share something, anything, so I force myself to continue. 'No, it's OK,' I say, and make myself smile. 'I was a bit of a nightmare teenager, to be honest. Bit of a handful. I fell out with my mum. Don't blame her at all . . .'

'Misspent youth, huh?' He narrows his eyes, grinning. 'Always thought there was something mysterious about you – a few skeletons in the cupboard maybe. In a good way, of course.'

He refills my glass and, thankfully, changes the subject. As we finish the meal he talks about what it was like growing up in London, and about being a student at Saint Martins. He's funny and takes the piss out of himself and the more I laugh, the more I relax.

'And that,' he says, finishing his story, 'is why I can't even smell Jack Daniel's now without wanting to go and lie down in a very dark room.'

I smile, 'I'm a bit like that with vodka,' I say, then try not to think about the last time I'd drunk it. Our eyes meet, a silence falls, a new intimacy lingers in the air between us. He has refilled my glass and as I take another sip he says, putting down his spoon, 'I seem to be doing all the talking. You're very good at listening to my rubbish, but I don't know anything about you.'

'What do you want to know?' I ask, my heart instantly sinking.

He shrugs. 'How did you come to move to London, did you study here?'

And I don't know what to say, because I'm not going to talk about why I left Fremton and what I was like when I first moved here – because there's nothing to tell. I have no funny stories to share, no friends to talk about, no wild anecdotes to recount, none that I could possibly tell him, anyway. I look down at my plate.

'OK,' he says at last, getting up. 'None of my business, I guess,' and he begins to clear the dishes away. And just like that the warm, intimate vibe between us slips away and the awkward, puzzled silence grows and I desperately try to think of something to give him, anything to make him sit back down and look at me the way he had been a few moments ago, but my mind is entirely blank.

And so on a desperate impulse I get up and I go to him and I do what I have always done in this situation, the only thing I know that works: when he turns to me in surprise I put my arms around him and kiss him. For an awful second I think he's going to resist, but to my relief he begins to return my kiss and I'm so thankful that I respond more passionately, running my hands over his body, pressing myself against him, and when, momentarily, through the woozy fog of alcohol Connor's face swims horrifyingly into view, I kiss James harder, using every ounce of strength I have to push the memories away and with urgent fingers begin to undo his belt, his flies, until suddenly he puts his hand on mine and he pulls away. 'Um . . .' he glances at me, and I feel a hot, stinging slap of embarrassment.

There's an awful silence. Mortification rises in me. I look away as he does himself up again. 'What's the matter?' I mumble.

'Nothing,' he says. 'I'm sorry, I just – I wasn't expecting it, I don't know, I . . .' He moves away. 'Do you want coffee? I could make us coffee . . .' He goes to the kettle.

I stare at his back. 'No,' I say at last. 'No. That's OK. I guess I'll – I better go. It's getting late.'

'No, look,' he says, 'please stay. Have another glass of wine. Or a coffee. Please, sit down.'

But I gather up my coat and bag. 'It's OK. I'd better get back to Maya. I better go. Thanks for dinner.' And as I hurry off down the hall I hear him calling me one last time, but I don't reply, just quickly leave and close the door behind me.

When I emerge into the night I pause for a second at his gate, my eyes closed tightly as embarrassment crashes over me. When I open them again a movement across the road startles me. A figure on the other side, half hidden by a parked van, suddenly turns and disappears off down the street. The road is unlit and I can't make out if the person is a man – or a tall, broad woman. For some moments I stand there, frozen, before the thought of James coming out and finding me jolts me into action and I take off in the opposite direction, towards home.

Later, I lie awake in bed, listening to the night, my thoughts racing. Had it been Heather I'd seen? Had she come back? On impulse I get up, find my mobile and click open the internet. In Google Images I type the words 'Jennifer Wilcox' before pressing Search. I'm met with page after page of strangers' faces. After a few moments' thought I add 'Birmingham' and 'Methodist Church', and there she is, on the very first page: Heather's mum. I click on her image and I'm taken to a website for a church in a place called Castle Vale. Next to some information about a food bank is Heather's mother. She's wearing large, ugly glasses now, and her hair's grey and in a shorter style, but it's still her, those eyes with their expression of pious disapproval unchanged. Below her picture are the words: 'For more information, email Jennifer Wilcox', followed by a Gmail address. It's probably long out of date, I tell myself, but nevertheless I click on the link.

I write quickly so that I don't have time to change my mind.

Hi Jennifer, I don't know if you remember me, I was Heather's friend in Fremton, Edie. I live in London now. I'm sorry to contact you out of the blue like this, but wondered if you'd heard from her recently. We have been in contact, but I haven't spoken to her for a while and . . .

I pause, staring at the screen. And . . . what? *I think she might be stalking me?* Eventually, I add, a little lamely,

I'd like to talk to you about her.

My finger hovers over the Send button, and then, on impulse, I press it.

Before

It's on a Monday night that everything falls apart. I haven't heard from Edie all day, and I'm watching telly and picking at some cheese on toast, wondering where she's got to and hoping she's all right, when the doorbell rings. I jump to my feet and open the door, already laughing with relief, about to usher her in when I notice the expression on her face and it's only then that the smile freezes on my lips.

She pushes past me into the house, and we stand in the hall as she glares back at me, her eyes bright with fury. 'Edie?' I say hesitantly, but I know what's coming, that the happy, beautiful time we'd spent together is over.

She's about to speak but the sound of my dad moving about upstairs stops her and she takes me by the arm and pulls me roughly into the kitchen. 'What's the mat—' I begin.

'Tell me, again, Heather,' she says, 'about the time you saw Connor by the canal.'

'Um . . .'

'You could see them clearly, yeah? Him and this girl? You told me what she looked like, what clothes she was wearing.'

'Yeah . . .'

'And it was about seven? At night?'

I nod.

She narrows her eyes. 'It's pitch-black by seven, specially down there.'

'Well maybe it was a bit earl—'

'And you said she was tall?'

I can feel my heart thudding. 'I think so. Quite tall. Listen, Edie, what's—'

She snorts. 'Oh really? Because now I think about it, you said at the time she was quite short. Shorter than me.'

I shake my head. 'I don't . . . I can't . . .' I hate lying. I've never been any good at it. I feel confused and panicky. 'Edie, please—'

Her eyes bore into me. 'You said it was a couple of nights before we went to the pub together.'

Miserably, I nod.

'The thing is, Heather,' she says, and her voice is slow and deliberate, as cold as her stare, 'Connor was in Overton with Tully that night. He's got messages on his phone to all the others, telling them to get down there. He showed me them.'

'Um . . . maybe not a couple of nights before, maybe three. I don't—'

'Well, which is it? Two or three?'

My panicked mind is blank.

Her mouth falls open. 'Oh my God. He was right. You were lying, weren't you? Connor was fucking right! You made the whole thing up.' She takes a step nearer and I shrink away.

'No! No, I didn't! Edie, please, I—'

Her voice is suddenly a shout and I jump out of my skin. 'Tell me now. Did you lie?'

It's no good. It's finished. I drop my eyes and nod.

When I next look up the expression on her face makes me burst into tears. There's disbelief and shock there, but more than that, I have never seen her look so hurt. I reach out my hand to her. 'Edie, I'm so sorry—'

But she bats me away. 'Everyone at school said you were a weirdo. But I thought they were just bitches and you were all right. I thought you cared about me. That out of everybody, you were looking out for me.' She shakes her head, 'Christ. Do you even know what you've done? You've fucked up everything!'

I can barely look at her, can only stand there, miserably staring down at my feet.

'*Why*, Heather? Why would you do this to me? Because you want me for yourself? Is that it? I've seen the way you look at me. Christ you're disgusting. You are actually fucking disgusting. I will never forgive you for this. Never.'

The look of contempt and hatred she shoots me makes my heart shrivel and I sink into a chair, a crushing feeling in my chest as I watch her turn abruptly and walk out of the house, slamming the front door behind her.

I move from clock to clock, taking my time, locating each tiny key from its hook or ledge or cubbyhole and, carefully inserting it, turn it precisely the right amount so as not to overwind. With one finger I gently set each pendulum in motion, adjust the second and hour hands, before moving on to the next. I don't know exactly when I started doing this, but someone's got to: I used to hate Dad's clocks, but I hate their silence more.

As I hover in the upstairs hall I hear him behind his study door as he shifts in his chair, the radio playing something by Bach. I expect he's doing some marking, or else copying something down from his Bible; he seems to be doing that more and more these days. I find little slips of paper covered in his handwriting all over the house, but I don't even try to decipher them any more. I finish winding the last clock and slip back into my room. It'll be time to start dinner soon, but before I do, I find the bottle of vodka I've hidden beneath my mattress and take a quick gulp, then one more, before replacing the cap and screwing it on tight. It's been four months since Mum left, and three and a half since I last spoke to Edie.

Mum and I meet almost every week, at the café on the high street. We talk about her new job at the health centre and I tell her how I'm getting on at school. I don't tell her how I only do the bare minimum there now, that I sometimes don't bother going in, that I'm beginning to fall behind to such an extent I'm worried I'll never catch up. I want to tell her I'm sorry, that I know her leaving is my fault. But I don't, and we're both pretty relieved when it's time to go home.

I see Edie now and then at school, but we don't talk. If she sees me, she pretends she hasn't, turning abruptly away down a corridor or into a classroom, and I never have the courage to chase after her, to stop her, to make her see how sorry I am. I've written her a hundred letters, I've picked up the phone countless times, but in the end I never send them, I never dial the number I still know by heart. Instead, when lessons are over and I should be at home studying, I catch the bus to somewhere else, I walk around the shops, slipping whatever I can into my bag, stuff I think Edie might like, mostly. Or else I ride my bike to an off-licence on the edge of town, where if I time it so there's no customers, the man who works there will sell me anything I want, and never asks my age.

After a watery, windy spring the shock of heat seems to come from nowhere, the sun blasting down day after day, biting at my skin as I traipse from shadow to shadow. Dad's working from home today so I've been wandering around pretending to be at school since 8 a.m. I've been to the rec, and to the library, across the

231

motorway's overpass and back again, and I'm cutting back behind the hospital when the battered white car pulls up beside me, its engine growling, music thudding from its open windows, a male voice calling out my name.

I stop and feel an electric jolt of shock to see Connor staring back at me. 'You all right, Heather?' he says, his voice a slow drawl, his eyes hidden behind dark shades. Apart from the surprise of seeing him, I am, as usual, momentarily stunned by his good looks, so out of place here amidst Fremton's greyness, making my eyes flinch as though I've looked directly at the sun. Because there's always been something a little repulsive about his handsomeness too, something too brutal and cruel in his perfect features. Between his legs sits a bottle of beer and he takes it now and puts it to his lips, but I feel his eyes on me still, from behind the black shades, watching me.

And then I peer behind him to the back seat and see Edie there, with two other lads, and all thoughts of Connor are forgotten. A sensation as though I'm falling – a slipping down, losing grip kind of feeling. She glances at me, a quick, cool, hard stare, before turning away to look out of the window. 'You getting in or what?' Connor says, and I glance back at him in confusion. What can this mean? What could they possibly want? But I know I cannot and will not refuse: irresistibly I am drawn to where Edie is, the sight of her after so many weeks like water after endless thirst, and wordlessly I nod.

I have barely sat down in the passenger seat before Connor accelerates and we speed off, tyres screeching. My heart pounds as I pull the seat belt around myself. The air is thick with smoke and the sweet, sickly smell of weed, and I glance back at Edie again but she's still staring steadfastly out of the window. The two lads next to her are arguing about something I can't hear above the rap music that's blaring from the speakers.

Suddenly Connor speaks. 'You all right then, Heather?' he says. I don't like his voice with its local accent tinged with something I guess he's copied from a gangster movie, his mocking, over-confident tone that most lads round here seem to use, as if you're a bit stupid, or a bit deaf, or both.

'Yeah,' I mumble.

'What you been up to then?'

I shrug. 'Not much, school and that.'

He glances at me. 'Not been busy making shit up about people?'

I shake my head, clenching my fists tight.

'Because I know you like to do that.'

I don't reply and he laughs, an ugly, humourless noise. 'Cheer up, for fuck's sake. I'm only messing with you.' He doesn't say anything else after that, just continues to drink his beer and take long draws on the joint one of the others has handed to him, its end flaring and crackling as he inhales. We drive through Fremton and out the other side, Connor hitting the accelerator even harder as soon as we're on the bigger, less busy roads.

233

What's happening? Where are they taking me? Surely Edie wouldn't let anything bad happen? I turn to the back seat, but her closed, angry expression makes the words die on my lips.

Finally, on the other side of Wrexham, we turn off down a dirt track and up a steep hill and at last Connor slows down. The tape we've been listening to comes to an abrupt end and as the winding road takes us higher and higher the car is silent. I look around myself in confusion. What is this place? When at last we reach the top, Connor stops the car and we all get out. I trail behind Edie. I just need to speak to her, to make her see how sorry I am. Then she'll have to forgive me, she has to.

We pass through a copse and what's waiting on the other side makes me stop in amazement. I'd heard of the Wrexham quarry before, but I'd never been here or dreamt it was anything like this. An enormous jagged basin of white rock filled with water that's a strange unnatural green, a sheen of oil upon its still, rippleless surface. On the furthest side groups of local kids are getting drunk in the sunshine, music playing from their car stereos. Now and then one of them throws himself into the water, to a chorus of shrieks and cheers. I take it all in, the sun beating down on me, the sky an intense blue.

I notice that Connor and the others are talking to a group of people sitting beneath some trees a few yards away. Hesitantly I follow them, realizing as I draw closer that I recognize some of his friends from the party. I sit down in a scrubby patch of grass nearby and wait. Nobody looks at me, as though they've forgotten I'm here, and I turn my attention to Edie. She's wandered a little further away and is sitting by herself, staring out across the quarry. Occasionally she glances back at Connor, and she seems so sad and alone it makes my heart hurt.

I suddenly realize that the boy nearest to me is the one I'd met before in the square. Liam. He looks even younger without his hoodie, with his thin naked arms, his close-cut brown hair that shows the fragile curve of his skull, his pale, thoughtful eyes. I creep a bit closer to him, feeling a little better to see him here. 'How come there's no one in the water on this side?' I ask him when he looks up, nodding at a large red sign that says, 'DANGER: NO SWIMMING'.

He shrugs and says in his low, mumbling voice, 'Full of crap over here. People dump all sorts in it: shopping trollies, dead dogs – you name it. Supposed to be an old car wreck down there somewhere.' His eyes flick up to me from the joint he's rolling and away again. 'Some kid jumped in and got impaled on a pole a few years back. Sticking right up, it was, just under the surface.'

I shudder; open water terrifies me. At that moment Connor calls Edie's name and I see her look up eagerly with a hopeful smile. But when he speaks his voice is cold and flat. 'You bring that gear, yeah?' he asks her. She nods and throws him something from her pocket, and when he turns away again I see the disappointment on her face.

A few moments later she stands up. I'm not sure what she's doing at first, but then, as I watch, she slowly and deliberately pulls her top off, standing in her bra for a second or two, before kicking off her flip-flops and wriggling out of her skirt. I can tell she knows she's being watched. Finally, when she's only in her underwear she lies back down, stretching out, her eyes closed against the hot sun, her long hair spilling around her shoulders. It takes my breath away to see how beautiful she is, her long, slender legs, her small, perfect breasts, like a model from a picture in a magazine. When I glance back at the others I see that they are watching her too. No one speaks.

Suddenly she props herself up and turns to me and my heart leaps. 'You not sunbathing then, Heather?' she says.

I look at her in surprise. 'I haven't got my swimmers,' I stammer.

Her voice is cold. 'So? Haven't got mine, have I?'

I'm conscious that the others are listening, and I look away in embarrassment. But when I next glance up, she's still staring at me, her eyes challenging. 'What's the matter? You too stuck up to get your kit off or something?'

I shake my head. 'No, but . . .'

'Go on then, do it.'

I hesitate. Is this what I need to do to make it up to

her? To make her forgive me, love me again? I would do anything to make that happen. A long moment passes.

'Do it,' she says again.

Slowly, my cheeks burning, I stand up. I pull my top up and over my head and quickly sink back to the ground, my arms folded tightly across my chest, the sun biting into my naked white flesh.

'And the rest,' she says, nodding at my legs. 'Not going to get a tan with them on, are you?'

Reluctantly I get up again and undo my jeans, losing my balance and almost falling over as I slide them down my legs. I hurriedly sit back down, knowing how awful I must look compared to her. When I look up our eyes lock.

And then, in the silence, Connor speaks. 'Now that's what you call a proper pair of tits, ain't that right, Edie?' He pauses before adding casually, 'Not like your fried eggs, are they?'

In the loud laughter that follows mortification sweeps through me and when I glance up at Edie I see the humiliation and fury in her eyes. Abruptly she gets to her feet and storms off to the edge of the quarry, slides down one of the large white rocks and disappears.

At first I don't move. I've made everything worse. Everything is even worse than it was before and now she hates me more than ever. What if she's fallen in? At last I get to my feet and follow her, not even caring about the view Connor and his friends must have of my bottom. When I reach the edge I peer over and see that she's a couple of metres below, sitting on a ledge, her feet dangling above the water. Clumsily I lower myself down to her, the gritty surface of the rock scratching at my skin.

'Edie,' I say, a little breathlessly. 'Please, Edie.' But she continues to stare down at the water. 'I'm so sorry about what I did,' I tell her desperately. 'You've got to forgive me.'

She looks at me then. Now that we are so close I can see that she has lost weight and there are deep shadows beneath her eyes; unhappiness radiates from her. Finally she speaks, spitting her words out at me, each one sharp as a tack. 'I'll never forgive you,' she says, getting to her feet. 'You're a fucking bitch.'

I gasp and tears fill my eyes at her look of disgust. 'You're pathetic,' she says, her eyes travelling over my body. 'Look at the state of you.'

I scramble to my feet and reach out to her, grabbing her by the arm, trying to stop her from leaving. 'Please, Edie,' I beg. 'I didn't mean to do it, I'm so sorry—'

What happens next is definitely an accident. She whirls round so quickly, and she's so angry as she shouts, 'Get off me, Heather, just leave me the fuck alone.' She doesn't mean to push me into the water, I'm sure she doesn't. But still I topple and fall backwards off the ledge. I hit the surface with a loud slap, the shock of freezing cold knocking the air from my lungs. As I fall through the green, murky water I think about what Liam had told me, about the cars and the dead dogs and the boy who

238

died, and I kick and kick until at last my head bursts up through the surface, into the sunshine again, and I'm gasping for air.

I swim towards the ledge where Edie is standing, and for a moment, just for a moment, I see the relief on her face before she turns away and begins to climb back up to the top. With difficulty I haul myself out, scrabbling about on the rocks before finding a foothold and following her. I'm only a little bit behind her when I look up and see Connor there, staring down at the two of us and smoking a cigarette, the oily green surface of the water reflected in his shades.

They drop me off where they found me. As I watch them drive away I think about Edie, and why they picked me up, and what it could possibly mean, but mainly I think about how unhappy she seemed, and how horrible Connor was to her, and I think about how she needs me now more than ever.

That night I dream about the quarry. But this time, I don't fight my way back up to the surface; my head doesn't break up into the warm sunlight. Instead I continue to plunge deeper and deeper until suddenly it's no longer my body I'm inhabiting: I am my sister, I am Lydia. The water begins to fill my mouth, my nose, choking me until I can't breathe. As I sink lower and lower the awful, burning pressure in my lungs builds and builds until I wake to darkness, to dizzying panic,

239

my face wet with tears, my breath ragged gasps. *Lydia.* Grief floods me: how frightened she must have been.

We had been camping in the Brecon Beacons, near where we lived in Wales. A little site next to a lake with a scattering of tents and caravans, a few communal wooden buildings. One morning I woke early to see Mum gathering her things for the shower block and when she saw me she put her finger to her lips and whispered, 'Stay here.'

Dad was fast asleep, snoring in his sleeping bag, but almost as soon as Mum had zipped up the tent behind her, Lydia had woken too. 'Hebba!' she said, smiling up at me.

I glanced at Dad and, just like Mum had done, put my finger to my lips. 'Come on.'

We had crawled out into the misty, early morning sunshine and gone down to the shore of the sparkling lake and looked at the boats tethered to the jetty. 'Me boat, me boat!' she said, hopping about in excitement.

I knew we weren't allowed. 'No, Lyddy,' I said, but held her hand as we paddled in the lacy ripples of the lake's shore, the hem of her nightie and the cuffs of my pyjama bottoms growing heavy and dark in the lapping water. Near us, a blue-and-yellow dinghy bobbed gently.

Lydia held out her arms to it, looking back at me, her round, cornflower blue eyes beseeching. 'Me boat, me boat!' she said again.

I'd hesitated, glancing back at the silent tents. What fun it would be! In that moment all the reasons why

240

we shouldn't had disappeared. 'OK,' I said and using all my strength had lifted her into the dinghy, before hopping in myself. I guess it was our weight and movement that had set it loose and I hadn't noticed we had become untethered until we were a metre from the jetty. I'd grabbed hold of the oars, immediately dropping one into the water, and began chopping so inexpertly with the other that we just moved further and further from the shore. I started to panic. Mum would be so cross. We drifted closer towards the centre. Lydia saw my face and began to cry, 'It's OK, Lyddy,' I said.

But she must have felt my anxiety because she got up and walked towards me, her arms outstretched. 'Want to go back. Want Mummy.'

'No,' I shouted. 'Sit down, sit down! It's not safe!' And she had started back in shock, crying even more because I'd shouted, and that's when she'd lost her balance and fallen in.

I didn't know what to do. Shock and terror had paralysed me at first. She flailed about for a few moments, her head bobbing in and out of the water, crying and swallowing and spluttering, her white nightie ballooning around her, and then she had disappeared. I wasn't a very good swimmer, the worst in my class. I couldn't see her, couldn't reach her. I should have jumped in after her, I should have, but I was too scared. I hadn't realized I was screaming until, far away, on the shore, people began to run from their tents. I saw my father leaping into the water and beginning to swim, while I'd sat in the middle of the lake and screamed and screamed, and knew that she was gone.

It's about four the next afternoon when I arrive at the Pembroke Estate. I stop at the bottom of Connor's tower and stare up at the rows and rows of black windows, wondering which one of them is his. It strikes me that he might be up there right now, staring down at me, watching me, and I shiver, looking around myself at the concrete outbuildings, the garages and bin sheds. A dog tied to some railings barks unceasingly up at the sky and a child throws a football at a wall, over and over, *thwack thwack thwack*. I take a deep breath and walk towards the lift.

When Connor answers the door I don't say a word, ignoring the flicker of surprise and then the smirk on his face as I walk past him up the hallway to the living room. Several of his friends are sprawled across the sofa, armchair and floor, music thudding from the speakers. Edie sits in the corner and when she looks up, her expression doesn't alter. She squints at me for a moment, before her head falls and she goes back to watching the muted TV screen. Everywhere you look there are cigarette papers and lighters and pipes and bags of weed. I take a seat on the sofa next to Rabbit, who's bending over a line of white powder on a CD case. On the floor by my foot I notice a small bag of white pills.

I turn my attention back to Edie, whose eyes are closed now, her head lolling on to one shoulder, and I wait. Someone's got to look after her; someone's got to make sure she's OK. I won't let Connor destroy her. I will not let that happen. I see him, standing in the doorway looking in at us, his cocky smile, his cruel green eyes, and a pure, white-hot hatred sweeps through me. I clench my fists tighter and tighter, as the seeds of an idea begin to take root in my mind.

After

We stand at Monica's back door, looking out at the communal garden. 'What a tip,' she says, kicking at an abandoned armchair, its guts spilling foam and rusty springs on to what might once have been a lawn. It's viciously cold today; icy and bleak, the trees black and skeletal against a flat white sky. I look at a sodden mattress rotting beneath a mountain of rubbish and I shiver, wishing Monica would hurry up and close the door so we could return to her cosy flat. But she's warming to her theme. 'It's a disgrace,' she goes on. 'Why haven't the council been to sort it yet? They need to pull their finger out. I'm going to complain.'

'Yeah,' I say. 'Good luck with that.' The cold bites into me and I blow warmth on to my fingers. 'Christ, Mon. Let's go back in. I'm bloody freezing.'

'Why don't we do it ourselves?' she says. 'You, me,

and the boys – see if we can rope in some of the other flats too?'

'Um . . .'

'Yeah,' she says, enthusiastically. 'We'll get the council to take away all this crap, then we can start turning it into a proper garden again.'

'Well,' I say slowly, 'that might . . .'

She turns to me impatiently, 'Don't you think it'd be nice to have somewhere Maya can play?'

I look at her eager face and cast my eye over the garden again, seeing it now through her eyes: cleared, growing, with flowers and a lawn, Maya playing in the sunshine, and I smile. 'Yeah,' I tell her, 'it really would.'

She nudges me. 'Could even get that fella of yours to help out.'

The familiar hot creep of embarrassment returns at the mention of James and I look away and mumble, 'I already told you, he's not my fella.'

'We'll see.' A sudden icy rain begins to fall, and at last we return to the flat. We find Billy sat at the kitchen table, Maya perched on his knee as he tinkers with a part from his motorbike. She looks up and smiles when she sees me, a line of black grease streaked across her cheek. It's warm in here with the rain pelting at the windows, the radio playing a Lady Gaga song that Monica hums along to as she puts the kettle on and washes up some mugs. I take a seat as Ryan appears and hands his brother a spanner, the two lads conferring intently as they work.

As I watch the boys I wonder how it must have been for them, to have grown up the way they did; how it is that they turned out so well despite the things they must have witnessed, all the violence they'd seen. It occurs to me that the goodness in their mother must have been enough to outweigh the evil in their father, and my thoughts turn to Heri. He'd been a good man, I remind myself anxiously, and I hope with all my heart that it's him who Maya takes after, and not me.

'Earth to Edie?'

I look up, startled. 'Sorry, what?'

Monica laughs. 'I was saying, why don't you and Maya come to us for Christmas Day? It'll just be me and the boys, but you're welcome too.'

'Really?' I say. Uncle Geoff had already told me he'd arranged to spend the day with old friends. 'I didn't know if you'd be back in touch by then, you see,' he'd added apologetically and I'd felt a fresh wave of guilt and reassured him that Maya and I would be absolutely fine, that we'd see him on Boxing Day instead. I smile at Monica. 'That'd be amazing! Are you sure?'

She laughs. 'It really won't be, but yeah, of course.' She lowers her voice. 'Ryan and Billy haven't had a decent Christmas for a long time, I want it to be special this year.'

I'm so touched I have to swallow hard before I reply, 'I'd love to. It'll be great.'

She smiles. 'Yeah, it will, won't it?'

*   *   *

The next morning, after weeks of freezing rain I wake to a December Sunday morning so unseasonably mild that I step out on to the roof and blink up at the hazy blue sky in astonishment. Below me the quiet streets and dew-soaked gardens glisten expectantly in the sunshine and I bundle Maya into her buggy and set off for the park. Warmed by this bright, beautiful sunlight my fears about Heather begin to recede. There had been no more phone calls since the night I went to James's, and Jennifer had never replied to my email. I feel a tentative flicker of hope: perhaps it's all over, after all.

The park's already busy when we arrive, people emerging like moles from their burrows, smiling their surprise while their kids charge around without their coats. I take Maya to the swings and she laughs so delightedly that a man walking past stops and smiles. 'Now there's a happy little face,' he says, and I feel an almost overwhelming rush of pride as I think of how far we've come, Maya and I; what a distance we've travelled together since those first few grim months of her life.

Later, as we sit together on the grass, I spy a grey-haired woman sharing a sandwich with a little boy and as I watch, the image of my mother's face flickers across my mind. A memory comes to me of one of the last times we spoke. I was standing in our old front room, Mum sitting on the sofa, her crutches propped up next to her. She was smoking a cigarette, hair done and lipstick on her face even though she hadn't stepped foot outside for months. She was crying, and I was refusing to look at her. 'Edie,' she said. 'Please talk to me.'

But I'd cut her off. 'I'm fine,' I snapped. 'There's nothing to talk about.' I turned back to staring out at the street.

'But you look bloody terrible! You're never here, I don't even know what you're doing or where you're going half the time.' Her voice had been desperate.

My eyes had swum with tears and for a second I imagined telling her everything, begging her to help me, to make it all go away before it was too late, to put a stop to Connor and me. But the moment passed and instead I turned and said furiously, 'There's nothing wrong! Leave me alone.' And I walked out of the room, and out of the house, slamming the door behind me.

'Come on,' I say to Maya, pushing away the rush of sadness and regret, 'let's go to the shops, shall we? Buy us something nice for lunch.' When I put her in her buggy I look at the shiny black eyes gazing back at me and feel my heart tighten with love.

And then, near the gate, I see James cycling towards us. Hurriedly I lower my head and pray that he won't spot me, but a few seconds later I look up to see him slowing to a stop right beside us. 'Hi!' I say too brightly as he gets off his bike.

'Hey,' he replies, and there's an awkward silence before we say at the same time, our voices clashing jarringly, 'How are you?' and, 'Yeah – fine, fine.'

He's wearing big, Fifties-style glasses today that I'm vaguely aware have become fashionable recently. A mortifying memory of our evening together flashes into my mind and I stare hard at the ground.

'All set for Christmas?' he asks.

I nod. 'I'm going to Monica's for lunch, actually. Should be nice.'

'Yeah? That's . . . great then,' and there's another painful pause as we continue to avoid each other's eyes.

'Well . . .' I say at last, 'better . . . you know, better go.'

'Right. OK.' And I think I'm going to get away with it until he suddenly says, 'Look, can we . . . can I talk to you for a moment?'

We go to a nearby bench and at first neither of us speak as Maya looks gravely from one to the other of us from her buggy.

'I've tried to ring a few times,' he says.

I glance away. 'I know. I meant to get back to you . . .'

'I'm sorry that things went a bit weird the other week.'

'Honestly, please don't worry about it. It was my fault, it wasn't . . . I don't think I'm really your type, am I?'

He laughs, and it's a nice laugh, deep and warm. 'Trust me, you're anyone's type, look at you. I was just a bit taken by surprise, when you . . .'

I feel myself flush. 'Yeah,' I say quickly, looking away.

'It's just that I've been single since I split with Stan's mum, I wasn't expecting—'

'What?' I ask. 'That I'd jump on you? Make a holy show of myself? Yeah, I get that. I felt like a big enough twat at the time, so please don't feel you have to go on about it.'

'Sorry,' he says. 'Been feeling a bit of a twat myself, if that's any consolation.'

We sit in silence for a while until at last I sigh and say, 'Are they even real lenses in those glasses of yours?'

He grins. 'You think I'm a pretentious tit, don't you?'

'No,' I say. 'Of course not.' And when he raises his eyebrows at me, I bite back a smile and say, 'Well, yeah, maybe a little bit.' We both look down at our feet and laugh.

'How's Maya been?' he asks after a few moments.

'Yeah, she's been brilliant.'

He looks down at her. 'She's lovely.'

'Nothing prepares you, does it?' I say. 'For how much you love them. I look at her sometimes and think, wow, she's just the best thing that's ever happened to me. And it's crazy how much they love you, too, isn't it? How they look at you and need you and love you no matter what. I get these mad rushes of happiness sometimes – never felt like that before, never thought that I could.' I stop, suddenly realizing that he's staring at me. 'What?' I ask.

He smiles. 'Nothing.' He takes his glasses off and, after considering them for a moment, chucks them on the ground. And then he leans over and kisses me, and it's different, this time; it's OK.

I leave him sitting on the bench, promising to call him soon. By the time I reach my road I have to keep my face turned from passers-by because I'm smiling so much and I don't even notice the police car parked outside our building until I'm nearly at the door. It's only then that I see Monica on the front step talking to a couple of officers. I sprint the last few yards, pushing the buggy in front of me.

'But what are you going to do about it?' I hear Monica asking as I reach her. 'He's not supposed to come anywhere near us! Surely there's something you can do?'

The first officer, a woman, is blandly soothing. 'As we've already said, Ms Forbes, we'll be looking into it.' Monica laughs in bitter disbelief as the officers move off towards their car. 'We'll be in touch,' they say, in a way that I guess is supposed to be reassuring, before getting in and driving away.

She turns to me then and the expression in her eyes makes my heart lurch. 'What happened?' I ask, but instead of answering she leads me wordlessly into her flat.

I gaze in at what was previously Monica's well-ordered home. Somebody has completely ransacked it. Pictures have been ripped from the walls, furniture smashed, mattresses slashed, cupboards emptied. Everything I look at as I make my way carefully through the wreckage

252

has been destroyed. Ryan and Billy stand in the midst of it all, ashen-faced.

'Jesus Christ,' I whisper, when I can speak. 'Who did this? Are you all OK? Was anyone hurt?'

She turns a kitchen chair the right way up and sinks into it. 'We weren't in. Got back from the shops and found it like this.'

I stare at her. 'And do you . . . I mean, was it him? Phil? Did anyone see anything?'

'Of course it was him,' she says angrily.

'Did he take anything?'

She shakes her head. 'Only my phone.'

And looking at her pale, pinched face I feel her terror, suddenly. It's as if I can taste it, touch it, understand it in a way I hadn't before. 'But how did he get in?' I ask. 'This place is like Fort Knox.'

Billy hangs his head. 'I forgot to lock and bolt the back door after letting the dog out.'

'He must have come over the garden wall,' says Monica, and I look around at the damage and mess as an icy chill creeps up my spine. No one speaks for a long time. 'I'll make a cup of tea,' I say at last. 'Billy, have a look on your phone for a locksmith.'

When he doesn't reply I glance up at him and realize he's barely heard me and it strikes me suddenly how very young he is, this tall, well-built seventeen-year-old, as he stands there with his arms wrapped around himself, his eyes flitting anxiously from his mother to the chaos surrounding him. 'Billy,' I say, more gently now, going

253

over and putting my hand on his arm, 'go and call a locksmith.'

Later we sit in tense silence while Monica smokes cigarette after cigarette and bites at the loose skin around her thumbnail. 'He's messing with my head,' she says suddenly, grinding her cigarette end into an overflowing ashtray. 'It's a warning, that's what this is – letting me know that he's still around, still watching me.'

'The police will find him,' I say. 'They'll get him for this.'

She shakes her head. 'They're useless. He doesn't give a shit about them anyway, that's why he's done this in broad daylight. Maybe when he's finally killed me they'll take some notice, but until then it's: "Don't worry, we'll look into it."'

Her landline phone rings and we both jump, staring at it mutely for a few seconds before she pounces on it. I can tell that it's the police. She talks in tense monosyllables then listens silently to what they have to say before slamming the phone back down in disgust.

'Reckon they've talked to him and he's got an alibi,' she tells us. 'Says he was nowhere near here and he's got a list of witnesses to prove it. They searched his place for my mobile, but there's no sign of it.' She thumps the table. 'Who else would it be? Who else is going to do this? Of course he's got an alibi. He's not that bloody stupid.'

'What else did they say?'

'Nothing. Just that they're "satisfied he wasn't involved".' She shakes her head. 'Christ, I hate him. He's loving this, knowing he's had this effect on me.'

I look from Monica's face to Billy's, and feel a familiar dread begin to build inside me.

When a couple of hours later I return to my flat, I lie down and try to take a nap while Maya sleeps. But it seems as though the second I close my eyes and start to drift, I'm hit by a memory of that last night in Fremton so vivid and disturbing that I wake with a pounding heart, my body shaking, my skin damp with sweat. I had seen myself running from the quarry, the surrounding, darkening fields pressing in against me, my lungs screaming for air. But the faster I'd tried to run, the slower I became, my legs growing heavier until I could barely move them at all. I'd looked over my shoulder and cried out in fear to see Connor following behind. I'd turned back, renewing my efforts, trying in vain to make my legs move. And then there, ahead of me, was Heather, slowly walking towards me, her eyes fixed on mine. Closer and closer she came, the smile on her face making me scream and scream in horror.

When my heart finally calms I lie awake, still far too upset to sleep, the sick, frightened feeling refusing to leave me until, desperate for distraction, I reach for my phone and turn it on to find an email waiting for me.

Clicking on the unread message icon I see Jennifer Wilcox's name and with trembling fingers I open it and read the four lines of type.

> Edie. From your email I gather that you have been in touch with Heather. I would like to talk to you if that is the case. I can come to London this weekend, if it's convenient. Perhaps we could meet some-where near Euston station. Let me know. Jennifer

Outside my window the sun disappears behind a cloud and, just like that, spring turns to winter again.

Before

No one talks much in the hot, messy lounge of Connor's flat; mostly they play computer games or watch TV and smoke weed. I don't know what I'm doing here or why I've come, not really, or even what I'm expecting to happen. I just want to make sure Edie's OK, because she hadn't seemed it, at the quarry – she hadn't seemed OK at all.

When Connor comes in and calls Edie's name she jumps up eagerly and goes to him, smiling in relief as he pulls her down on to his lap. When my eyes eventually drift up to his face I flinch as I meet his hard green stare. Slowly, his eyes still fastened on me, his hand moves upwards until it disappears beneath Edie's short skirt. I quickly look away, staring out of the window while my cheeks burn.

Outside, the sun blazes in the cloudless sky, belting

down upon the motorway, and I wonder about them, all those people in all those cars as they leave Fremton far behind, on their way to someplace else, someplace better. I glance back to the room, to this ragged band of strangers suspended up here with me in this hot, stuffy flat, and I try to make sense of how I came to be here, how it came to be that I should end up here too.

'Heather,' Connor says, breaking me from my thoughts. 'Get me a beer from the fridge.'

I don't reply.

He raises his voice, just a fraction. 'Are you fucking deaf?'

I glance at Edie but she ignores me and a long, uncomfortable moment passes before I reluctantly get to my feet. Self-consciously I pick my way through the bodies littering the floor, gingerly stepping over legs and ashtrays and empty cans until I reach the door. In the kitchen where hot sunlight pours in through smeared glass and the floor feels tacky beneath my feet, I bend down to a tiny fridge. A sour, stale smell hits my nostrils as I open it and quickly pull a can free. And when I straighten up again, Connor is standing behind me.

'You all right there, Heather?'

Wordlessly I hand him the beer and he takes it from me, popping open its ring pull and taking a long swig, not moving from his position, nor dropping his eyes from mine. Suddenly he takes a step towards me and I hurriedly back away until I feel the knock of the sink's hard edge against my spine. He sniggers, and placing his beer can on the table comes closer still and, leaning forward, his hands grip the sink so I'm trapped between his arms. His face is inches from mine and I can smell the beer and cigarettes on his breath as he murmurs, 'What you doing here, Heather?'

My mouth is very dry. 'Come to see Edie,' I whisper.

'Yeah?'

I nod.

'You fancy a bit of that, do you?' He smiles. 'That it? That why you were chatting shit about me? Want her for yourself?'

'No,' I say. 'Let me go. I want to go home.'

'I don't like people telling lies about me,' he goes on, his face moving a fraction closer. 'You listening?'

I feel my scalp creep and still he doesn't move or drop his gaze. I see something so dark and disturbing, so devoid of warmth in his eyes that fresh fear pulses through me. It's like looking at the green, oily surface of the quarry, its secret deathtraps looming suddenly into view. And as we stare at each other my expression must alter, showing him what I have understood, that I've seen through to his lonely, rotten core, because in that instant the hatred in his eyes deepens, sharpening its claws and baring its teeth. My lungs empty of air.

'Connor?'

I cry out with relief to see Edie appear in the doorway behind him. She looks from one to the other of us and as Connor straightens up I quickly move away from

259

him. 'Edie, come home with me,' I say desperately before Connor can speak.

She shakes her head but doesn't answer. I see her hesitation and for a moment a faint hope climbs inside me. 'Please, Edie,' I beg, 'I'm scared he's going to hurt you. I'm so worried for you, you've changed so much, you look so awful . . .'

'You better shut your mouth,' Connor warns.

'You could find someone else,' I blurt, ignoring him. 'Someone nicer—'

'That right, is it?' he interrupts. 'Not good enough for stuck-up little cunts like you? That it?'

Edie still hasn't spoken and I have to swallow hard to clear the lump in my throat when I see the desperation in her eyes. I turn back to Connor's hateful face, and say, quietly, 'Yes.'

He makes a lunge and I just have time to hear Edie shout, 'Get out of here, Heather, get out,' and see her step between us before I make it out of the kitchen and out of the flat, slamming the door behind me. I hurtle down six flights of stairs until I reach the bottom and I don't stop running until I've left the estate behind.

I stay away from the flat after that, brooding on the plan I had begun to form and spending my time hanging around at the end of Edie's street, hoping to catch a glimpse of her and reassure myself that she's OK. But it's not until a few weeks later, at the beginning of August, that I see her again. I'm sitting in the town square, eating a Greggs sausage roll and wondering if it's too early to go and hang around outside her house, when I spot her walking past on the furthest side. I get to my feet and watch as she approaches the payphone outside the police station. As she digs out her purse I make a large loop round and duck behind the phones' shelter, and there I wait, straining my ears to listen.

'Connor?' she says, her voice muffled. 'It's me.'

I hold my breath as she falls silent, listening to him speak. Then, 'No, Connor, please baby. No . . . no, I don't want to . . . I don't want to.' She begins to cry and I ball my hands into fists. 'That's not true,' she says. 'Listen to me . . . I . . . but I do! I do love you. I love you so much! You're all I have, Connor, why don't you believe me? I'd do anything for you.' She falls silent again, and then, eventually, reluctantly, says, 'OK. Yes . . . OK, I will. I promise.' She hangs up the phone, and I watch as she slowly makes her way back across the square.

I'm on study leave from school, and I sit with my father in the kitchen as he tips baked beans on to some burnt toast and passes me my plate before retrieving a hardback book from his jacket pocket and opening it to read. Within seconds he's absorbed and I watch him silently for a while. Since Mum left, a kind of peace has settled between the two of us. I leave him to his work and he in turn takes no notice of what I do, accepting without question that it's my schoolwork I'm preoccupied with while I'm alone up in my room. And although this is a relief after living with Mum's constant, critical scrutiny, it also leaves me with an unsettling sense of freefall, as though I'm about to step off a very high cliff and there'll be no one to catch me when I land.

Suddenly Dad looks up from his book, catching me staring, and I watch as he mentally fumbles around for something to say. After a long pause he murmurs, 'It might be a good idea to go over your UCAS forms this evening, Heather. You shouldn't leave it too late.'

I manage to nod and, satisfied, he returns to his book. As my beans go cold I let myself imagine saying, 'Actually, Dad, there's no point in applying for uni, because I haven't a hope of getting the grades I need anyway.' So far I'd managed to fob my teachers off with tales of illness and 'trouble at home'. But there was a sense of things unravelling, of the lies I'd told spinning out of my control. My parents and I have talked about my plans to study medicine since I was eleven. They've been putting money into my uni fund for years. And I had always studied as hard as I possibly could, desperate not to disappoint them, even paying my birthday and Christmas money into the post office account myself. Still I allow the fantasy to run in my head, how easily I could blow the world wide open with a single stroke; tell Dad about the awful grades I've been getting, how I've ruined everything, force him to see me – really, actually see me – for once. But of course I don't. Instead

I go back to thinking about Edie and the last time I saw her.

After the phone call in the square, there'd been no sign of her for a week. Anxiety had nagged at me every day. What had Connor wanted Edie to do? A dull foreboding had grown inside me and I'd stepped up my surveillance of her house, spending longer and longer at the end of her street, waiting for her. And then a few days ago, when the afternoon had begun to stretch into evening and I was about to give up and go home, I'd seen her approach and watched as she'd let herself in.

Quickly I'd followed her, slipping through her side gate into the tiny scrappy garden. Hearing raised voices I'd crept up to the kitchen window and peered in. Edie's mum had her back to me but her voice was loud and clear. 'You're a bloody liar,' I heard her say. 'I phoned the school and they said you haven't been in today, or to any of your classes this week!'

Edie was staring at her feet and she'd looked so thin and tired that my heart had hurt. Her mum must have seen it too, for her voice had softened. 'Edie, I'm worried about you. There's something wrong, I know there is. Please talk to me.'

To my surprise, Edie sank into a chair and put her head in her hands. Her mother and I both watched as her shoulders began to heave. 'Oh, Mum,' she'd said when she could finally speak. 'I just . . . it's all just so . . .'

Silently I'd urged her, *Tell her, Edie, please, tell her.*

'What's the matter, Edie?' her mum had said, going to her and putting a hand on her shoulder. 'Come on, love, it can't be that bad, can it?'

Edie had looked up, an expression in her eyes as though she were pushing a lorry up a hill. I'd held my breath as she'd opened her mouth to speak.

'Is it a lad? Is that it?' her mum had gone on. 'It is, isn't it?'

And silently Edie nodded.

'I knew it,' her mother said triumphantly. 'I bloody knew it! *That's* why you haven't been going to school! Oh God, Edie, don't be a bloody fool, don't let a lad screw your life up the way I did! You want to be like me? Pregnant at seventeen? Your life over? Don't make the same stupid mistakes I made!'

And just like that, the shutters in Edie's eyes had come slamming down. 'That's all I am to you, isn't it?' she'd said. 'A stupid bloody mistake! Well fine, maybe I'll do what Dad did and leave too.'

She'd stormed from the room, her mum following awkwardly on her crutches saying desperately, 'Edie, I didn't mean it like that, you know I didn't!' But Edie had run from the house, leaving her mum and me to stare after her in the silence.

It's this I'm thinking about when Dad stands up to clear our plates away. I haven't touched my own lunch, but he makes no comment as he scrapes the cold mess into the bin. As I'm about to mutter something about homework and leave, the doorbell rings. We look at each other uncertainly for a moment or two before I go to answer it. When I open the door, there, standing on the front step, is Edie.

After

I get to the café before Jennifer, a greasy spoon on the Euston Road. I've missed the morning rush of commuters and, apart from a couple of builders with their tabloids and fry-ups, I have the place to myself. While I find a seat, awkwardly manoeuvring Maya's buggy and cursing myself for bringing it, there's a flurry of activity as the Italian owner bears down on us, scooping Maya up and cooing, '*Ciao, bambolina!*' while he whisks her away to the counter and, before I can stop him, presents her with a cupcake thick with chocolate icing. Maya's face lights up, and she sinks her two tiny new teeth into it with such a look of bliss that the café owner and I both laugh. And when I next look up, Jennifer is standing in front of me.

I'm unprepared for the effect it has on me, seeing her again. I'd met her only a handful of times back then, but instantly I'm sixteen again and standing in her kitchen. Despite the eighteen years that have passed she still has that same cool demeanour, the same air of disapproval.

'Edie,' she says, and awkwardly I half stand.

'Hi, Jennifer,' I say, and the fear that had begun to swill around in my gut since I'd agreed to come today gathers strength: How much does she know about what happened? How much had Heather told her? Nothing, surely? *Surely* nothing? 'Please, sit down,' I say nervously, almost sending a bowl of sugar flying. 'Can I get you a coffee?'

She nods and takes a seat opposite me while I order from the girl behind the till. 'You have a baby,' she says, when I've sat back down.

'Yes, this is Maya,' I tell her, 'she's eight months old now and—'

But Jennifer interrupts me. 'You said you've been in touch with Heather?'

'I . . . yes.'

'You've seen her?'

I nod. 'She stayed with me for a while. I . . . I was struggling a bit with Maya and she . . . looked after us.'

Jennifer's eyebrows shoot up. 'Really?'

I hesitate. 'When did . . . I mean, can I ask, when did you last see her?'

She doesn't answer at first, and then, not quite meeting my eyes, says, 'About a year ago. It was the first time in seventeen years.'

I look at her in surprise and she says defensively, 'I suppose you know about all the trouble we had before she left Fremton?'

'Trouble?' I say, my stomach churning. 'I – no, what do you mean?'

A silence. 'Well, it was . . . you see . . .' She falters, and for the briefest moment I glimpse a flash of an old, long-buried pain before the shutters fall once more and she says tightly, 'I'd prefer not to discuss all that, if you don't mind.'

We drink our coffee. 'When did she leave Fremton?' I ask.

Jennifer purses her lips. 'When she was seventeen.'

A year after I did.

She sighs. 'And then, just over a year ago, there was a phone call. From a hospital.'

I stare at her. 'A *hospital*?'

'A psychiatric hospital. Somewhere in London. I believe she'd been living in hostels for a time before she was admitted.'

I shake my head. 'I don't under—'

'Heather had always been a rather . . . highly strung child. I suppose her difficulties became more pronounced after her sister died, and later, when she . . . well, after all that dreadful business before she left.'

'What . . . business?' I force myself to ask again, but Jennifer ignores me.

'The doctor who rang told me she'd had a nervous breakdown,' she goes on, quietly. 'They wanted us – her father and me – to go and see her.' She sniffs primly. 'Brian and I had reconciled by that point, you see. The doctor thought it would be useful for the three of us to undertake . . . family therapy, I suppose you'd call it.'

'And did you?'

Her gaze drops to her cup and for a second the old Jennifer vanishes and someone far more vulnerable takes her place. I realize that she must be almost seventy now and for a second my nervousness is replaced by pity.

'I did, yes. Her father felt it would be too much for him, so I went alone.'

I nod. 'And . . . how was it?' I ask.

She sighs. 'Awful, actually. Heather had made it abundantly clear what she thought of her father and me when she'd left home all those years ago. She attacked me, in fact. Smashed up her father's clocks. She was quite out of control.'

I am too shocked to do anything but gape at her.

'And at the hospital, she left me in no doubt that she still felt the same. The way she spoke to me was completely unforgivable.' Her face is flushed a deep red, and I see that her hands are trembling. She glances at me angrily. 'Her father and I had only been acting in her best interest back then, after all.'

As I watch her pull herself together I try to make sense of what she's told me. Quietly I say, 'She thought you blamed her, for what happened to her sister. She thought you felt it was her fault.'

She drains her cup of coffee and replacing it on the

table considers it for a long time, then says softly but very clearly and with infinite sadness, 'It *was* her fault. I did blame her.'

'But it was an accident,' I say, 'a terrible, tragic accident.'

'Is that what she told you?'

I shake my head in confusion. 'She said Lydia fell into the lake.'

Jennifer doesn't answer for a moment. And then, choosing her words carefully, says, 'I think Heather probably convinced herself that what happened was an accident. But I don't believe it was.'

'But why on earth—'

'Heather was very jealous of Lydia. Horribly so. And she'd always had a temper. She would fly off the handle about every little thing. She would lash out at Lydia sometimes and barely know she was doing it. One time I watched her from my kitchen window push her off the garden swing, then she lied about it.' She stops and her eyes are bright with emotion. 'I had to watch her every single minute. The night before Lydia drowned there had been a scene. A huge tantrum, Heather saying that I didn't love her – that I loved Lydia more. She became completely hysterical, it took hours to calm her. And then, the next morning . . .'

Her words hang in the silence. My thoughts chase round and around. 'Did you ever tell Heather that? That you thought she'd killed her sister deliberately?'

There's a long pause, before she says very quietly, 'I

271

tried for many years to convince myself that it had been an accident. I never spoke about it to anyone. But when I saw her at the hospital, when she was shouting and raving at me, so out of control, I saw it: I *knew* it. I knew what she was, what she was capable of. And suddenly I couldn't keep quiet about it any more. So I told her. I told her I knew that it had been her, that it had been her fault Lydia had died.' She looks at me with defiance, as though daring me to protest.

'What did she say?' I ask.

'She went crazy. She screamed and shouted, clawing at her skin and drawing blood with her nails. She had to be sedated and I was asked to leave.'

I'm silent as I digest all this. At last I say, 'Jennifer, why did you want to meet me today?'

'I wanted to tell you to be careful.'

My eyes shoot to her face. 'What do you mean?'

'I've seen for myself too often how unpredictable she can be when she loses her temper. But in the hospital, it was worse. She'd changed. She was so out of control, so angry. I was frightened of her. Very frightened. Just be careful, that's all.'

When I return to my flat an hour or so later and see that my door is ajar I know with cold certainty that Heather has been there. The door's easy enough to push open if it's not Chubb-locked so I do it instinctively whenever I leave the house. I'd done it this morning as usual – I *know* I had. Fear grips me. Is she in there? I

272

stand outside and listen. Nothing. Maya squirms impatiently in my arms and I push the door open and step inside.

The flat's empty, but I can smell her, I'm certain of it: I can smell Heather. I walk from room to room, my scalp prickling, but nothing has changed. And then, suddenly, standing in my hallway, I look up, and my heart freezes. The sliding hatch to the loft, where I'd put all Heather's belongings, has moved. Just a fraction. I stare at it uncertainly. Had I closed it properly, before? I was sure I had. I stand very still, listening. Nothing. You're being ridiculous, I tell myself. You can't get up there without a chair or a ladder, and if someone was up there, the ladder would be down here.

I sit with Maya and try to tell myself that I've imagined it; that I had left the door unlocked myself, had not completely closed the hatch. I hold my breath and listen but there's only silence. You're going mad, I tell myself, you're paranoid, that's all. On sudden impulse I drag the stepladder from the cupboard, and in one quick movement pull the loft door back into place. I stand there staring at it for a long time, unease twisting inside me.

I barely sleep that night. Instead I lie awake, alert to every tiny sound and when I eventually drift off I dream so vividly of Fremton, of Heather and of Connor that I wake again, my heart racing. As soon as the first light trickles in beneath my curtains I get up, dress quietly so as not to disturb Maya, and sit in the half-light of

273

the kitchen drinking coffee, my head banging, staring out of my window until the sun rises. When Maya wakes I dress and feed her, carefully lock the door behind us, then take her with me to the ground floor. I knock on Monica's door, praying that she'll already be up, and relief floods me when I hear her begin to draw back the bolts.

She looks shattered when she opens the door. 'How are you?' I ask as she leads me to the kitchen.

'Knackered.' She yawns and puts the kettle on. 'I'm not sleeping at the moment. I just lie awake, listening to every little sound, imagining that it's Phil.'

I glance around the room. Even though the flat's been tidied there's still evidence of the break-in: broken furniture, pictures that had been smashed now missing from the walls, a door off its hinges. Monica makes the tea and as she passes me my cup she sits down and looks at me properly for the first time. 'You don't look too clever yourself. You all right?'

I stroke Maya's hair. 'I'm fine,' I lie, swallowing hard. 'Just a difficult night with this one, she couldn't sleep either.' I make myself smile. 'Should have brought her down here, could have kept each other company.' And at that moment, to my surprise Monica begins to cry, and for a second or two I freeze in indecision, clueless as to what I should do. She doesn't bother to wipe the tears from her face but sinks her head into her hands in a gesture of such defeat that I get up and walk around the table to her, and put an awkward hand on her shoulder.

274

I want to tell her that I understand what it's like to not be able to sleep at night, to be frightened in your own home. I want to confide in her about Heather, sympathize with her, give her comfort and have her comfort me. But of course I don't. She's frightened of a violent man who has physically harmed her. Heather has never attacked me, never tried to hurt me in any way. And yet I do fear her; I am more frightened of her than I have ever been of anything or anyone in my life. At last I whisper, 'Monica? Don't cry, please don't cry.'

She doesn't answer at first, but instead scrabbles around for a tissue and blows her nose. 'I'm so sick of it,' she says at last. 'He's still doing this to me, you know? Trying to get into my head. Still trying to control me. When's he going to leave me alone?'

'I don't know,' I say miserably. 'I guess if he does something else the police will have to—'

She cuts me off impatiently. 'The police? What can they do? They don't give a flying fuck.' She sits up and wipes her eyes, staring at me angrily. 'When he was pissed out of his mind he'd come home and pick a fight then force me to do whatever he wanted. He made me feel like nothing, like I was nothing. Now he's doing it again. Making me feel like this in my own home, making me feel like I'm nothing again.'

I put my arms around her and feel my own tears begin to fall as I say, 'Oh Monica, you're not nothing. You're not nothing, Monica, you're not.' And as I hug her tightly I try to quell the horrible, sickening thought

275

that it was Heather and not Phil who'd been responsible for wreaking such havoc in Monica's home – that all she was going through now was down to me.

PART FOUR

Before

I'm so surprised to see Edie on my doorstep that at first I can only stare at her. 'Do you want to come in?' I say at last.

She shakes her head, and not quite meeting my eyes, mumbles, 'I want you to start coming to the flat.'

I gape at her in astonishment. 'Why?' I ask. She shrugs but doesn't answer. I think of the phone conversation I'd overheard in the square. 'Did Connor tell you to ask me?'

She glances at me, then quickly away again. 'No, course not.'

I think about this. 'I don't want to,' I tell her. 'I don't like Connor. He scares me.'

She doesn't speak for a moment or two, and then says simply, 'Please, Heather.'

'But why?' I ask.

Her eyes fill with tears. 'I just need you to come to the flat,' she says.

'He's made you come, hasn't he?'

'No,' she says, then adds, 'he'll be nice to you, I promise. He's not going to do anything.'

I hear my father moving about in the kitchen down the hall and I know that I don't have a choice, not really. Edie needs my help, she needs her best friend to help her, and no matter how much I hate Connor, that's what I'll have to do. 'OK,' I say.

She smiles in relief, making my heart lift, despite everything. 'When will you come? Will you come tomorrow?' she asks.

'Yes,' I say, 'all right.'

'Do you promise?'

She looks so like a little girl, her eyes so pleading, that for a second she reminds me of Lydia. 'I promise,' I say.

She nods and turns away, hurrying off down the front path, the gate swinging shut behind her.

And so I keep my promise. I go back to the flat the next day, and the day after that, and I keep on going round there until pretty soon it's as if I've always been a part of it here – have always known this crowded, stuffy room with its worn, dirty carpets and its sour smells and thudding music, have always been familiar with the faces that find their way here day after day, like me.

For the most part Connor leaves me alone, as if it's

enough at least for now that I have done what he wanted by coming back, though for what reason, I still don't know. Sometimes I'll catch him looking at me, as though smirking at his own private joke. 'Heifer,' he'll say, because that's what he calls me now, 'pass me that lighter' or 'move your fat arse', but mainly he ignores me. And so, too, does Edie, as though the moment on my doorstep when she'd cried and pleaded had never happened, her eyes skimming over me, darting away whenever I try to meet them. I don't mind: at least if I'm here I can watch over her, make sure she comes to no harm. I feel as if we are all waiting for something, although I have no idea what.

Sometimes I come for an hour, sometimes the whole afternoon. Just enough time to reassure myself that she's OK. Every morning I pack up my school bag and say goodbye to Dad, then I go and sit in the rec and wait until enough time has passed and I think someone will be up and about in the flat, and then I make my way over there, knocking on the battered blue door, steeling myself for whatever mood Connor might be in, wondering if today's the day he'll let me know exactly why I'm here.

This morning when I arrive at the estate Connor and several of his friends are spilling from the lift, Edie hanging on to Connor's arm, her face lit with excitement. They're all very drunk and I'm struck by the strangeness of seeing them out in the world like this, the sunlight revealing the pasty hollows of their faces, their dirty clothes and lank hair.

'Heifer!' Connor says when he sees me, letting go of Edie and putting an arm around me. 'C'mon, we're going on a little trip.'

I shrink from his touch and his arm tightens, pushing me forward so I stumble. 'Come on, fuck's sake,' he says irritably, already moving away, and I trail after them. We drive to the quarry in three cars, me in the back of Connor's, squashed between the one who's called Tully, the Welsh one they call Boyo. Music blasts so loudly from the speakers it hurts my ears and the countryside rushes past in a yellowy green blur. I stare down at Boyo's hands resting on his knee, his fingers short and dirty, the nails bitten to the quick, LOVE and HATE inked on to his knuckles.

When we reach the quarry we join a group already sprawled in the shade of some trees, far away from the people sunbathing and swimming on the other side. I find a spot at the edge of the group, as near to Edie as I dare, though she pretends she hasn't seen me. Connor's loud and expansive today, swigging from a bottle of whisky, cocky and aggressive as he jokes with his friends. And it's as though the others, feeding off his mood, become louder and wilder too, the atmosphere in the close, warm air prickly and unpredictable.

Suddenly Connor looks over at Edie. 'Go and get my fags,' he says, slinging his car keys at her so hard that she ducks out of the way just in time and they land in the scrubby grass behind her. I reach for them and for the first time in ages our eyes meet. 'Edie . . .' I say.

282

Her eyes are hostile as she holds out her hand. 'What?'

'I . . . are you OK?' I want to tell her that I know about the fight with her mum, that I know how unhappy she is, but of course I can't.

'Give me the keys,' she says flatly.

'I—' But she snatches them from my hand and turns away.

The morning passes slowly. I watch without really paying attention as a skinny, weasel-faced boy named Niall shows Connor the contents of a holdall. I catch a glimpse of a jumble of electrical equipment: a laptop, a DVD player, a couple of cameras and mobile phones. Connor pulls out one of the cameras and laughs. 'Nice one,' he says, before turning to point it at Edie. 'No don't, I look awful!' she giggles, waving her hand in front of her face. He takes a picture then tosses the camera down carelessly in the grass, turning away again. And there it stays, until after they are all far too drunk to remember it, and I slip it into the pocket of my jeans and take it home with me.

Months later, when I take the film to be developed, besides the endless shots of an elderly Chinese couple's barge holiday, there she is, Edie, laughing at the camera, her hand a pink blur in the foreground, and there I am sitting just behind and staring away in the direction of the quarry. I will study it endlessly, in the months and years that follow; that smile of hers, the expression in those large brown eyes, trying to see if I can find any clue, any warning of what was to come.

After

James and I sit on a bench by the sandpit, watching Stan build a castle for Maya. For the first time in days I feel myself begin to relax. I huddle deeper inside my coat and blow warmth on my hands as James joins the kids and enthusiastically tries to help, adding pebbles and twigs to Stan's creation, suggesting turrets and moats. At last Stan turns and rolls his eyes at him so witheringly that I laugh out loud, a little giddy with the relief of being out of the flat.

Since I'd returned home last week and found my door unlocked, every moment that I spend there sees me jumping at the slightest noise, the sound of footsteps on the stairs sending me into a blind panic, Jennifer's warning ringing in my ears. But today, right now, I feel OK. There's something about James that makes my fear and paranoia feel smaller, somehow, less insurmountable.

Since we'd kissed in the park we had met for drinks and dinner a few times and I'd begun to look forward to our time together, to miss him when he wasn't around.

I suddenly realize that he's speaking to me. 'Sorry, I was miles away, what did you say?' I ask.

He grins. 'I was just thinking about your drawing, wondering why you stopped doing it.'

I shrug. The truth was it reminded me too much of the person I used to be, before Fremton, before Connor, when I was still a kid, and saw the world so differently. The few attempts I'd made as an adult, producing the sketches James had seen in my flat, had only made me feel sad, reminding me of what I'd lost.

'You're wasted as a waitress, I reckon,' James says. 'Your stuff was really good.'

'Maybe you're right,' I say and turn back to watching the children, hoping that the subject will be dropped.

We leave an hour or so later and when James says goodbye he adds, 'How about lunch tomorrow?'

I smile. 'That'd be nice, maybe Monica will have Maya for a couple of hours.'

He nods. 'Great.' And I feel again the pull of attraction as he holds me in his gaze.

The kitchen fridge ticks loudly in the silence as I pour myself another glass of beer. For the tenth time since I put her down for the night I go to check Maya as she sleeps in her cot then check my front door to reassure myself it's securely locked. I pace around the small space of my kitchen, restlessly going from the window to the table and back before fetching another can of beer from the fridge. I have started to drink again recently – something I hadn't done since leaving Fremton. But lately, the evenings here alone with Maya have felt too long to endure completely sober. Desperate to distract myself from thoughts of Heather, I go to my bookshelf and search for my old sketchpad and pencils.

I stare down at the blank sheet in front of me. It's been so long since I attempted to draw anything that I feel too nervous to try, and for a long time I look at the empty white paper, unsure of how to begin. At last I take a deep breath and, my hand feeling heavy and clumsy, pick up a pencil.

I start by drawing Maya, the easiest subject to begin with. My hands move slowly at first but soon gather speed as I become engrossed in recreating the exact expression of her eyes, the way her black curls fall against her cheeks. Soon I'm so absorbed that when Maya murmurs in her sleep across the hall I look up in surprise, and realize that for the past hour or so I had entirely forgotten myself. Next I draw Monica sitting, in my mind's eye, at her kitchen table, Benson & Hedges in hand, the tattoos that twist and wind their way along her arms gleaming behind the cloud of smoke curling from her cigarette, her eyes, bright and candid, gazing coolly back at me. Another hour passes as I work through sheet after sheet, drawing now an enchanted forest for Maya, its trees and hollows alive with animals and birds.

And when I finally put down my pencil I'm filled with a sense of satisfaction I'd almost forgotten I was capable of.

It's nearly midnight and I'm about to go to bed when my mobile rings, shrill and shocking in the silence. Perhaps it's Monica, or Uncle Geoff, I tell myself nervously as I look over to where it lies on my kitchen table. Some sort of emergency that's made them call so late. I pick it up, not recognizing the number that flashes on the screen. 'Hello?' There's no one there. 'Hello? Hello? Who is this?' Nothing. But I can just about make out the sound of someone breathing. 'Hello?' I sense the other person listening to my voice and fear drips icily through me. 'Go away!' I shout. 'Leave me alone!' Impulsively I fling the phone away from me, watching it clatter to the floor. Almost immediately it begins to ring again. I stand and watch it buzz and vibrate upon the lino before I run to it and turn it off.

The narrow pub table is all that separates us, our empty lunch plates and glasses littering its surface, the tips of our fingers almost but not quite touching. I had been laughing at something James had said a moment before, but now a lull falls upon our conversation, the noises of the busy pub rumbling on around us. The late afternoon sun shines through the window in two gold bars across his face, his eyes glowing brown and amber in its light. There's a small scar at the bottom of his chin and I imagine myself reaching over and touching it,

288

feeling the soft bumps and grooves with my finger. The air between us crackles, waits. 'Shall we go?' he says, and wordlessly I nod. In the street as we walk his hand casually brushes then catches mine and the electric charge that shoots through me makes my skin tingle.

When we reach his house I hesitate. 'Well . . .' I say. 'I guess I better . . .'

He smiles, still holding my hand, and pulls me gently towards him. 'Come in,' he says.

And here we are, in his kitchen. Suddenly unsure, I walk to one of his paintings and pretend to look at it for a while. I don't hear him follow me until he's there, turning me around, lifting my chin and kissing me, pushing me against the wall, wrapping his arms around me and pulling me until I'm hard up against him and his lips are on my neck, my mouth, and I don't know what I had expected, but not this urgency, this passion, or that my body would respond with such strength. My lips brush his jaw, I breathe in the scent of his neck, and his hands are up beneath my top now, unhooking my bra, and I'm surprised at how much I want him, as if my body has taken over and I can think of nothing other than having his naked skin against mine, and I haven't felt this way, this desire for someone since . . . since him, since Connor . . . And everything stops.

'What?' he says, pulling away to look at me, a little breathless.

Connor's face, Connor's eyes, Connor's lips. It takes

everything I have to push him from my mind. 'What?' James asks again, his brow furrowed in concern. 'What's wrong?'

I shake my head. 'Nothing,' I say firmly. 'Nothing.' And he smiles again and pulls me towards the stairs.

In his bedroom we kiss as he begins to undress me and together we sink on to his bed. I reach out to unbuckle his belt but again I freeze. Suddenly Connor is everywhere: his cold, watchful presence lingering in every corner, his scent on James's sheets, his taste on James's lips. Fear paralyses me. It had been different with Heri and all those others before him, where sex had been about nothing more than the physical, but here, now, with James, something has changed. I close my eyes tightly against the memories but there's no escape. There I am again as darkness falls upon the quarry, where everything around me is panic and confusion, the horror of it, the belief that I would not, could not survive what was about to happen. I open my eyes and stare into James's worried face and realize that I'm shaking.

'Hey,' he says, 'hey, hey, Edie, it's OK, it's all right.' He puts his arms around me and holds me closely as I tremble against him, cold with fear.

The rain has begun to fall heavily by the time I walk home from James's, and I wrap my coat tightly around myself, pulling my hood up against the downpour. Then, as I near the park, something catches my eye and I stop.

The road is badly lit here but I can still make out a figure hurrying away from me, towards the park's gate. A sudden fear claws at me. It's Heather – the trudging gait, the shoulder-length hair, the broad build, it's definitely her, I'm certain of it. I call her name but my hoarse, fearful voice is whipped away by the wind. I hurry after her, calling her again, but she doesn't stop. I break into a run and just before the park's gates I reach her. Adrenalin surges through me as I put a hand on her shoulder and she stops and turns. And there we stand, looking into each other's faces, the rain pouring down on us. The sight of her like a punch to the throat. I can hardly believe that it's her, that here she is, in front of me at last.

Her expression is unreadable as she stares back at me. 'Heather,' I say, my voice ragged, breathless. 'Heather, I—' but at that moment she turns again and runs off into the park, its darkness swallowing her instantly. I stare after her, knowing I should follow, entirely unable to move. I think of Monica's flat, smashed to bits. I hear again Jennifer's voice: '*Be careful, Edie.*' The thoughts chase around and around as I remain there, frozen in indecision, before fear gets the better of me and I turn back towards home, to where Maya is.

That night as soon as I get into bed, the phone calls start again. Each time I pick up and say Heather's name the line goes dead until at last I turn it off, throwing it across the room as though it were a grenade. I watch it as it skids across the kitchen floor before coming to a rest beneath a chair. And then I go back to bed and pull the duvet tight around me, knowing I won't sleep tonight.

Before

We are about to leave the quarry and go home when the fight breaks out. The heat that's been steadily building all afternoon has reached boiling point and we're sluggish and silent as we sit around in the dust. Even Connor's good mood has gradually soured beneath the sky's hard blue glare. Thick yellow smoke hangs motionless in the air around us and my burning eyes drift to where Liam sits nearby, making some sort of pipe with a plastic bottle, foil and a Biro, his brow furrowed in concentration, his hands deft.

At that moment he looks up, glancing around himself and patting his pockets. 'Anyone got a light?' he asks. And that's how it begins.

Connor, a few metres away, holds up his lighter and as Liam raises his arm to catch it, Connor throws it hard at his face. A nasty little smile plays around his lips and there's a scattering of laughter.

Liam blinks, rubbing his forehead, 'Come on, man,' he says mildly.

But next Connor picks up an empty cigarette packet and aims that at his face too, and this time the laughter's louder. 'Connor, fuck's sake,' says Liam. But his protest is met by more missiles and soon Connor is throwing anything he can get his hands on: an empty beer can, a bunch of keys, one of Edie's kicked-off trainers. Liam bats them all away. 'Fuck off,' he says quietly.

'Awww, what's the matter?' mocks Connor. 'You gonna cry?' He turns to the others, 'Look at the face on him!' And then he throws Edie's other shoe.

That's when Liam says it, his eyes lit with temper. 'I said fuck off, Connor!' He rubs his face where the keys have made a nick in his skin. 'Go on! Why don't you go down Happy Pete's and fuck your mum.'

The silence that greets this is absolute. I look from face to face in confusion, alarmed by the sudden tension in the air, but everyone's staring hard at the ground. Liam's so livid I can tell he blurts out what he says next without thinking. 'Hear she only costs a fiver these days. Give her one from me while you're at it.'

I look at Edie, but she's staring down at her hands, her face rigid. Nobody moves. Connor gets up and his eyes are blank; he doesn't even look angry. But he crosses over to Liam in two seconds flat and I see the panic on Liam's face as he realizes what's about to happen. He scrambles backwards, trying to get up, but it's too late: Connor picks him up by the scruff of his T-shirt and punches him, one quick, hard fist square in the middle of his face, and Liam's nose seems to explode with blood.

And he keeps on punching him. Over and over. Nobody moves, nobody stops him. It's like something out of a dream, entirely surreal on this beautiful summer's day, all of us frozen, watching. Liam doesn't make a sound at first; the only noise is the dull thump of fist hitting flesh. I watch, horrified, unable to move or think or do anything but stare at the blood that's pouring from Liam's mouth. At last Connor drops him and I think, that's it, it's all over, but it's not, because now Connor begins to kick him: in the face, in the ribs, in the stomach, while Liam makes awful animal howls of pain. Edie and I jump to our feet, screaming for Connor to stop.

At last he does. He looks down calmly, blankly, at Liam lying broken and bloody on the floor and then he turns away, saying 'Get him out of here,' to no one in particular. Three of them drag Liam into one of the cars, his broken, battered body, his swollen, bloody face.

After

The street beneath my window is empty and still, in silent wait for the day to begin. A fox streaks across the pavement, something small and unidentifiable clamped between its teeth. I stand by the window looking out at the pale blue dawn and wait for my daughter to stir. I'd woken earlier as though bursting up through the surface of dark cold water, wide awake and alert in an instant, a nameless dread making my heart race, and when I'd found my phone and turned it on, there had been twenty-two missed calls and three voicemail messages, each of them silent.

Maya gives a cry from her cot and I go to her, scooping her up in my arms and holding her to me tightly. 'It's OK, baby,' I murmur. 'It's all going to be OK.' After she's eaten I get dressed and quickly gather her things. It's time to find Heather, it's time to make this stop.

'Could you look after Maya for a while?' I ask, when Monica answers my knock.

'Sure,' she says, looking at me with concern. 'Are you OK?'

'I'm fine.' I try to keep my voice level. 'It's just that something's come up. I hate to ask, but it's important.'

She takes Maya from me and nods, and I'm grateful when she doesn't ask any more questions.

As I walk up to the park I scan the faces of the few people that I pass. Is she nearby? Is she watching me right this moment? I find a bench and pull out my phone. My heart pounds. A fine, icy rain begins to fall as I find Heather's number and press the Call button. When I hear the ringtone I grip my mobile tightly, half willing her to answer, half terrified that she might. The automated voicemail kicks in and I take a deep breath and speak. 'Heather,' I say. 'It's me. I know that you've been calling me. Come and meet me. I know you're nearby. We need to talk about what happened in Fremton.' I think for a second and then add in desperation, 'Please, Heather. For God's sake, you've got to stop this. You've got to leave me alone. I'll be in the café at the top of the park. I'll wait for you.' At last I hang up and putting my head in my hands I sit there for several minutes, the rain soaking me. I know she's close. I can feel it.

The café's quiet when I arrive so early on a Saturday morning: a few exhausted-looking parents with newborn babies, a jogger or two. I take a seat where I have a good view of the door and, placing my phone on the table in front of me, I wait. Half an hour slides slowly past. The café begins to fill up. Where is she? Has she listened to my message? Is she on her way? A single, razor-sharp image from that awful, long-ago night returns to me, and I take deep breaths, trying to quell the dizzying panic I feel.

'Are you OK?' The waitress is looking at me with concern.

I make myself nod. 'I'm fine. I'm fine.' With a sympathetic smile, she moves away and I look at the clock above the till. An hour and twenty minutes since I first called Heather's phone. The thought of returning to my flat, of continuing to live with her shadowy, threatening presence, never knowing when she's going to reappear, leaves me in despair. I think about how Monica's flat had been broken into, ransacked, destroyed. What does she want? What does she want from me now?

Another half an hour passes before I accept she's not coming. I'd been stupid to think that she would. Suddenly I long to see Maya's face. A fresh anxiety grips me. I had left her with Monica to keep her safe while I confront Heather alone. But what if she's gone there? What if it's Maya she wants to harm? Snatching up my phone I leave the café at a run, heading back into the park, the quickest route to my street. As I pass the bench I'd been sitting on I make frantic, desperate plans: once I've got Maya from Monica's I'll pack a bag. I'll phone Uncle Geoff and ask if we can stay there for a week or two – just until I've made Heather meet me, just until I've made her stop. *And what if you don't make her stop?* The thought hisses through my garbled thoughts as I quicken my pace. *What if she keeps on and on? What if she attacks you? Harms Maya?* Then I'll have to make her stop, I tell myself desperately. I'll just have to make her.

And suddenly I feel a hand gripping my shoulder.

Before

I lie awake and listen to the night, trying not to think about what had happened at the quarry. But every time I close my eyes I see Liam's bloody, broken face, hear the sound of fist hitting bone, Liam's howls of pain. For a brief and horrible moment I imagine it's Edie lying there in Liam's place and I sit bolt upright, gasping at the thought. I have to get Edie away from him. I have to get her away from Connor. Something awful is coming. I can feel it.

Eventually, in the early hours of the morning when the dark hangs close and thick, I turn on my bedside lamp and sit staring at the shadows that are thrown upon the walls, my thoughts chasing each other, always returning to the same one certainty: I must save her; I must save Edie. And when I think of Connor, the hatred I feel for him builds and expands inside me, an

301

all-encompassing loathing that makes my heart clench like a fist, my veins fizzing with a kind of violence. The plan I had been formulating since the day I first went back to the flat returns with renewed strength. It's the only possible solution, and as I sit there in the lamplight on my little single bed I'm filled with a jittery, heart-pounding excitement. Because it's the only way; the only way to get Connor out of Edie's life for good. Only I can save her. And now that I have made my decision, it's impossible to imagine the future any differently.

The hours are long and silent while I make my plans, adding to them, fine-tuning them until they're real and certain. When I eventually fall asleep it feels as though a few seconds have passed before I'm blinking awake to bright sunlight and the sound of my father calling me to breakfast. I get up, at first bleary-eyed and dis-orientated and then, in an instant, alert with adrenalin when I remember the decision I'd come to a couple of hours before.

In the kitchen Dad puts some cornflakes in front of me and disappears as usual behind his paper. Radio 4 burbles quietly in the background and for once I'm grateful for his lack of attention as I sink into my own thoughts. I grow hot and cold, feel myself trembling all over as the enormity of what I plan to do hits me. Do I dare, I ask myself, do I *really* dare to do it? And the answer comes back, *Yes*. I have no choice, after all. Edie needs me to take care of her, needs me to do this for her. Fear mixes with excitement. I'm deep in thought when Dad lowers his paper. 'Aren't you hungry, Heather?' he asks.

I look down at my untouched breakfast. The thought of eating is impossible. I push my bowl away and shake my head, waiting for him to turn back to *The Times*. But instead he continues to watch me. 'Is there something wrong?' he asks.

The question startles me. It strikes me that I can't remember my father ever directly asking me how I felt before, about anything. He usually prefers to keep our conversations to the godly or the academic. He sighs and folds his newspaper, putting it down on the table in front of him. I stare back at the brown bushy eyebrows peppered with grey, the beaklike nose, the hazel eyes. *My* eyes, I realize suddenly. I had never noticed before that, for all our differences, our eyes at least are the same. I think of the bright, intense blue of my mother's, the same as Lydia's.

'Heather?' he says again. When I don't reply he says quietly, 'I saw your light on, in the night.'

I nod, sliding my gaze away from his. 'I couldn't sleep.'

'I expect it's been difficult for you,' he says, his voice strange and thick, 'what with . . . your mother . . .'

I'm hit by a rush of emotion, tears stinging my eyes.

'Well, anyway,' he hurries on, 'I might not be as . . . what I mean is, I'd like to think you felt able to confide in me, if you . . . erm, felt it . . .' he pauses, 'necessary.'

I have no idea what to say. I think about when Lydia

died, the chasm that had opened between my parents and me. How many years I'd wanted either of them to see someone other than the person responsible for her death. And now it's too late, it's all too late. At last I clear my throat. 'I'm fine, Dad,' I say. I get to my feet, and to my surprise my voice comes out clear and strong. 'I better be going. Don't want to be late for school.' As I pass him I pause, and on impulse reach out and briefly pat his arm; our eyes meet and something passes between us, almost as though we both know that this will be the last time we ever touch.

I go straight to Edie's street. Her house is dark and silent with every curtain drawn when I arrive. I look at my watch: 8.30 a.m. The morning has that cool, waiting, dew-soaked stillness summer mornings have before the heat falls. As I hesitate, a woman's voice shouts out down the road, 'Come back here, Ahmed, you little shit,' while a man standing on his step dressed in boxer shorts smokes a cigarette and eyes me sullenly.

When I put my hand to the knocker it sounds like gunshots in the morning quiet. A long moment passes and then another before Edie's mother finally opens up, her face pale and drawn. 'She's not here,' she says immediately. 'She didn't come home last night and you can tell her from me that she's still only seventeen and I'm going to call the police if she doesn't—'

'Listen,' I interrupt and she stops talking in surprise. 'Listen to me, please. I need to see her. It's very important. Tell her she needs to meet me. I'll wait for her. Six o'clock tonight at the old dairy. Tell her I'll be there.'

'No, you listen. I don't know—'

'It's very important that you tell her. The old dairy. If she's not there tonight I'll wait for her, every night until she comes. Tell her.' And then I turn away.

After

The man gripping my shoulder is stocky and well built. I stare at him in astonishment. When I try to pull free his hold tightens. 'All right, Edie?' he says.

My shock deepens. Who is this? How does he know my name?

He grabs hold of my arm and starts walking, half dragging me along with him.

'Who . . . what do you want?' I stumble over my feet, and in my panic try to search for possibilities. Had Heather sent him? I pull away. 'Get off me!' Wildly I look around me, but this part of the park is empty. I think about screaming and as if reading my mind he stops and yanking me closer, roughly puts a hand over my mouth. Terrified, I stare back at him. Shaven-headed, in his forties, a wide flat face with small dark eyes. I look down as he reaches inside his jacket and my heart stops when I see the knife concealed there. The world falls away from me. *Maya*, I think. *Don't hurt me, don't take me away from Maya.* I give a small cry of horror.

He puts one hand around my throat. 'Listen . . .' he says, in his thick South London accent. 'You do as you're told and nothing's going to happen. I just want to see her. All right? I just want to talk to her.'

Who? What? My mind spins in confusion. 'Leave me alone,' I say, desperately trying to twist out of his grasp as he begins to pull me again in the direction of the main gate. But his grip's so strong that the pain in my elbow is now excruciating, as though the bones might shatter beneath his fingers.

He continues talking as if I hadn't spoken. 'Know you're tight with her. The two of you. Very cosy. Always round each other's flats. Seen the texts you sent her when I took her phone. Watched you together. Thick as thieves, yeah?' He nods, his small eyes dark little holes. 'All you got to do is get her to open the door so I can talk to her. Then that's you done. Just need to have a word with her. Need her to listen to me,' he nods to himself, satisfied with his plan.

And then the penny finally drops. 'Phil,' I whisper. 'You're Phil.'

He doesn't reply. He's dragging me along again, and though it's broad daylight, and the street's fairly busy, he's clearly and terrifyingly unconcerned. Violence radiates from him, buzzing and fizzing behind his eyes like trapped electricity. Passers-by glance up in surprise when they see us, but quickly look away and hurry on, their expressions suddenly masked, unseeing: don't get involved.

I think fast. 'Phil, listen,' I say, trying to sound reasonable. 'I can tell you're angry, I know that—'

'You wanna get that door of yours fixed,' he interrupts. 'Get anyone coming in, lock like that.'

The break-in at my flat, it was him. Reason escapes me, fear returns. 'Let me go. Please, *please*, Phil.' I think about the scar on Monica's back, and my blood turns to ice. 'Listen—'

'Why don't you shut the fuck up?'

Only one couple, emerging from their house, tries to intervene. 'Um, excuse me,' the man calls out nervously as Phil drags me along. 'Are you all right?'

'No,' I call desperately, twisting towards him, but Phil yanks my arm so violently I cry out in pain.

When we reach my building he pushes me up the steps, causing me to stumble. 'Open the door,' he says.

'Look, don't do this,' I plead. 'She's not in: Monica's not in anyway.' At this he grabs hold of my head and smashes it against the wood. Pain shoots through me. He pushes his face into mine and the expression in his small, dark eyes silences me.

'You got a little one, yeah?' he says to me. 'Seen you with her. You get me into Monica's flat – hear what I'm saying? Get me in there and I won't come back for you.' He pulls his knife out and holds it to my neck.

As I scrabble about in my pocket for my keys I try

desperately to think of what to do. I only have a matter of seconds. I have to keep him away from Maya and Monica, and this is my last chance to stop him. In my fear I try to focus. He loosens his grip on my arm a fraction as I put my key in the lock and turn it. When I push the door open a crack and he begins to follow me I kick backwards with all my might, trying with my foot to push him back down the steps so I can get through the door alone. But it's like kicking at a brick wall. He doesn't even falter. Before I can do anything else he launches himself after me, pushing me into the hallway and slamming the door behind us.

I hear Maya crying from somewhere inside Monica's flat and I cling on to it, focus on it, trying to think clearly. If I do one good thing in my life it will be to protect my daughter. After all the damage I've done, the mistakes I've made, it's only Maya that matters now. Suddenly Phil puts his hand over my mouth and twists my arm behind my back. The pain is horrible. His hand shifts to my windpipe and he presses with such force that I think he'll break my neck. As I choke and struggle for breath he hisses into my ear. 'This is what you're going to do, you fucking little bitch. You're going to knock on that door and get her to open it. If you say anything about me, I'll kill all three of you, OK?'

I nod and feel the point of the knife dig into my neck. He pushes me towards Monica's door and with a shaking hand I knock. From inside, Maya's cry grows louder. A few moments later I hear Monica's voice. 'That you,

Edie?' she calls out and then, 'Shush, Maya, Mummy's here.' She pauses, and I hear the uncertainty in her voice. 'That is you, isn't it, Edie?'

And I think about how much I love Monica, the first real friend I've had since Heather. Tears fill my eyes. I don't reply. Again I feel the blade of Phil's knife against my skin. 'Yes,' I say, but too quietly and I feel the tip of the blade pierce my skin, blood trickling down my neck. 'Yes,' I say more loudly. 'It's me.' Phil clamps his hand over my mouth, and I hear her on the other side beginning to pull the bolt back. I feel him tense with anticipation. My heart pounds in my ears, a second passes and then another and I hear the first lock begin to turn. In his eagerness his fingers loosen a tiny fraction. As Monica turns the second lock I jerk my head away and have just enough time to scream, 'Don't open it!' I hear Phil's cry of rage before pain rips through me, and then . . . blackness.

Before

She doesn't come the first night. I wait and I wait while the sky turns purple and gold, the twilight seeping into the dairy's derelict corners, the broken brick walls growing blurry and indistinct, the trees beyond it darkening, thickening. The grasshoppers' shrill chirping builds to a crescendo and somewhere behind me comes the faint sound of children calling to each other from the streets of Tyner's Cross. The scent of the evening deepens, musky and sweet. Seven o'clock comes, then eight, the long grass whispers in a sudden breeze and I think about Edie and I think about Connor and the blood roars in my ears and still she doesn't come.

I wait the next night, and the one after that, and then, on the fourth, as I make my way through the field, I see her: a small figure sitting on the furthest wall. Five to six, the sky still a bright clear blue, the heat still

313

punishing. I see there's something very wrong long before I reach her. My heart races and I quicken my pace, tramping through the grass, kicking it away from me. When I reach her she's half-slumped, her head bowed to her chest, her eyes closed. I kneel before her and take hold of her arms. 'Edie,' I say, 'Edie, are you OK?' When she doesn't respond I shake her, my panic rising. 'Edie,' I say, 'what have you done? What have you taken? Please, Edie, wake up.'

She raises her head and slowly her eyes focus on me. 'Heather,' she says, and starts to laugh, a hysterical, high-pitched giggle. 'Hiya, Heifer,' she says and falls against me. I grip her shoulders and hold her upright, and when I look down I see a scattering of tiny needle marks along the insides of her thin arms. 'Edie,' I say, my eyes filling with tears, but at that moment she reels away from me, and vomits long and hard into the grass.

I stroke her back until she's finished and when she's finally stopped I gently lift her up and help her over to a place in the shade, and she sits obedient as a child on the grass, her back against the wall, her head on my shoulder.

'Edie,' I whisper. 'You have to get away from him. You have to.'

I brace myself for her anger and denial but to my surprise she only says, very quietly, 'I can't.'

'But look at you, look what he's done to you.'

She begins to cry. We sit in silence for a while and I feel something of the old closeness between us. I savour

314

it, closing my eyes to hold it tight. 'Edie,' I say after a long moment. 'Has he . . . has he ever hurt you?' I hold my breath but she remains silent. I begin to wonder if she heard me, and then I feel her head move against my shoulder as she nods. I put my arm around her and hold her to me, while white-hot rage flashes through me. I picture Connor's face and want only to annihilate it, claw at it with my fingernails until it's a bloody mess. I could kill him. I know that with absolute certainty. If I saw him now, I could kill him.

After a few minutes she wipes her eyes and sits up a little. 'He doesn't mean it,' she says. 'He can't help it. Sometimes I do things, say things that make him . . . you don't understand, Heather. You don't know him. How lovely he can be. He loves me. He really loves me.'

I bite my tongue and will her to keep talking.

'If you knew the things I know . . . about his child-hood and stuff, the things he's told me . . .'

I think about what Liam had said about Connor's mum but then I think of Liam's battered, broken face and I start to feel sick again. 'I don't care,' I say hotly. 'I don't care about him. I only care about you! Look!' I say snatching up her thin wrist, holding it up to show her the needle marks. 'You know this is wrong. You know it is! You've got to stop seeing him, you've got to get away from him!'

'How can I stop? How can I?' Her voice rises. 'He's here, everywhere I look there he is.' Tears pour down her cheeks as she gestures at the towers. 'I can't, I can't

315

get away from him. He's in my head, always. There's no way out. It goes on and on and on.'

I pull my arm away and kneel in front of her, staring at her fiercely. 'I can stop it,' I tell her. 'I can make it stop. You just have to listen to what I say. You have to do what I say, and it can all be over.'

She stares at me. 'What are you talking about?'

'Think about how you wanted to go to art school and move to London. Think of the life you could have. You're scared of him. I know you are. Well, aren't you?'

Through her tears, Edie nods.

Tentatively I move closer to her. I take her in my arms and hold her, breathing in the dirty, greasy smell of her hair, feeling her thin body limp against mine. 'I can make it all stop.'

She sniffs. 'How?'

So I take a deep breath and I tell her. At first her eyes widen in disbelief. 'Are you mad? No way!'

'Listen to me,' I say. 'I can do it. You just have to leave it all to me. Think about it. Is there any other way? Do you want him to be doing this to you in a year's time? In two years' time? This is the only way out. I'll take care of it all.'

She leans forwards, her head on her knees. 'Oh God. Oh God oh God oh God.'

She begins to cry, great heaving sobs, and I wait. When she's finished, she sits up, her eyes fastened upon the three towers. After a long time I finally hear her say it. 'OK,' she whispers. 'OK.'

'Good,' I say, my heart pounding, my thoughts racing. 'OK. Good. You need to go home now, go home and get some sleep. And then you call me. You call me when you're ready. OK?'

She nods.

'OK?' I say. I grab hold of her hands and look deeply into her face. 'I'll be waiting.'

'Yes,' she says, and the expression in her eyes as she stares back at me is half terror, half hope.

After

I lie on the hospital bed as the doctor examines me. A short, cheerful Australian, he smiles happily at me as he peers at my cracked ribs, split lip and black eye, nodding sympathetically when I wince at his gently probing fingers. I wonder what he thinks about how I ended up here – I have clearly had the living daylights beaten out of me – but if he passes any judgement, he doesn't let on.

It seems I've been lucky. The police had been here earlier, informing me gravely that they'd got to me just in time. Closing my eyes against the pain, I manage to sit myself up in the bed. 'So I can go?' I ask the doctor.

He nods. 'There's not much else we can do for you here now the concussion's gone. Just take it easy and continue with the painkillers and you'll pretty much heal yourself.'

At that moment the door opens and Monica appears, holding Maya in her arms, and there's something about the sight of my daughter, with her outstretched arms and little cry of recognition, that totally undoes me. I clasp her to me and finally allow myself to cry. After a few moments Monica puts her arms around me too, and I feel overwhelming comfort to smell her familiar scent of shampoo and cigarettes.

When we release each other she sits on my bed and gives me a tentative, anxious smile. 'How much do you remember?' she asks.

I stroke Maya's hair. 'Everything until I shouted out to you. What happened? I guess you called the police?'

She nods. 'Yeah, but one of the neighbours already had, apparently, some couple up the road. So they arrived pretty quickly, thank God.' I stare at her, trying to take it all in, and see that she's struggling not to cry. 'Christ, Edie, it was so awful. Standing there on the other side of the door, listening to him do that to you.' She reaches over and takes my hand. 'I'm so sorry.'

'It's not your fault.' I squeeze her fingers. After a silence I ask, 'So what's happened to Phil?'

'The police have him. I just got off the phone to them.' She shakes her head as if she can't quite believe it. 'This time they've got witnesses, Edie. They've got GBH, they've got a weapon with intent. They reckon they've got enough on him to lock him up again.' She pauses and looks at me searchingly. 'Edie, they went through his phone and he had your number on it, must have got it when he stole mine from the flat. Apparently he'd been calling you. Why didn't you say anything?' She waits for me to answer.

'I don't know,' I say at last. 'I guess I . . . I guess I didn't know it was him.'

'I'm so sorry you got mixed up in all this. You'll never know how grateful I am for doing what you did,' and then she puts her arms around me and holds me tightly again.

After the cab has dropped us home from the hospital, Monica fusses around me, settling me on to the sofa, making lunch for the three of us, and asking me repeatedly how I am. It's something of a relief when at last she goes to her own flat. My ribs and jaw ache horribly and I feel fragile and raw, but more than anything I just want to be alone with Maya, to let it sink in, finally, what happened to me.

At first I drift around the flat in a sort of daze and it's not until I've settled Maya down for her nap and I'm washing up the lunch things that it hits me all at once what happened. I see again Phil's small dark eyes, feel the pressure of his grip on my arm, the moment outside Monica's door when he'd knocked me to the ground. Without realizing it, I've drifted back into the living room, and I'm staring unseeing out of the window when a woman's laughter from the street scatters across the silence and I jump nervously. Gingerly I put my fingers to my ribs and wince. I go to the sofa and lie down, closing my eyes and gradually, like silt rising to a river's surface, through all the dark, murky pain and shock of Phil's attack, I recall the single, amazing fact that it had been Phil, not Heather, who'd been in my flat, who'd smashed up Monica's flat and made all the phone calls to my mobile. *It hadn't been Heather*.

Before

Edie phones the next afternoon. 'Are you OK?' I say, relief flooding me when I hear her voice. 'I'm so glad you rang.'

'Yeah,' she says, but her voice is strange and flat.

'Are you . . .' I hesitate. 'Are you ready?'

'Yes,' she says. 'I'm ready.'

'Where shall I—'

'At the quarry. Meet me at the quarry. Tonight, at eight.'

I think fast. 'The quarry? But—' I stop, I don't want to say anything that might make her change her mind. And if meeting at the quarry is the only way she can arrange things, then that's where it'll be. 'OK,' I say. 'The quarry. That's fine. I'll see you there.' She falls silent and I listen to her breathing. 'Edie?' I say. 'You're doing the right thing. This is the right thing to do. You'll see. It's all going to be OK.'

Later, I sit in my bedroom and wait. From out of the silence, all around the house, the clocks strike five. Three hours to go. I glance around my room, at everything so familiar, every object and piece of furniture seeming to take on new significance now that I know that this time tomorrow the world will be so very different. With shaking hands I pull out the black cloth bag I'd hidden beneath my mattress. Through its fabric I feel the outline of what's inside and my courage nearly leaves me. Perhaps it's not too late, I think wildly. Perhaps it's not too late! I could stay here, call it off, I could retake this year of school and start again. But I know that I'm fooling myself. I have to do what needs to be done and afterwards Edie and I will be together, just the two of us, we'll be together for always.

At seven o'clock I tell Dad I'm meeting a school friend and, my heart in my mouth, the black bag under my arm, I set off. From the high street I catch the first bus to Wrexham and when it drops me off twenty minutes later I begin the walk towards the quarry. The heat is ferocious, on either side of me empty fields vibrate with grasshoppers, my thighs rub together with each step, the bag bounces against my hip, my own breath is loud in my ears.

When I come to the familiar turning I check my watch: a quarter to eight. My insides fizz with nerves. I begin to walk up the dirt track, climbing higher and higher, my chest tightening and tightening, until, at last, here I am. The quarry. On the far side of the still, green water the local kids are packing up their cars and calling their goodbyes. The sun is swollen and pale in the darkening sky that's streaked with red and gold. I round the corner and there she is, waiting for me. Edie. My heart leaps. She's here. It's happening, it's really happening. 'Edie,' I call out to her, raising my arm to wave, and then, suddenly, I stop. Because behind her, stepping out from the copse, are Connor and his friends. All of them. Fear like a knife cutting through the centre of me. I look back to Edie, to the expression on her face, and my heart breaks.

After

Monica scrapes the last of our Christmas lunch into the bin before returning to the table and flopping down next to me. 'I've never eaten so much turkey in my life,' I tell her. 'You'll have to roll me out of here.' She smiles and lights a cigarette and we sit in peaceful silence for a moment or two, drinking our wine while Maya, in her high chair, throws pieces of food down to the waiting dog, laughing gleefully each time he catches something in his mouth.

'Thanks for today, it's been so great,' I tell her.

'It's the least I can do, you know that. After what you did—'

I roll my eyes, 'Oh God, don't start all that again!'

She laughs but then asks anxiously, 'You sure you're OK, though? Are your ribs still sore?'

'I'm fine,' I tell her firmly. 'Honestly. Stop worrying.' A second later, Billy and Ryan appear.

'Look at you two winos,' Billy says. 'Are we ever going to have our Christmas pud?'

Monica throws a cracker at him. 'Get it yourself, lazy arse!'

He shakes his head sorrowfully and turns to me. 'See the crap we have to put up with, Edie?'

I laugh, silently marvelling at the change in Monica and her sons. Since the moment Phil was put back in custody it's as though they stand taller, surer somehow, a lightness and energy in their eyes that had not been there before. I want to tell Monica that this is the best Christmas I've had for a long time, that being here, included in her family like this, means more to me than I can put into words, but at that moment Monica turns to me and smiles and I realize there's no need, that somehow she's already guessed. 'Come on,' I say instead, getting to my feet and lifting Maya from her chair. 'I want to give you your present.'

In the living room I kneel down by the tree and retrieve the parcel I'd put there earlier. I sit with the boys while Monica unwraps it. Once she's pulled it free from its red shiny paper she stares down at the drawing I'd had framed for her. 'You did this?' she asks, stroking the glass. 'Seriously, you did this yourself?'

I laugh, embarrassed. 'Yeah.'

She crosses the room and places it carefully on the mantelpiece before coming back to the sofa where the four of us look at it in silence. It's of Monica and the two boys and I'd worked on it for days. 'You should do this for a living,' Monica tells me.

'Yeah, right,' I say.

'No, seriously! Bugger waitressing.'

I feel myself blush and remember how James had reacted a few nights before, when I'd shown him the pictures I'd been working on over the last few weeks. He'd examined them intently before turning to me and saying, 'You could make a career out of this, you know.' When I'd protested, he'd said, 'Why not? I'm sure you'd get work as an illustrator.' And even though I knew he was being ridiculous, that people like me don't do things like that, nevertheless for a moment I'd let myself imagine a future very different from the one I'd long resigned myself to.

It's late afternoon when the intercom buzzes and I jump up to answer it, knowing it will be James come to have a drink with us after spending the day with Stan. I find him on the doorstep holding a bottle of Champagne under each arm, smiling back at me. When I go to him he puts his arms around me, the bottles clunking together behind my back as we kiss. As I lead him into the flat and introduce him to the others, happiness flips and somersaults behind my ribs.

I'm impressed and a little envious of how easily James manages it, this business of meeting new people. He's chatting now to Ryan about his motorbike and I watch how attentively he listens and asks questions, and when Billy makes a joke, his laugh, deep and sudden, fills the room. I see with a shock of clarity the possibility of falling in love with him, not right this minute, but some time, the days and weeks ahead tumbling inevitably towards it, something shimmering and indistinct yet unmistakably there in the future, and the old voice inside me that would normally tell me to run as far away as possible is silent for once.

I'm shaken from my thoughts by Monica nudging me and handing me my drink. 'It's nice to see you so happy, love,' she says, and I put an arm around her waist and smile.

We're settling down to watch a film an hour or so later when James grimaces and brings Maya over to me. 'Think this one might have an extra Christmas present for you.'

I take her from him and laugh. 'Lucky me.' Gathering up my bag I head for the door. 'I left the nappies upstairs. Might as well change her there, won't be a tick.'

And then there they are, those last few moments after leaving Monica's flat, as I run up the stairs with Maya in my arms, carelessly passing all those familiar doors with their scuffed, white paintwork, their brass letters, the sounds and silences seeping from beneath each one. I will replay them so many times in the weeks and months to come, those final brief minutes before everything changes. And I notice nothing different when I push open my door, the flat in the same disarray I'd left it in as I'd rushed to get ready for Monica's Christmas lunch only a few hours before. I suppose I'm too busy seeing to Maya, my mind too full of James to register the closed kitchen door.

The nappies and mat are already out from this morning's change, and I lie Maya down and do what I have to do on autopilot. When I've finished I leave her sitting on the floor. 'Just going to wash my hands,' I tell her. 'Don't you crawl off anywhere, I'll be right back.'

Later I will estimate that I spent less than thirty seconds in the bathroom: rinsing my hands under the tap, running my fingers through my hair and quickly checking my make-up before turning off the light and leaving again.

And yet when I return to the living room, Maya is gone.

In confusion I walk into the kitchen and what I find there makes my blood freeze. A sensation of falling, the world rushing away. The window is wide open and, standing out on the flat roof of the bedsit below, at its furthest edge, looking down over the gardens and houses and streets, is Heather, with Maya in her arms.

For a long moment my shock is so absolute that I can neither think nor move. It's only when Maya turns and peers at me over Heather's shoulder that I am at last jolted into action, crossing the room and climbing out on to the roof, senseless with panic. Every instinct tells me to run to Heather and snatch my daughter from her, but instead I force myself to walk very slowly towards them.

Heather seems unaware of my presence, continuing to stare out across the rooftops below and though I feel as though my heart is in my throat I make myself speak. 'Heather,' I say.

When she doesn't reply I take a step and then another towards her, until I'm only a few metres from her and she turns and we regard each other at last. Even through my panic I can see that she looks terrible, as though she's been sleeping rough for weeks. Her face and clothes are filthy, her hair lank and matted, and there are deep shadows beneath her eyes. But it's the eyes themselves that frighten me the most, the way they stare at me so dully, as though she barely knows where she is or who I am.

Now that I'm closer I see with fresh horror how near she is to the edge of the roof. Behind her is a sheer drop, the ground at least seventy feet below. I silently pray for Maya to remain still and dare not move a muscle myself. I force myself to speak in a low, calm voice. 'Heather, please give her to me.' I reach out my arms very slowly. 'Give Maya to me, please. Now.'

At that, she looks down at Maya and finally speaks, her voice vague. 'I missed her, I missed her so much.'

I keep my arms outstretched, fighting the impulse to run and grab my daughter. My heart thumps painfully. 'Please, Heather. Give Maya to me and we can talk.' When she doesn't move I'm unable to hide my desperation. 'We'll talk, I promise. You and me. We'll sit down and talk properly together – you can hold Maya as long as you like, but let's please go back inside.'

She shakes her head. 'No, I don't want you to have

332

her. It's not right.' She looks down at Maya and strokes her hair tenderly.

At this a sudden anger gets the better of my fear. 'Heather, I'm her mother. She needs me! Give her to me now.'

She glances at me. 'You? She doesn't need you.'

I'm silent, terrified of saying the wrong thing, of making the wrong move and causing her to fall. A cold wind begins to pick up around us, the two of us so alone up here surrounded by this vast and empty sky. 'Heather, please—'

'Why did you do it?' she asks suddenly. She looks at me directly then, and I find I cannot meet her gaze and have to look away. So here it is: here it is at last.

'I don't—' I begin. I stare at the ground for a long moment, the words gathering in my throat are both too much and not enough. I notice that I'm crying, and wipe the tears away angrily.

'Why, Edie?' she says again.

'Heather, don't do this. Give me my daughter back. Give her to me!' In desperation I step towards her so that I am as close to the edge as she is, only a metre between us now. I don't dare to come any closer. In her arms, Maya, entirely unperturbed by her predicament, plays with Heather's hair.

'You were my friend. Why did you do it, Edie?'

I shake my head, and cannot answer her.

When I look back at that summer it's with a sick sort of disbelief at the person I'd become. It had happened so gradually that I hadn't even noticed how cleverly, how completely Connor had begun to destroy me. The drugs had gotten harder, more frequent – most of the time I was either high or crashing down, or drunk. I seemed to spend every second trying to keep him happy. Even towards the end, things could be OK: he could be loving and gentle, telling me I was the only good thing in his life, and at these times I'd be elated. And then from nowhere a thick black cloud would descend and it was as though a stranger appeared in his place.

He controlled everything I did. I'd dress the way he wanted me to, barely speaking in case I said the wrong thing. By the end of that summer I was in too deep to claw my way out. It had become normal, to sleep with his friends if he told me to, to think, instantly, that it was my fault when he hit me, humiliated me, used me.

The night I met Heather at the old dairy, I'd been lower than I'd ever been. Earlier that day we'd got drunk at the flat and he had lost his temper, punching me hard between the shoulder blades before kicking me out of his flat. Heather had made it seem so simple. She had it all planned out. She was going to take the money from her uni fund and the two of us would run away together. We would go to London, start a new life, away from Fremton, away from Connor. We would be happy. She had seemed so full of hope and certainty when I had been so broken and desperate that for a moment I had believed her: the tiny part of me that knew Connor was destroying me, knew he would only get worse and worse, had glimpsed a way out.

And when I left Heather that night I had carried it with me, that hope. She was right: I had to get away from him. The fact that she believed in me, would do this for me, had been a jolt out of the helplessness I'd felt for so long. I went home and resolved to do what she said. I stayed away from the flat for two days. I didn't drink, I didn't take drugs, I didn't call him. And I felt better, I really did. I felt stronger and even more convinced that leaving Fremton with Heather was the right thing to do.

On the third day I got up and got dressed and around noon I left my house to go to the phone box to call her, to tell her that I was ready. I remember so clearly how calm I'd felt, aware of a faint hint of freshness in the air as though that long, stifling summer was finally about to end. And then, at the end of my road, I had turned the corner to find Connor's car waiting for me.

Here, on the roof, Heather says, 'I trusted you. I loved you.'

I want to put my hands over my ears, to block out her voice and the memories. But in her arms is Maya, and beyond them is a seventy-foot drop, so I swallow hard and force myself to nod. 'I know,' I say.

I used to think Connor was telepathic. It was as if the moment I reached the end of my rope, began to pull away, he always somehow knew. And then it would

335

start, the contrition, the promises, the affection and love I'd been craving. That night he begged me to get in his car and he told me how sorry he was, how much he missed me, how he'd kill himself if he lost me. He cried and talked about how fucked up he was, how no one had ever loved him before, and I fell for it, the way I always had. I really believed I could save him. If I could show him just how much I loved him, if I could only stop annoying him, we would be happy. We sat in the car and talked and talked and by the time he drove me back to his flat it was as if the last few days had never happened. Heather, her plans, my resolve all disappeared.

Most of that first night is a blur. I was so happy. The flat was full of people as usual but Connor looked at me as if I was the only person there. In the early hours I curled up on his lap and felt the first woozy rushes of the E I'd just taken. He had his eyes closed, his fingers tapping to the music playing on the stereo, and I'd looked into his face and could hardly believe how beautiful he was. 'I never would have gone with her, you know,' I murmured. 'I'd never have left you.'

He opened his eyes. 'What?'

'Heather,' I said dreamily, laying my head against his chest, breathing in his scent. The colours and sounds of the room had begun to bend and warp, my arms were weightless, every limp, slow movement they made followed by a trail of light. 'Got all the money from her uni fund, hadn't she, so we could run away together.' Someone handed me a joint and I took a long draw, saying sleepily, 'Supposed to call her, tell her where to meet me.' I kissed his lips. 'Silly Heather. Why would I want to do that, why would I ever leave you?'

I must have taken myself off to Connor's room at some point and slept for several hours because when I woke up it was long after midday. I stumbled into the lounge and found that most of the people from the night before had cleared off, just a few comatose stragglers remaining. By contrast Connor was full of energy, pacing around the flat on his mobile, talking quickly, his eyes bright and intense. 'Yeah, mate, yeah. Come round. Niall's coming, and all that lot. Be a laugh.' I wondered if he'd even slept yet.

It was impossible not to get caught up in his good mood and when he passed me the bottle of vodka I'd taken it, not caring that I hadn't eaten anything or drunk anything that wasn't alcoholic for twenty-four hours. I didn't even care that the friends he'd invited over were the ones I didn't like much; the older, rougher ones who brought with them the harder drugs. We started doing lines of coke and smoking something that made my head roar and my heart ricochet around my body. But I was happy. I was with Connor and nothing else mattered.

'We should fuck her up.' We were half lying on the sofa together, watching someone called Jonno cut out lines of white powder.

'What? Who?'

He passed me the vodka. 'Heather. We should fuck her up. Fucking busy bitch. Need to teach her a lesson.'

'Yeah,' I said, not paying much attention, thinking he'd lose interest soon.

But he didn't. He kept on about it. 'Who the fuck does she think she is? Trying to come between us all the time. Trying to split us up. Go on, you should phone her. Say you'll meet her.'

'No, baby,' I said, 'let's leave it. Just stay here and have a laugh.'

But he kept on and on. And the more wasted I got, and the more he talked me into it, the more I got caught up in his plan. Because he was right, wasn't he? Heather *was* always trying to split us up. Why would she do that when he made me so happy? As I listened to him, an anger of my own began to rise inside me. I'd actually nearly done what she said! I'd nearly left Connor behind and gone with her! I grabbed hold of that anger, let it grow until it had silenced the faint, small voice that whispered something very different. It was a laugh, that was all, a joke. We'd mess with her head, Connor said, teach her a lesson. I didn't want this new happiness between us to end. I didn't want to do anything to stop him loving me.

So I went along with it. I called her from Connor's phone, while him and the others listened in silence, the music turned off.

Through Tyner's Cross we hurtled, into the town, past the marketplace and the pubs and the empty shops. Then on to the open roads, nothing but fields on either side of us, going faster and faster, hedgerows

338

and road signs and other cars blurred flashes as we passed. I leaned out of the window and screamed and laughed into the wind. We all felt it, I could tell, like we were flying, like we were on top of the world and in this car, between the six of us, it was pure speed and energy and excitement. I wished we could go faster and faster, I didn't care if we crashed, I didn't care about anything but the inside of that car, hurtling through the empty winding roads, nothing on either side of us but fields.

We got there before her. The others waiting in the trees beyond the clearing, the quarry darkening beneath the sinking sun, the kids on the other side packing up and driving off, the rumble of car engines and shouts of goodbye carrying across the water to where we stood. And then there she was, her face lit with happiness to see that I had come. I saw the bag under her arm, knew that it was full of money, her plan for us to run away together shining in her eyes. Her joy lasting for only a moment as she looked beyond me, and realized what I'd done.

It happened so fast. She turned, tried to run, but they were all too quick for her, moving in a pack. I couldn't stop laughing suddenly, a panicky hysteria surging up and spewing out of me. She tried to break free but we had her surrounded and every time she tried to get past us someone would push her back into the centre. A crazy, frenzied game of British Bulldog. We were getting nearer and nearer to the edge of the water. I remember her grim desperation, our shouts and jeers, how I laughed and laughed.

I don't know which one of us shoved her in. She fell backwards in slow motion, limbs splayed as she went down, down into the water. As we waited for her head to break up through the surface I looked at Connor, at his face, alight with something I'd not seen before, and I felt the drugs and the vodka and the adrenalin charging through my veins and I told myself it would be OK, that it wasn't that bad, just another crazy, drug-fucked night that would be over in the morning, all over in the morning and we'd get up and go on again like yesterday and all the days before that. It was a laugh, that was all, it was just a big joke.

She pulled herself out, water rolling off her sodden clothes, panting cries of shock. I thought that it was over, that we had played our trick and taught our lesson and we'd be on our way. But he hadn't finished with her, Connor; he hadn't finished with her at all. When he moved towards her, she tried to run again but the others, they followed him, did as he said, her screams of NO NO NO NO NO lost beneath their jeers. And as they egged each other on I stood there, watching, as Connor started to undo his flies, as he shouted at the others to hold her down, her screams now the sound of every and all terror. I watched him, Connor, my Connor, my love, and I did nothing. And then I turned and I ran.

*　　*　　*

Here on the roof Heather doesn't speak for a long time, and when she does the wind nearly carries her voice away. 'You did nothing, Edie. You watched what he did to me and you did nothing. I saw you. I saw in your face that, even then, it wasn't me you were thinking about, it was only him and you.' She watches me impassively for a few moments. 'I was going to have a baby,' she says.

I close my eyes. 'Oh, no. Oh God, Heather, no.'

'I don't even know which one of them was the father. When they were finished with me, when they'd all had their turn, they drove off.'

I nod.

'I didn't have it,' she goes on. 'They wouldn't let me, my parents. They made me get rid of it. She came back to us, my mum. Moved back in.' She looks at me. 'Isn't that funny? In a way, what happened brought them back together. They wanted to deal with me, my baby, together.'

'Did you tell them?' I whisper.

She shakes her head. 'They weren't interested in why I was pregnant . . . only that I was.'

In the following silence, far above the world that presses on regardless, I remember Jennifer saying in the café, 'We were only doing what we thought was best for her.' I think of the intervening years between Heather leaving Fremton and the night she ended up outside my flat. I think of her at sixteen, having an abortion, dropping out of school, leaving home alone. But I force myself to push the thoughts away. I look at my daughter in Heather's arms and know I have to focus on Maya – I have to do everything I can to keep her safe. I need to keep Heather talking. 'Why did you come looking for me, that first time?' I ask her.

Her reply is almost lost in the wind. 'I wanted to die. I had tried and tried for so many years to get over what happened, but in the end I couldn't. It just got too hard. I took so many pills, so many, I wanted it to be over.'

'Yes,' I say softly, and I think about what Jennifer had told me about visiting her in hospital. 'But why did you come to me?'

'Because of my mother.'

I shake my head. 'Jennifer? I don't understand.'

She frowns and shifts Maya's weight in her arms, unconsciously leaning a fraction closer to the edge, causing a silent scream of terror to rise up in my throat. 'She came to see me at the hospital and she said . . . she said . . .' Her voice is a stricken whisper. 'She said she knew I'd murdered Lydia.'

'Oh, Heather . . .'

'She said she'd always known it. That she'd kept it secret all these years, but ever since Lydia died, she'd known I'd done it deliberately. That I'd pushed her in.' Her face crumples in pain as she remembers. 'But I would never have hurt her! I loved her more than anything. I didn't push Lydia, Edie. I wouldn't!'

I remember the things Jennifer had said about her daughter, the monster she'd painted, and as I look at

Heather now, I know that she's telling the truth. 'I know, Heather,' I whisper. 'Oh, Heather, I know you didn't hurt her.'

Her eyes search my face. 'I would never hurt anyone. All I ever wanted was for people to like me. Sometimes I'd get upset . . . I'd get upset and suddenly I wouldn't know what I was doing, I'd get in a state and lose control, but it was never . . . I would never hurt anyone on purpose! And Lydia fell, there was nothing I could do! She just fell!'

My eyes fill with tears. 'I know, Heather, I know that, I do.'

'You were the first person who liked me, who didn't treat me like a freak. You were everything to me.'

Maya squirms in her arms and I let out a cry of fear, but Heather doesn't seem to hear me as she goes on.

'My mum said that everything bad that had happened to me since Lydia died was because of what I'd done. That God was punishing me.'

'Heather—'

'And I thought, could it be true? Is *that* why they did it? You, Connor and the others? Because God wanted to punish me? Do you think that's true, Edie? Do you?' She searches my face, her expression as confused as a child's.

Mutely, I shake my head.

'Then why did you do it, Edie?' Her eyes meet mine, her words cold and deliberate suddenly. 'You brought me to them. You tricked me. And then you watched it happen, and you ran.'

'I don't know. I don't know!' Panic grips me as she shifts Maya in her arms. 'Heather, please!' I cry. 'I don't know.'

She stares at me silently and after a while her expression changes, as though she sees something, understands something for the first time, and I feel as though she can see right inside me, to the truth of me. 'It was because you're cruel, Edie. Because you have no goodness, no heart. It wasn't my fault at all, was it?'

'Please, Heather, whatever I've done, I'm begging you, please don't hurt Maya.'

She looks lost in thought, and then she gazes down at my daughter. 'Hurt her? I love her. I love her so much. I missed her. I just wanted to see her again.'

'You can,' I say quickly, eagerly. 'You can see her whenever you want. But come away from the edge. I'm frightened. You're frightening me. Give her back to me.'

'To you?' She shakes her head. 'No. I don't want you to have her. What has she done to deserve that?' Her eyes are full of tenderness as she murmurs to Maya, 'It's too bad, isn't it, my darling, it's too hard.' She turns to look down at the gardens far below and says, 'I've tried and I've tried but it's just too hard.'

Cold horror washes through me. She's going to jump, I realize. She's going to jump with Maya in her arms. I need to stop her. I need to stop her from jumping.

Thinking fast, I say in a rush, 'You're right, Heather. You're right.'

She hesitates. 'What?'

'I am cruel. I don't deserve Maya, I'm no good for her. You,' I tell her, nodding madly, 'you should have her, not me.'

'Me?' She looks at me with incomprehension. But when the meaning of my words sinks in, something changes in her eyes. She looks down at Maya. 'Me?'

'Yes, you have her. You look after her. You're right. She'd be better with you. Better without me.' My words are garbled, desperate.

I see the possibility dawning on her face, a new future she'd never considered before, and for a second something like joy flickers in her eyes. And then she looks at me sharply. 'I don't believe you.'

'Don't jump, Heather! Please, please don't jump!' I beg.

She looks away and says with utter hopelessness, 'Why not? I am so tired of it all. All I wanted was for you to love me, Edie, to be my friend. I tried to get over it, what happened. For years and years I tried. But it got harder and harder.' She gazes down at Maya before continuing very quietly, 'They found me. At the hostel, they found me unconscious and took me to hospital and then my mum came and she said what she said.' She looks at me. 'When I found you again, and looked after Maya, it was the first good thing I'd had. And now that's over too.'

345

Maya begins to cry and struggle in her arms, reaching out for me. My heart lurches, fear grips me. 'It doesn't have to be,' I say quickly.

Then, as Heather watches, very slowly I inch forward until I'm at the edge too. I look down at the ground far below. If I jump, Heather won't. It is the only way I can think of to ensure she doesn't do it. And as I look into my daughter's face I know that I would die rather than take that risk, that if Heather did jump, and took my daughter with her, I wouldn't want to live anyway.

And isn't Heather right, after all? Isn't it true that I don't deserve her? That it would be better for Maya without me? If I died it would be the end of it; all the guilt would be over.

I take a step forward, the tips of my shoes peeping over the edge. I look at Maya, and I can hardly see her for my tears. Silently I say goodbye to her. I take a breath. And then, somebody calls my name. I turn, and through the open window I see Monica standing in my kitchen.

Heather gazes at Monica as though emerging from a dream. She looks down at Maya, screaming now in her arms, then at me standing on the edge of the roof, and seems utterly confused, as though she has no idea what has happened, what has led us to this. I stare mutely, pleadingly at Monica, and very slowly she crawls through the window until she is out on the roof with us. She speaks very gently. 'Heather,' she says. 'Give Maya to me.'

At first it seems as though Heather hasn't heard her. Monica takes a step nearer, her arms outstretched. 'Give her to me, Heather,' she says more firmly, 'there's a good girl.'

But instead of replying, Heather turns her back and walks away from me to the far corner of the roof, still dangerously close to the edge. I watch helplessly as she holds Maya tightly, her face entirely blank. But although I'm almost senseless with fear, Monica doesn't falter, her voice low and steady. 'Heather,' she says again. 'Whatever this is, whatever has happened, Maya needs to be safe now.'

I see Heather listen to her, and I hold my breath, praying wordlessly.

'You are very upset, I know, I can see that,' Monica continues, 'but this isn't the way to make things better. Maya hasn't done anything to hurt you, has she? Has she, Heather?'

Heather shakes her head a tiny fraction, and a tendril of hope unfurls inside me.

'I want to help you, Heather,' Monica says. 'I want to listen to you. But you have the chance now to keep Maya safe. Because she's only a baby, isn't she? Isn't she, Heather? And she trusts you to keep her from harm. Bring her to me, Heather, so that she's safe. Will you do that for her, Heather? Please?'

A long moment passes. It hangs in the balance, what

347

Heather will do. And then, at last, Heather turns, and slowly, mutely, steps towards Monica. She passes Maya to her and I let out a long, painful gasp of relief. I take my daughter from Monica and fall to my knees, crying into Maya's hair.

But Monica doesn't move. 'Why don't you come in, Heather?' she says. 'It'll be just you and me. We can talk.' She speaks with infinite gentleness, as though to a small child, and for a moment I think Heather is going to do as she asks, but instead she takes a step backwards, and then another, and I let out a stifled scream of fright. But Monica doesn't waver. 'Come in now, Heather,' she repeats. 'Come in and let me help you. I'd like to help you, if you'll let me.'

At this, Heather stops, her face crumples, and she begins to cry.

'Heather,' I beg, 'please . . . please, Heather.'

Monica takes a step forward and holds out her hand to Heather. There is absolute silence, the world waits. And then, finally, Heather takes it. Together they climb down into the kitchen, and, overwhelmed with relief, I get to my feet and follow them.

James stands in the door staring back at us, his face blank with shock. 'What the fuck? Shall I call the police? Who is this?'

After a silence it's Monica who answers him. 'This is Heather. Edie's friend.'

But when Heather next speaks, it's to me. 'Tell them

what you did,' she says. 'You were my friend. Tell them. Tell them what you did.'

'I'm sorry,' I cry, clasping Maya to me and sobbing. 'I'm so sorry, there's nothing I can do about it now, there's nothing I can do!'

'What is this about, Heather?' Monica asks. 'Let me help you. Tell me what's wrong.'

And so she does. She tells them everything. I can't look at Monica or James while they listen to her story. I sit on the floor of my kitchen and hold Maya to me as Heather tells them what I did. When she's finished, Monica turns to me. 'Is this true, Edie?' she asks, and finally I nod. She gapes at me, shocked and bewildered. 'But . . . didn't you call the police, tell somebody . . . ?'

'I . . . I . . .'

But Heather interrupts me. 'She told me not to tell.'

Monica stares at me in disbelief. 'You told her not to tell anyone? *Why?*'

'Monica,' I say desperately, 'I can explain, I . . .'

I hear the phone ringing as though from somewhere far away and pull the duvet over my head, sinking back into my pain, my bruised and battered body curled tightly in the position I have lain in for the past three nights and days.

At first I'd tried to struggle free, kicking and punching with a strength I never knew I had, but the more I fought the more forcefully they'd held me. I could hear myself screaming, my hysterical NONONONONO like something not a part of me, a sound I'd heard myself make only once before, the day my sister died. And then it was as though I left myself, floating away until I was looking down from far above, watching it happening to someone else, limp and passive as they finished what they'd set out that day to do.

When at last it was over, when they'd all had their turn and driven off, I had stayed in that strange and disconnected state and I'd thought about my sister, about the moment when she'd fallen, back, back, back into the water, how I'd not been able to save her. And then I thought about Edie, how the moment I'd realized what Connor was going to do, I'd screamed for her to help me and in my panic and my fear had turned to her and seen the way her eyes were locked on him, and I'd known then, even before she'd turned and run, I'd understood that it was only Connor she could see, and it always had been.

And all at once, I'd returned to myself, all feeling and sensation coming back to me in a sickening rush, and that was when I'd heard the awful endless high-pitched scream, like an animal, going on and on and on, and realized that it came from me.

Here in my room the distant ringing of the telephone stops abruptly and I hear only the slow, rhythmic sound of my own breathing, in and out, in and out, and I hold my breath, because even the sound of myself disgusts me now. Sometimes, since it happened, I leave myself for hours, drifting far away from this body lying

350

motionless upon this bed. I have not eaten, nor talked, nor barely left my room in days.

A knock on my door. 'Heather?' I open my eyes to see Dad's face, his pleading, anxious eyes peering at me as he says, 'It's Edie on the phone. I don't know what's happened, but please talk to her, Heather, please.' He has barely finished speaking before I've leapt out of bed, running to Dad's study, shutting the door in his face and grabbing at the receiver, so desperate am I to speak to the one person who can help me, who can tell me what to do, how to stop this awful gutting, choking pain.

'Edie? Edie is that you?'

'Yes.'

I can barely speak for sobbing. 'Where are you? You must come back, you must help me. Please, Edie, please help me.'

But her voice is flat and cold. 'I'm in London. Heather, you must listen to me. You can't tell anyone. Do you understand?'

'But—'

'I mean it, Heather. Do not tell anyone. If you do, I'll be dragged into it too. I'll be a witness.' For the first time her voice cracks. 'He'd kill me, Heather. He'd find me and he'd kill me and then he'd kill you too. I'll tell them that you're lying, that you've made the whole thing up.'

I sink to the floor, struggling to breathe, dizzy with shock, certain that I'm going to be sick. 'But, Edie, I can't, I don't . . . please, Edie, you've got to help me.'

Edie's voice cuts through mine. 'If you love me, you'll

keep quiet. If you talk about this to anyone, I'll never forgive you. Do you hear me? I will never fucking forgive you.'

   And then she hangs up.

In my kitchen, so quiet now you could hear a pin drop, Heather tells Monica what I'd said to her that day, and when she's finished, Monica's expression when she looks back to me has changed from bewilderment to disgust.

After

The train pulls out of Euston station and the woman opposite me takes a paperback from her bag and begins to read. On my lap, Maya sucks on a breadstick, looking out of the window as the world slips past. A recorded announcement tells us that the buffet carriage is situated at the rear of the train, and we begin to pick up speed. Soon inner London turns into pebble-dashed suburbia until at last the final loose strands of the city's outskirts, with its industrial estates and depots and warehouses, peter out into green fields.

On the rack above me sits a small suitcase. A dog-eared newspaper left by someone else lies on the table in front of me but the words swim before my eyes and once again my mind begins its sickening replay of Christmas Day.

After Heather had finished her story a stunned silence

had fallen. For a moment, nobody had spoken or moved. Unable to look at Monica or James, I could do nothing but cling to Maya and cry. Finally, Monica had gone to Heather and put her arms around her. 'Ssshhh,' she'd soothed. 'It's OK now, it's all going to be OK.' And then she had taken Heather's hand and led her out of my flat. She didn't look at me as she passed me by.

James had stared at me, open-mouthed with shock. 'Edie?' he said. 'I don't . . . Surely this can't be true?' But I could only nod, and after several silent seconds he had left too. And then I had sat down at the kitchen table with Maya, and waited for Christmas Day to pass.

An hour or so later the train stops at a small rural station and a crowd of teenagers get on, clutching cans of beer, traipsing noisily down the aisle, swaying and laughing as they go. Maya, who had fallen asleep somewhere near Birmingham, stirs briefly in my arms but quickly settles again, leaving me to gaze out of the window, hardly seeing the countryside that's flashing past. Suddenly the train enters a tunnel and I find myself faced with my reflection, staring into my own eyes for a moment or two until the train emerges once again into daylight, and I vanish once more.

On Boxing Day morning I'd gone to stay at Uncle Geoff's, leaving almost at the crack of dawn to avoid the possibility of bumping into Monica – I couldn't bear to have to face again her hard, cold stare of contempt. Despite my uncle's kindness, the passing of those icy late-December days and endless nights had seemed interminable, a horrible reminder of the last time I had run there to hide. And then, finally, I had come to my decision.

On my way to the station this morning, I'd made one final stop. When James had opened the door we had stood in silence for a long moment. I saw a flash of sympathy in his eyes and I had clung to it desperately. 'Are you OK?' he asked quietly, and I had nodded. He had stroked Maya's cheek and I'd been overcome with loneliness and longing.

'I wanted to say goodbye,' I said, and he had nodded, but didn't ask where I was going. Behind me the taxi's engine growled.

'Have you seen Monica?' I asked at last.

'I've spoken to her,' he said. 'She gave me her number. I guess I just needed to talk to her.'

'How is she?' I asked, tears stinging my eyes. 'How's Heather?'

And he had told me how Monica had taken Heather in, had found her a refuge to go to in the New Year, somewhere they could help her. 'She's a good person, Monica,' James had said.

Shame had slammed into me. 'Yes,' I'd whispered, 'she is.' And then, with nothing left to say, I'd turned and walked away.

The train pulls in at Wolverhampton and Maya and I get off to wait for a new one to take us on the last leg of our journey. Half an hour later we chug slowly through countryside that becomes increasingly, sickeningly familiar with every passing minute. I grip the table in front of me, trying to keep the waves of nausea at bay. I feel Connor's presence getting nearer and nearer, not just a memory, an intangible monster from my past, but a real person, existing in the world somewhere close. I remember the morning I'd left Fremton for good, just before dawn as the first light had bled into the sky, and as the train pulls into Fremton station I begin to shake so violently that I can barely stand.

As Maya and I walk along the familiar streets I feel a growing panic as memory after memory slams into me: the town square where I'd met Connor that first time, the pubs and off-licences we used to go to, the road that leads to Braxton Field where the fun fair came to town. In the windows of small, black-bricked houses, tired Christmas trees stand, bedraggled beneath wreaths of sagging tinsel. Torn wrapping paper trails from over-stuffed wheelie bins. The pavements are mostly empty in this cold, end-of-year mid-morning, but I fearfully scan the face of every passer-by. Does Connor even live here any more? Do any of them? As I approach Tyner's Cross I see the estate looming ahead, its three towers glowering down at me, and the closer I get, the noise of the motorway grows louder, like the warning growl of some unseen beast.

At last I reach my mother's street. I pause at the gate and see that nothing whatsoever has changed; the peeling paint on the door is the same shade of lemon, the same curtains my nan had once chosen hang at the windows still. I make myself approach and knock on the door, fear pounding through me.

When my mother sees me standing there her mouth falls open in shock. We consider each other for a long, silent moment, until her gaze falls from my face to her granddaughter's and for an instant, in the shadows of her hallway, I see her eyes flicker with a sudden light. At last I begin to speak and I don't stop until I've finished the speech I'd rehearsed on the long journey here. Her face betrays no emotion as she listens, but at last she nods and after a second or two I hand Maya to her before I turn and leave.

Retracing my steps through the quiet streets I reach the market square and stand for a while, taking in the empty shops and spray-painted statue, the air of sudden abandonment. And it seems as though the very second I look up at the sky, snow begins to fall, thick and white and fast, filling the world with a soft blue light. I walk on towards the large red-bricked building on the farthest corner of the square and I pause for a moment on its steps, until finally I go in, the door of the police station swinging silently shut behind me.

Acknowledgements

My thanks to: my agent Hellie Ogden at Janklow & Nesbit (UK) – without her vision, hard work and all-round brilliance, this book wouldn't exist; my excellent editors, Julia Wisdom and her team at HarperCollins in the UK; Danielle Perez and her team at Penguin Random House in the US; Kate Stephenson, Claire Paterson, Emma Parry.

I am also indebted to my friends Alex Pierce, Steven Regan and Justin Quirk for their many readings of the work in progress, their wise advice and endless encouragement.

Finally, but most of all, huge love and thanks as ever to David Holloway.